THE HOUSE OF ILYA

By, Richard Leslie Brock

About the Author

Richard Brock uses his academic disciplines in Classical History and Folklore and Mythology along with his military experience in Alaska and over 1,000 miles on the Pacific Crest Trail for this book.

Contents

The House of Ilya

Chapter 1, SAINT PETERSBURG RUSSIA, 1782

Five-year-old Anton Niktovich sat at the dining room table and surveyed the battlefield that lay in the valley before him. As a fire crackled inside the deep green malachite fireplace, smoke from musket fire shrouded the soldiers. Armed troops painted in bright red enamel lined up shoulder to shoulder in rows on one side surrounded by crumpled napkins and strewn silverware. These were the soldiers of the Russian Imperial Army.

On the other side was a group of Polish volunteers called the Bar Confederation who had grown weary of Russian meddling in their homeland and rebelled. The Poles were painted bright blue and were fewer in number than the Russians. He knew the story of the battle from his father who had been given a first-hand account from Company Commander Kutuzov, a family friend. The war had been fought and won by the Russians just five years before Anton had been born. Thus, the suppression of the Polish revolt was not some remote historical event. It was connected to his life and to his Russian identity. As he mused on what it meant to be Russian, light snow began to collect on the window overlooking the Neva River behind him.

Hearing embedded cues in his father's voice about the combatants, he knew he was supposed to favor the triumphant Russians and disfavor the rebellious Poles, many of whom were punished for their insurrection with death or exile to Siberia after their defeat. Pleasure in their vanquishment dripped from his father's lips as he uttered the dreaded word "Siberia."

But in his young mind, Anton was puzzled at his father's antipathy for the Poles. Not only were the Poles outnumbered, they also seemed to be justified in defending their homeland from the more powerful invading army painted in red. Anton could not yet answer this question to his satisfaction. Instead, he maneuvered his blue soldiers into a flanking move and killed all the Russians every time he played the game. It seemed the fair thing to do.

Among the hundreds of brightly colored soldiers scattered across the table, he had a favorite. Somehow, this tin soldier had escaped being painted during its manufacture in Nürnberg and if one were to name its color it would have been silver. Anton could not remember if this soldier came in the box of red soldiers or the box of blue ones. No matter, it never seemed to fit on either side of the battlefield anyway. Anton solved the contradiction by rendering it into a scout that roamed the wild hills and valleys of the padded furniture and over the rough-hewn parquet floor made with spruce hauled in from the Siberian Taiga that lay in patterns beneath the dining room table.

One day his father noticed the lone-soldier hiking along the lumpy leather armrests of his favorite chair.

"Which army does this silver one belong to?" he asked after picking it up to inspect it.

"Oh, he's just a scout, father."

"Yes, but for which army son."

"He's just a scout," he answered with a wrinkled brow. He was annoyed that his father did not understand that the job of a scout had nothing to do with taking a side.

Smiling at the naiveté of his adopted son, Leonid Niktovich, an Admiral in the Imperial Navy, recalled the day that he and his wife took a summer journey to a church orphanage in Zaporizhia. It was a small town on the Dnieper River that lay a few miles north of the river's outflow into the Black Sea. After four miscarriages that had nearly cost his wife her life, adoption was now their only pathway to have a child and an heir. But a secret adoption was needed to ensure that the child would be graced with a noble birthright. Thus, they chose to adopt far from their home by feigning a need for an extended stay at a sanitarium on the Black Sea for her fragile health. Months later, they would return as the joyous parents of the child.

As his wife cradled the infant, Leonid Niktovich turned to the nurse.

"Do you know if he came from a Russian family?"

"I'm sorry sir, we don't know. The child was found on the steps of the orphanage carefully bundled in a wicker basket. But he does have the blue eyes, fair skin, and hair of a Russian, doesn't he?"

"Yes, but were there any other clues you might have overlooked - a symbol, a marking on the basket, a piece of traditional clothing, a note?"

"Nothing but this, sir," she said as she pulled a wide red sash from the closet behind her. "I forgot about it until just now when you asked. It was wrapped tightly around the basket to ensure the baby was secure in it. Whoever did it seemed to care about the safety of the child."

"This is a man's sash," said Leonid as he stretched it out between his upraised hands—"a Cossack sash."

"Yes sir. It would seem so."

"A Don Cossack, perhaps?"

"No sir. Not with a sash like that. This child came from a Zaporizhian."

"The ones who claim to see the future?"

"Yes, sir. Pagans, shape-shifters, and sorcerers all," she answered disapprovingly as the cross hanging from her neck swung from side to side. "And vicious too!"

Anton's father returned his mind to the present and surveyed his son's battlefield on the dining room table again still wondering what his son meant by not having to choose a side. He had no answer. But Admiral Niktovich concluded that his son would eventually learn that everyone has to take a side in matters of life and death, war and peace, justice and injustice—even a scout. He trusted that The First Cadets would rectify his confusion.

Chapter 2, THE FIRST CADETS, 1794

Gregor Ivanov was an upper-classman with a penchant for abusing younger cadets or anyone else that happened to be smaller than him. Though seventeen year old Anton Niktovich had never been the target for Gregor, Anton often saw him tormenting other boys including a boy named Alek. Alek was one of the few upperclassmen that Anton knew. He was the best chess-player at the academy, and he was Anton's friend. But he was also the most picked-on boy in school due to his small size and his bookish ways. Anton often played chess with him late at night in the dorms or the library. His many losses to Alek validated Alek's reputation for his prowess at the game—he was only able to beat Alek once. Other than chess, outwardly they seemed to have little in common. But Alek thought he perceived something in Anton that Anton had not yet realized about himself. Feeling a bond, Alek often told Anton what he was thinking or reading about on any given day. It flattered Anton that Alek would share such thoughts with a younger cadet. One evening after a game of chess, Alek pulled a book out of his satchel after looking both ways to see if anyone was looking. It had a bland title: *Journey from Saint Petersburg to Moscow.*

"It's a banned book," he whispered. Empress Catherine herself banned it. Sent the writer to Siberia. Called him a Jacobin."

"Jacobin," he responded quizzically not knowing what a Jacobin was?

"Read it and you will see."

Anton read it by candlelight in his dorm to the annoyance of his roommates. He found the title to be a ruse. It was really a political essay written as satire, and it was critical of Russian nobility. Alek said it was written by a nobleman with a conscience. The book implied that being noble as a birthright was unfair—as unfair as being born into serfdom and held in it for life. Anton found the concept both troubling and amusing but ultimately unpersuasive.

Nobles are born noble because they are superior by birth, he thought. *Everyone knows that—everyone except Alek—do I miss something?*

The next morning, Anton returned the book to Alek. Moments later, he saw Gregor corner him down the hallway and slap his books to the ground, the sound of the books hitting the floor echoed down the hallway. As Alek bent down to pick them up and obscure the title of the banned book, Gregor gave him a shove and sent him sprawling to the giggles of several followers in his pack. Anton saw his friend try to rise up with his spectacles askew. But Gregor kicked him in the face while he was still on his knees shattering his glasses and cutting his eyelid so that blood flowed down his face.

The word "stop," suddenly escaped Anton's teeth's barrier before he could restrain himself. And with that word, the bully slowly turned his attention to the younger cadet. Now nakedly exposed to the bully, Anton could run or stand his ground. To Anton's surprise, he felt a confidence and strength building within—imminent punishment from Gregor notwithstanding. As Gregor advanced, Anton straightened his shoulders, lifted his chin, and looked proud, as the muscles in his arms swelled with blood, and he waited for whatever Gregor had in mind. The bully stepped over Alek like a gorilla as he advanced menacingly toward Anton who he knew was an underclassman. Taking slow, deliberate steps with closed fists, he came within inches of Anton's face, which despite his younger age, was nearly eye-to-eye. And when the bully looked into Anton's gaze, he saw no fear, only a quiet resolve. And just when he realized that this victim might fight back, Anton's knee struck Gregor's groin with such force that Gregor's overweight body collapsed at once as if he had been shot through the heart and crashed to the floor eyeball to eyeball with Alek whose bloody face managed a hint of a smile. No other blow was struck, but as Anton helped Alek up from the floor and collected his books, he looked forward to the day that the First Cadets were rid of Gregor Ivanov. Gregor's dejected sycophants walked away and left their heretofore hero alone as he writhed and groaned in pain and cradled his testicles with both hands.

"Thank you," said a battered Alek over the moans of Gregor. Thank you for taking my side. No one has ever taken my side."

"You are welcome, but I didn't take a side. I just did what was right."

"Well, anyway. You are a good friend, Anton. So, thank you again."

"Yes, well, let's get you to the infirmary. Your eye doesn't look good - chess after dinner?"

A New Headmaster

The graduating class of the First Military Cadets in St. Petersburg was abuzz. A rumor was circulating that war hero Mikhail Kutuzov had been appointed as headmaster of the First Cadets, and he was to give an unscheduled address on the gun range the day before graduation. The venue was peculiar because speeches were never held there. Instead, they were always held on the Field of Mars parade grounds on the other side of the Neva River. In contrast to the pomp and circumstance that the Field of Mars afforded, the range was nothing, but a dusty field filled with spent lead and the remains of perforated targets that blew back and forth like the ghosts of imaginary soldiers.

Despite being a military academy for young boys born into landed nobility, not all of the cadets were destined for the military, and many had never even fired their muskets for practice. Some were taking classes in art, languages, and literature. In any case, it was an accepted fact that most of the cadets were more skilled at polishing their boots and shining their brass buttons for parades than getting their uniforms dirty on the shooting range.

Beside their annoyance with the hastily scheduled address by Kutuzov, some cadets gossiped about the Headmaster's rumored appearance. After all, he had been shot in the head in two different battles. One went straight through his left temple and exited the right. The other entered his right cheek exiting the back of his head and leaving his right eye badly disfigured. Most mortals would have expired from the first round. Many of his rivals even discounted his survival. Yet it was hard to dispute the many paintings of the hero that showed his injuries in ugly detail. The French surgeon who treated him said each bullet should have been a death sentence by all the rules of medical science. Despite that, he survived both shots to the head. And although everyone knew of his famous name and of his storied penchant for vodka and his predilection for young girls despite his ugly scars, only a few had seen him in person.

Known to be a brilliant military tactician, only a few of his colleagues knew of his ambitious plans to change the way battles were fought. What neither the cadets nor their aristocratic parents could have divined, was that he was determined to demonstrate this change of warfare on the firing range on the day before graduation. But that was not all he planned for that day. Included in his theme of change, he would also announce radical changes to the Academy itself.

The Long Rifle

When the date arrived for the Headmaster's address, the twenty-two graduating cadets were assembled with their muskets on the large open grounds that lay behind the Menshikov Palace where the First Cadets barracked. Most of the students fidgeted with their muskets having seldom fired them during their time at the Palace. All were children of nobles from St. Petersburg or Moscow, and the purpose of the school at the time was to mold them into what they were reputed to be by birth—nobles.

Military training was subordinate to cultural pursuits, although it was offered to those who aspired to become military officers. Civilian teachers taught all the subjects in the liberal arts including music, linguistics, drama, literature, science, and philosophy. Upon Kutuzov's arrival as headmaster in the spring of 1794, it was expected that he would make changes. After all, he had risen to the rank of Major General, he had the ear of Tsar Paul, and was used to doing things his way.

Most of the cadets standing at ease on the Menshikov Palace grounds waiting for Kutuzov to arrive were happy they were graduating and anxious to get the General's speech behind them. Nestled among the group of graduates, at the request of Kutuzov, was Anton Niktovich. He was an art student whose interests flitted between learning languages like French and German, the native languages of Siberia, and being fascinated with the adventure he believed the military might provide. The very word *military* equaled adventure to young Anton. And adventure was always twinkling behind his eyelids. It hovered over the brightly colored tin infantry soldiers that he pushed around the battlefield of his childhood even though Anton always saw himself off to the side or maybe in between the battling warriors. After all, he saw himself as a scout.

The cadet leader assembled the graduates in the large open area behind the palace and stood them at-ease with their Muskets at rest. Soon after that, a portly man in full-regalia riding on a muscular white horse entered the field through a gate at the right wall of the Palace. It was Kutuzov riding his snorting mount. He approached the cadets accompanied by the sound of the clopping cadence of his mount echoing from the walls. Once he was in position, the cadet leader called the students to attention. Kutuzov rode by the line of cadets showing only the unscarred left side of his face to his hushed audience. Occasionally he touched his hat in a condescending salute to them until he came to Anton. There, he halted his horse for a moment; gave him a proper salute, held it, and then clopped past the line of cadets to the gate on the opposite wall of the palace.

As he paused his snorting horse at the gate, the cadet leader called out: "shoulder arms," then "left-face," then "forward-march."

And with that, the line of armed cadets filed out of the Palace grounds dodging horse apples behind Kutuzov's mount and headed toward the open fields and the shooting range near the sea.

Arriving at the range, the cadet leader ordered that the muskets be unshouldered and stacked militarily. Then he directed the cadets to fetch fresh targets to replace the perforated ones that had succumbed to the damp sea breeze. Having completed their task, they reassembled in front of Kutuzov who was still seated high above them on his saddle. This was his first speech to the cadets since his recent arrival as headmaster late in the school year. His goal was not to impress this group of cadets. It was to begin a quiet launch of a message of change and distribute it like a virus so that the change would be from within. Always a tactician, he knew that these cadets would tell their noble parents, their siblings, and others of his message thus distributing the news and paving the way for acceptance by the administrators of the First Cadets. It was his way of setting an expectation. It was also the first salvo of his campaign to change infantry tactics forever.

"Men, and I call you *men* because you are now of age, we have fought our wars in the same inelegant manner for centuries. By unspoken agreement with our enemies, we have lined up our respective infantries and asked them to fire their muskets in the direction of the opposing forces sending a wall of lead their way. Then we would wait for a reciprocating volley from the other side and then we would count the dead. How many did we strike? No matter, we would say. If we hit enough of them, we will have won the battle. If not, we will have lost. But there is another way."

He nodded at the cadet leader who then ordered the students to get their muskets, load them, and form a firing line facing the twenty-two targets. Each target was shaped like an opposing soldier and together they formed an enemy skirmish line arrayed against the cadets. Four additional targets were isolated to the right and set a hundred yards further out toward the sea.

"Ready – Aim – Fire," called out the leader.

A blast of white smoke billowed forward as the muskets fired off in a stuttering out-of-sequence cacophony. After it cleared, the leader sent a cadet out to inspect the targets.

"Target one," yelled the cadet: "no hits."

"Target two: no hits."

"Target three: one hit."

He went on until he tallied the total damage to all the targets which added up to four hits out of the twenty-two.

"Niktovich," yelled Kutuzov, turning to look directly at Anton and displaying his mangled eye to him: "fetch your rifle."

"Yes, Sir," answered Anton, who strode past Kutuzov's mount and the shocked cadets.

Why was this underclassman even among us, they wondered?

Anton ignored the stares and retrieved his prized American-made Kentucky Long Rifle given to him by his Uncle Sergei who had returned from a diplomatic mission to Boston soon after the start of the American's revolt against British rule.

"Fire when ready," urged Kutuzov.

Anton set about placing the rifle butt on the ground, took out his powder horn, loaded the charger, and then poured the powder from the charger with its measure of gunpowder down the muzzle. Reaching into his leather pouch, he pulled out a ball and wrapped it with an oiled patch and set it at the opening to the muzzle. Then, he removed the wooden ramrod from the weapon, rammed the oily wrapped ball to the bottom of the barrel, and then placed the wooden ramrod back into its tube. After pulling the hammer back to the first position, he reached again for his powder horn, poured a small amount into the pan and the touch hole that led to the gunpowder sitting under the ball at the bottom of the barrel, tapped the pan to spread the powder, and covered it with the frazzle shield. After pulling the trigger back to the second position, he was ready to fire.

“Sir: requesting your permission to steady the rifle on this tree given the yardage?”

“Go ahead, son.”

Lifting the rifle, he balanced the barrel on a branch, took three breaths, exhaled the last and held still with his lungs empty, aimed at one of the four distant targets, squeezed the trigger, and fired. He repeated the loading and firing sequence three more times. Having practiced this load and shoot maneuver often under the supervision of his father, he loaded, aimed, and fired four rounds in two minutes as a wide-eyed and stunned group of jealous graduates stood in awe.

“Company leader, report on the targets,” commanded Kutuzov.

Running at a sprint while holding on to his sword and scabbard clattering against his legs, he reached the targets two-hundred-yards away. Out of breath, he yelled out the results haltingly such that he could barely be heard by the group two fields away.

“Target one, through the heart.”

“Louder,” boomed Kutuzov.

“Target one: through the heart, Sir.”

“Target two: through the head.”

“Target three: right lung.”

“Target four: through the head.”

Kutuzov may have retired from the battlefield to take over the First Cadets, but he was not done with influencing the Imperial Army's war tactics. His point with the demonstration was to change the long-held habit of firing walls of metal balls at the general direction of the opposing soldiers, and, replace that tactic with a focused and targeted approach. No longer would each side line up, fire, and hope for the best from inaccurate musketry. Henceforth, in Kutuzov's point of view, infantry would be armed with riflery that could take aim at specific targets and deliver lead with accuracy so deadly that it would take out the entire line of soldiers and, particularly their officers, with one blast.

A pleased Anton walked back toward Kutuzov who was smiling ear to ear and beaming out of his good eye. As he leaned over in his saddle toward Anton, the leather squeaked under the strain of his weight and his horse took a step to counter the load. Quietly he spoke:

"Good job son. Say hello to your father Leonid, and give your Uncle thanks for the long-rifle. Did I make my point?"

"Yes, sir, I think you did."

By the start of the following school year, Kutuzov had implemented his radical change to the Academy and fired all the civilian teachers. They were replaced with military officers who only taught military topics. And he continued to influence the Russian Imperial Army with fresh ideas about tactics and strategy.

Anton would be the last cadet to graduate from the Academy with a major in military strategy and tactics and minors in art and languages. But despite Kutuzov's re-focus on military matters at the Academy, he was astute enough to understand that some military missions required more than just ability to fire a weapon or obey a command. And in Anton, he recognized a young man destined for special missions.

Chapter 3, ANTON'S FIRST MISSION

After graduating from the First Cadets, Anton spent a year in the Russian Army as an intelligence officer deciphering indigenous Siberian languages at an institute in St. Petersburg. Then, in 1799, Kutuzov received a request from Alexandr Baranov who asked for a military intelligence officer with language skills to engage a tribe that had become troublesome. Baranov had been recently appointed as the Chief Manager of the Russian-American fur trading company. This company had been granted a monopoly to hunt, gather, and trade valuable furs with China, and it had the support of the Emperor and the support of the Imperial Army and Navy which were all keen on establishing a colonial presence in the Americas.

The company was most active in the new land called Alyeska, and Baranov needed a man who could quickly decipher the language of the mighty Tlingit tribe which ruled a fur rich island the Russians called Sitka. A man with Anton's skills could learn their ways, earn their trust, and help Baranov secure his trading post on Tlingit land. The only presence on the island was a weak post built as a small fort. The land was sold to Baranov by a Tlingit chief in 1799 to the disdain of other tribal leaders. This chief had sold him the land in return for

Baranov's promise that the trading post would benefit the Kiks.ádi clan of Tlingits whose main village lay a few miles south of the post. The easily assailable walls of the little fort were built with thin twenty-foot vertical logs. The perimeter of the fort measured a mere fifty by seventy feet and was poorly defended.

What Baranov planned to do beyond erecting this small beachhead on Sitka he did not confide to Anton. But the Tlingits quickly became suspicious of Baranov's motives and had harried his men with their arrows as they constructed the post that Baranov called Fort Saint Michael. Not to be taken lightly, the Tlingits were a powerful group that had confidently ruled Sitka and surrounds for thousands of years. Two earlier attempts by Russian squads to enter Tlingit territory by force were foiled. Neither party was ever heard of again. Weak and short of men, Baranov had reluctantly conceded that in the short term, diplomacy would be his only means of establishing a presence on Sitka if he wanted to expand fur trapping on that island.

The Tlingits, whose name translated to *the people of the tides,* were a sophisticated people. They had developed effective body armor and battle tactics sufficient to wipe out any Russian attempt at a forced occupation of the island. And they had the manpower, technology, and even modern musketry that had been supplied by rivals to Russian ambitions. Those included the British Hudson Bay Company and the Americans. Thus armed, Tlingits were a formidable threat to Baranov's small contingent at Fort St. Michaels. Therefore, whatever presence on the island that Baranov hoped to achieve would only be by the grace and consent of the Tlingit. And Baranov hoped Anton would be the man that could obtain that consent. He had the unique skills to learn their language, document their customs and manners, map their villages, use his skill at art to sketch the features of the land, and garner Tlingit approval of Russian activity on their island.

Anton's adventurous spirit relished the idea of living among savages as a scout or perhaps a diplomat between opposing sides. Confident in his noble birth and European superiority, he aimed to make short work of his mission and could find no reason to fear the savage Tlingit despite the begrudging esteem held for them by his superiors. He quickly informed Kutuzov that he would accept the mission. That evening, while a quarter moon shone down on the rooftops of St. Petersburg, he dispatched an acceptance letter to Baranov ensconced on an island in the Bering Sea. It would arrive six months later. At the same time a young woman danced alone by the light of the same moon six-thousand miles away in the Taiga forest that surrounded Petropavlosk.

Chapter 4, JOURNEY TO THE PACIFIC

Anton immediately set about readying for his land journey to the Pacific side of the Asian Continent. Travel by sea was not possible due to the perpetual ice in the Arctic waters north of St. Petersburg. Thus, Anton was faced with an adventurous but arduous winter journey that would begin on Christmas day. He took a full day to prepare. He decided to wear his army uniform for the first leg of the trip. It advertised his authority as an army officer and promised favored treatment of him along the way. For ease of carrying, he packed all the layers of clothing he would need to withstand the sub-zero cold in a seaman's bag. In a leather valise he packed a supply of paper, pens, ink, and charcoal he would need for his sketches of the land and the people.

He used another bag to pack a bearskin blanket to use while sleeping on the way or in stop-overs at hostels or the mail posts offering accommodations. The bags would stow well on the different types of transport he would be taking including a fast horse-drawn carriage, horse-drawn sledges, and horseback for the final leg. He packed his Kentucky long rifle in a purposefully crude and thus inconspicuous pine box along with a supply of lead balls, gunpowder, and a powder horn full of gunpowder. He wrapped the box in oiled canvas to protect it from the weather.

He carried two .32 Caliber overcoat pistols on either side of his fur-lined winter coat for the entire journey to protect against highwaymen. The normal targets for these robbers were mail carriers carrying gold, furs, silver, tea, or other valuables from the Far East. But they were known to attack the nobles and military officers on principle. That made Anton, in his army officer uniform, a target.

Though the journey would be long and tedious, he would use the time to plan his strategy to win over the Tlingits. Through his birth, Anton inherited a belief in the superiority of the white man over the savage and was confident he could persuade the Tlingit that it was hopeless to resist the Russians and to accept their small presence on their land. Still a naïve young man, he had never questioned the truth of that superiority. He believed that once the Tlingits fully realized the obvious preeminence of the Russian culture, that they would happily partner with the Russian America Company in the fur trade, and accept them on their land as a benefit.

The second part of his strategy was to rely on the universally held custom of hospitality among all peoples. While such rules of hospitality might be violated on occasion among some societies, most cultures felt obligated to protect visitors who posed no threat. That was why Anton purposely planned to live alone and vulnerable at an isolated unfortified outpost away from Fort St. Michaels. And while he would be armed, he would be one man among thousands of armed Tlingits. Under those circumstances, having weapons wasn't an effective defense. Tlingits could easily erase him from their territory at their will. But to harm such a hapless visitor would bring great shame upon them in most cultures, and his life would depend on his gamble that the Tlingits would feel that way too. The third part of his strategy was to earn their trust by learning their culture, learning the language, befriending them, and accomplishing his mission to placate this group of savages that were hindering whatever Baranov's strategic plan was for Sitka.

The first leg of his travel to the Russian Pacific Coast was from St. Petersburg to central Siberia. It would be a long trip of nearly four thousand miles. The only way to get there was by land travel over the Siberian Track which some called the Moscow Highway, and which others called the Siberian Route. Once in central Siberia, he would head to a small village established by Cossacks called Irkutsk. From there he would travel roadless territory via frozen rivers, frozen lakes, and overland horse-trails to Petropavlosk on the eastern coast of Russian Siberia.

He departed St. Petersburg on Christmas day. A swift Tarantass carriage carried him mail-post to mail-post along the Siberian Track. It stopped along the way for fresh horses. He slept inside the carriage except for an occasional stay at an Inn, postal station, or hostel.

The Siberian Track was the primary route for mail and parcels, including some shipments of high value originating from the interior of Siberia or imported through Siberia from China and Mongolia.

A week outside of Irkutsk after over two months of travel, a road-weary Anton was resting alone in the cabin when the carriage suddenly skidded to a halt when the driver pulled the brake and reigned in the horses causing them to whinny and rear up. Through the mist created by the heavy breathing horses, he saw two masked men shoot two of the troika of horses of a west-bound mail wagon coming towards his carriage and then turn their second pistols on the mail driver and the guard.

As Anton would learn later, among the mail shipment was a crate of raw gold carried from China as payment for Siberian furs. The gold was destined for St. Petersburg. As the highwaymen threatened with their pistols, Anton quickly reached into his winter jacket for his coat pistols, and held them cocked and at the ready in his lap after checking each frizzen for powder. One robber was yelling and demanded the crate of gold in broken Russian.

It was obvious that traders on the Chinese border had tipped off the highwaymen about this shipment of gold. Otherwise, how would they know this mail wagon was carrying the precious metal? The robbers seemed to be in complete control. But the postman suddenly pulled out his weapon and pointed it at the first robber's head before he could fire back thus creating a standoff with both men screaming at each other to drop their weapons. As the robber's horses nervously snorted and paced the icy ground, the other robber yelled out in his native language to the other and said:

"Shoot him in the head. Enough of this talk."

With that, a shot rang out hitting the postman between the eyes. Quickly following that shot the second robber fired on the guard striking him in the heart. Both were killed instantly and lay on the ground as their blood soaked into the dirty snow. After pulling their booty from the wagon, they remounted their horses, and each carried one end of the heavy crate by using the rope handles. Then they trotted menacingly toward Anton's carriage. When they reached it, they glowered at his driver and pulled their sabers with their free hands. Since they had unloaded their pistols into the postman, and the guard and had nothing left to shoot with, sabers were the only weapons they had left. Anton obscured his uniform with his winter coat and watched them from an open window. He held both pistols against the door, tracking them as they passed by. Dressed like most Russian peasants, they rode off but yelled "death to the Russians" in their native tongue as they passed.

Ob-Yeniseian, Anton thought: one of the languages close to Tlingit that he had been studying in the year after graduating the First Cadets. Seeing the carnage, he condemned them. *Savages,* he thought. *This country will be better off when they are converted to Christianity, and taught to speak Russian instead of their savage tongue.* Resist though they may, their destiny was inevitable as many older nobles in St. Petersburg counseled to young Anton.

He arrived in Irkutsk on February 15th after two and a half months on the Siberian Track. Leaving the

Tarantass carriage and the Siberian Track behind, he was now deep into the Siberian frontier. He traded his army uniform for the more practical provincial winter clothing. From Irkutsk, he traveled by a horse-drawn canvas-covered troika sledge on the Yakutsk Track over the Bratsky Steppe and arrived in Ust-Kut on March 15th. Ust-Kut lay on the west bank of the mighty Lena River. The frozen Lena wandered northeast and was a main route of travel to Yakutsk. It was usually frozen through the end of April, but not always. There were years when it thawed in early April. Several sledge drivers would not take him for fear of an early thaw and the risk that the ice would not support them all the way to Yakutsk. Each year two or three sledge drivers would die by drowning in the icy waters when they left too late in the season and their sledges broke through the ice and sank into the black waters below. But Anton finally persuaded a driver willing to take the risk after offering a higher price. Though he heard many loud cracks as the ice protested the weight of the heavy sledge and its troika of three horses, they traveled over 1,300 miles down the Lena and arrived in Yakutsk on April 15th. From there he would travel by horseback along the treacherous seven-hundred-mile Yakutsk-Okhotsk Trail to the coastal town of Okhotsk on the Pacific. He hoped to arrive there in early May 1800.

Chapter 5, THE COSSACK

Upon arrival in Yakutsk, Anton inquired at the local post about finding a guide to take him across the unmarked Yakutsk-Okhotsk Trail. The postman directed him to go up the main street to the livery. As he neared the stable, he saw a group of unsavory men leaning against a crude fence holding several horses. Anton guessed they were guides for hire and walked toward them carrying his luggage and gear. But before he reached them to inquire, a gruff voice called out behind him:

"Ilya take you."

Anton turned around and was startled to see a giant Cossack calling himself "Ilya." standing almost six and one-half feet tall with his hands on his hips wearing a long Cossack coat and a red sash. His towering hat made of from the skin of a Tundra Wolf and his piercing blue eyes and dauntingly large frame gave him a fearsome appearance. Anton estimated he was over fifty years old but had the bearing of a younger more vigorous man. Slung across the Cossack's back were a musket and a long iron-tipped lance. At his side was a curved sabre. Anton glanced over the other guides leaning lazily against the fence and sharing a bottle of vodka and was not impressed. Then he turned back to Ilya and looked him in the eye.

"You are sure you know the way?" asked Anton."

The Cossack growled out a "da, Ilya know," with an air of annoyance at the question and kept his hands on his hips as if he needed an answer soon.

"How much?"

After a short discussion, Anton had hired his guide.

True to his first impression, the Cossack spoke few words, and when he did, they came out as a growl. But after noticing Anton's army ring, Ilya was prompted to ask a question.

"You are soldier?"

"Yes, how did you know?"

Ignoring Anton's question, he simply stated: "Too bad."

"Why?"

"You see someday," he said as he took a swig from a silver flask then offered it to Anton.

"You drink?"

"No."

"You will," he predicted as he took another drink.

By the end of the fifteenth day of the month-long journey on the trail to Okhotsk, the Cossack had spoken no more than two dozen words with Anton. On the sixteenth day, they started to go higher into the mountains. It was then that the Cossack riding on the lead horse pointed to a ridge where a Roe Deer was eating grass from a patch of ground where the spring snow had already melted.

"Good dinner but too far," he said while breaking his silence but leaving his musket stowed.

"Maybe not," replied Anton as he dismounted and untethered his Long Rifle from his pack animal.

Loading it quickly, he was ready to fire shortly. The distant Roe felt no danger standing so far away and continued to munch on spring grass as Anton steadied the rifle on the rump of his saddle horse, took three deep breaths, exhaled, held, and fired. Almost a full second passed when the roe deer dropped to the ground, and Anton's saddle horse reared knocking Anton backwards into the deep snow behind him and covering his face and head with ice crystals. He looked like a snow-angel with a rifle. The Cossack laughed so hard he nearly fell from his saddle.

"Good shot boy. Good dinner tonight," he said between guffaws.

"Thank you," sputtered Anton, still trying to get to his feet.

"You drink now?

"No, I not drink now," mimicking Ilya's broken Russian as he finally gained his footing and replied. "I not drink now."

"You gut deer now?"

"No"

"Why not, your deer?"

"I don't know how," bellowed Anton feeling both angry and embarrassed.

"Too bad, I show."

After deftly gutting and sectioning the small deer, Ilya fashioned a spit over a crude fire pit made of random stones along the trail. After roasting a leg, he pulled a pot from his kit and sliced several slices of the meat into the pot with wild onions salt, pepper, and mushrooms along with a cup of fiery Chinese vodka. Then, without asking if he wanted it, he gave Anton a cup of vodka to drink. Weary from travel, hungry, and with the smell of good food cooking, he accepted the belly-warming drink with a thank you.

"I was soldier once," Ilya announced without explanation or warning as if it were adding to a conversation between them. "You like mushroom, Mr. Soldier?" he asked with a twinkle in his eye as he looked up from the fire that painted his face with a red glow?

"Da," answered Anton too quickly not knowing that Ilya had picked a special red and white mushroom along the trail.

"Why Chinese vodka?

"Chinese trade for Ilya's gold. Good vodka. Everybody like in Russia."

"You have gold?"

"Ilya find a little maybe."

Late in the evening, the pot of roasted venison and mushrooms had simmered down to a delicious smelling brew and Ilya served the stew.

"Good mushrooms," complimented Anton.

"Da, special," answered Ilya with a wry smile. "I learn mushroom from Yakut woman."

"Your woman?"

"Da. Good woman."

"And where is she now?"

"Dead."

"I am sorry. What happened?"

"Cossacks kill whole village. Long ago. You Soldier. You have woman?"

"No."

"You will.

Anton considered asking why Ilya should have such annoyingly strong opinions on his future but let it go.

They ate under the starlight with sparks popping from the dying fire rising to the sky and they would sleep in the open on the snow without a tent that night. Vodka warmed their bellies while Ilya kept half an eye on Anton until they both felt sleepy and bedded down. Anton kept his pistols under his blankets just in case someone of ill-will might be coming up the trail as they slept.

Soon Anton was in a deep sleep, but even in his slumber, he felt odd. The divide between sleep and awake, real and imagined, grounded and untethered addled his mind. He was not sure if he might just be hearing Ilya mumbling while drinking vodka by the fire instead of him dreaming his own strange thoughts with his mind in disarray. Finally, he succumbed to a vision no longer caring if he was hearing a story, a history, or just dreaming. Shivering in his blankets on the snow, he saw, or maybe he heard Cossacks on the march.

Cossacks with lances raised to the sky filtered through the frigid night on horses guided by starlight reflecting off deep snow while the Borealis spread a ribbon of green glow across the northern sky. It had been years since they marched in force against the Koryaks having subdued them long-long ago along with the other tribes like the Yakuts, Itelmens, and Chukchis. Empress Elizabeth herself had ordered they all be exterminated, and some were. But that was in the distant past. Now, when there was the occasional incident or even a small rebellion, the Cossacks always punished with cruel force to remind them of Russian rule, and the consequences of defying it.

This time it was about a young girl who was taken from her village by several drunken Cossacks to a lonely place by a river. After raping her, they slit her throat and threw her body to their dogs. Ten Koryak warriors tracked them down, found her body, and attacked the three Cossacks. Two were beheaded and brought back on pikes to the village along with the remnants of the young girl for her burial rites. The third Cossack was beaten, castrated, forced to eat his own testicles, and then tied to his horse which trotted back to the large contingent of Cossacks camped downriver. Before he died, he told of the attack by the Koryak warriors, and soon the whole troop of Cossacks was drinking, working up a blood-lust, and crying out for vengeance against the godless savages. Only one Cossack was against it. He was the largest and fiercest among them. He was also a Sorcerer who saw the future. And he forbade them to avenge the rapists.

The others ignored him and near midnight they rode out toward the village upwind to avoid alerting the dogs with their scent. Slowly, they walked with their horses as they neared the village. When they were close enough to charge, they mounted but moved slowly. As soon a dog would bark, or an alarm be raised, the Cossacks would gallop ahead, lances tilted forward, and impale anything that moved from dog, to Reindeer, to man, woman, or child. The massacre went on for nearly an hour in a din of triumphal whoops raised by the Cossacks over the moans of dying savages until the Cossacks were too tired to kill any longer and drank more vodka to sacrament their work.

Ilya the Sorcerer was the bastard son of a peasant mother from Zaporizhia and a Cossack cavalryman from the Caucasus. He surveyed the scene. The virgin snow covering the village grounds was trampled by the hoofs of the Cossack horses and stained by blood leaking from the dead and dying Koryaks. Ilya had always been a good soldier and always followed orders, but the murderous killing spree made him ill and he vomited his dinner of venison and the acidic greens culled from a reindeer gut on to the bloody snow. With his head and lance lowered, he pulled on his reins to turn his horse, return to their encampment, and leave the ugly scene behind him. He feared it would never leave his soul. As he wheeled his horse, a naked young girl stepped barefoot through the bloody snow into his path and held up a newborn infant. She pointed to her chest and then to his lance then back to her chest. She wanted to die. She and the infant were the lone survivors of their village.

As he sat in his saddle high above the girl, the infant let out a cry and several Cossacks came up behind them. One laughed.

"Kill her," he said as he took a drink of vodka from a bladder cut from a Caribou. "She's a worthless savage."

The girl ignored the taunts of the other Cossacks and kept her eyes on Ilya.

"Kill me," said her eyes, "take me from this tragedy" they seemed to say.

"If you don't kill her I will," said the other Cossack who leveled his lance toward the girl and the baby and spurred his horse forward.

Suddenly Ilya the Sorcerer pulled his saber, hoisted it high, and cut the Cossack's lance in half and the iron tip fell into the snow. The insulted Cossack looked confused. Ilya was the largest man in the unit, and not to be provoked without consequence. After a few tense seconds of indecision by the man whose lance was severed, the entire unit of Cossacks erupted in laughter. No one can predict how a Cossack will react to an insult from another Cossack. But by destroying his comrade's lance, he had insulted one of his own in front of his entire unit and a level of face-saving from the offended Cossack seemed in order. But the irony of a kindness given by Ilya toward a savage he was sworn to kill was somehow funny to the Cossacks. Soon they quieted, and the troop rode silently past him downriver toward their encampment. But none dared to look the Sorcerer in the eyes with his hack up so high. After they passed to leave only the sound water gurgling from the nearby river, Ilya stepped down from his horse, pulled a blanket out of his bedroll, and wrapped the girl and the baby. Then, he lifted them onto his horse and rode away from his comrades. The girl and the baby were sisters. The infant was called Kamak, and her sister was called Cheyvyne.

"How you sleep?" asked Ilya.

"Not good," answered Anton as leaned over and vomited his dinner of venison and mushrooms on to the snow next to his bedroll. "Not good."

"Cold water on face. Stream over there," pointed Ilya.

"You have a bad dream."

"Da," very bad.

"Did you tell me a story last night?" asked Anton.

"Story? Nyet, Ilya no tell story. Ilya sleep all night. Have best sleep for long time."

For days after the dinner of Roe Deer and mushroom stew, the Cossack went from taciturn to almost talkative, his tongue being loosened by his frequent snorts of vodka. When he was drunk enough, he sang. When he got more drunk, he told Anton about his life. Anton learned that Ilya lived with two young Koryak women on the outskirts of Irkutsk. But Ilya never said that either was his woman. He had belonged to a Cossack Cavalry unit until a few years ago, but now his main occupation was guiding rich patrons from Irkutsk or Yakutsk to Okhotsk. He also traded things with black-market traders that moved smuggled goods along the Amur River which bordered China and Mongolia. He had built a hostel for wealthy travelers coming to and from the west that he hoped would earn steady income. Anton also learned that, after the Cossack finished his task of guiding him to Okhotsk, he would be returning along this same route to guide a young noblewoman from Petropavlosk to Irkutsk. Once there, she would hire a carriage to take her along the Siberian Track back to St. Petersburg thus reversing the route Anton had just come by.

Except for Ilya's occasional singing or a random observation on wilderness that he shared with Anton as they traveled on through the mountains, they settled into a comfortable routine as they rode to the steady cadence of the horse's hooves punctuated by the occasional plop of horse apples on the trail. As the horses trudged forward, Anton noticed that every once in a while that Ilya would lean over on his saddle to pick a dry twig off a bush or tree, crush it, hold it up to inspect it, and then deposit it into his pocket. It happened often enough that he wondered just how big his pockets were and what the purpose was of his constant pruning of the brush. Now as they gained altitude, the trees began to thin and disappear as they passed above the tree-line and the snow became deeper and deeper.

Ilya continued to puzzle Anton. He had never known a Cossack that was not attached in some way to other Cossacks, especially to other Cossack Cavalry, or Cossack organizations called Hosts. He also wondered why Ilya lived in an isolated Siberian town with two

Indian girls. But mostly he wondered why the facts of Ilya's life that he did tell him so closely paralleled his terrible dream about the killing of the Koryaks. He put it off to the idea that Ilya had probably babbled pieces of the story to him along the trail, and he had not been paying full attention.

"You were in the Cavalry?"

"Da," grunted Ilya. "Thirty years in Siberian Host. My village called Pokrovsk on Lena River."

"You retired?"

"Quit."

"Why?"

"Ilya already take his eighty-one acres from St. Peter."

"St. Peter."

"Da. Government promise Ilya eighty-one acres for twenty-five years soldier."

"So, you did retire?"

"Nyet. Ilya take land by river before he quit. No kill Indians no more. No more forever," he said as he took a big swig from his bottomless silver flask, and then spat it out. "You drink?"

"Not now," said Anton as he mulled Ilya's pledge about not killing Indians anymore. *Anymore? How many had he killed?* His mind conjured infants hoisted on the long Cossack spears and felt his stomach turn a notch. It all reminded him of the tormented dream that came to him after their venison mushroom stew. Although he knew that the taming of Siberia had involved the near annihilation of savage tribes by Cossacks, the image of babies on spears brought the cruel reality home. He promised himself that his work with the Tlingit would be honorable. No babies on spears—savages or not he promised himself.

The next day, as the horses strained against the grade going up a steep almost treeless valley, Ilya pointed to the pass ahead and announced with some excitement: "storm come."

Anton squinted at the horizon and saw nothing, but Ilya picked up the pace. Soon they reached the only stand of trees to be seen for miles amid a pile of rocks and a flat spot for a tent.

"My place," said Ilya. "Good camp. You start fire, I make tent. Snow come."

"But it's spring."

"Da, big snow."

Ilya went about laying out the tent while Anton struggled with the fire. The small trees surrounding the flat spot had been picked clean of small branches for kindling by previous travelers leaving only the larger branches which would not ignite when Anton struck his steel and flint sparker. Anton's striking soon became frenzied as if he thought that he could overwhelm the branches into lighting, but it was futile. Ilya saw all of it from the corner of his eye, but let him struggle until the tent was erect needing only the guy-lines tied down. Then he strode over and dumped all the twigs and sticks he had been picking up along the way for days and dumped them in the fire pit.

"Kindling."

"Da," answered Anton barely looking up. His questions answered about why Ilya had been collecting twigs and stuffing them in his pocket for days.

An hour later they were covered in snow pushed by high winds coming over the pass. Anton was glad for the tent, and for the fire that cooked their second batch of venison gleaned from the Roe. This time Ilya did not add mushrooms.

"Chinese tea or vodka?" asked Ilya.

"Tea," answered Anton who had been missing his ritual evening tea since leaving St. Petersburg. "Why is the vodka Chinese?"

Trade with Chinaman for gold.

"Why?"

"Can't eat gold. In this land, tea is Ruble. Tea is food. Tea is drink. Poor Cossack punished for have gold, so Ilya trade gold for Chinese tea, Chinese vodka, and Chinese citronella. Then Ilya trade those things for other things Ilya need."

As the overland trip to the Pacific neared its end, Anton's brain was still addled by his dream, and how close Ilya's vignettes of his life fit his fitful nightmare.

"Ilya, I have a question.

"Da"

"When I awoke back on the trail and asked if you had told me a story about killing Koryaks, you said no."

"Da"

"Was that true?"

Ilya sat in silence for a moment, tugged at his beard, and appeared to be observing the stars. Then he answered firmly: "Nyet."

"Ilya a big strong Cossack but Ilya have sad story. Sometimes have to tell. Easier to tell story after mushroom and vodka soften head. Better as dream."

Anton noticed Ilya's eyes were wet as Ilya continued. "Sorry I lie, comrade. Now you know Ilya's days as soldier. May god forgive poor Ilya."

With that, Ilya seemed satisfied that the telling of his tale had done its purpose. Anton had no idea why he was the one chosen to hear it. Perhaps, he thought, Ilya the old soldier saw something in Anton the young soldier. Maybe it was the same as what Alek saw in him. In the dream, he called himself *Ilya the sorcerer*. Anton knew that Zaporizhian sorcerers, like shamans, claimed to see the future and peer deep into the souls of men. But perhaps it was nothing more than the idea that confession was good for the soul. Whatever it was, Anton took it as a kind of manly intimacy – a sharing of pain - the pain of guilt and death that formed a bond. *But I've killed no one,* he thought. *Why me?*

It had been a meandering five-month journey of over six-thousand miles first by Tarantass, then by overland trek on a sledge, then by sliding up frozen rivers on another sledge, and finally by following a seven hundred mile trail on horseback that took Anton across the whole of Russia to the shipbuilding port of Okhotsk. From there, he would board a vessel and voyage another thousand miles north to the Kamchatka Peninsula and the harbor town of Petropavlosk. There he would layover and rest a few days before taking his final voyage across the Bering Sea in mid-June to the land of the Tlingits on Sitka.

On their thirty-second day trekking by horseback over the mountainous Yakutsk-Okhotsk trail with Ilya, he came over a rise and saw the vast Pacific Ocean for the first time a thousand feet below the trail. He and the Cossack zig-zagged down the steep hills to a river drainage that led to a sandy beach then turned north toward the shipbuilding town of Okhotsk. There, they turned in Anton's horse and the pack horse at the livery. Soon a ship would take Anton to Petropavlosk a thousand miles to the southeast around the southern tip of the Kamchatka Peninsula, then north to Petropavlosk.

After a layover waiting for a vessel, a merchant ship from Boston that had sailed around Cape Horn stopped on its way to Petropavlosk, and Anton secured passage. Using gestures and a few words in Russian, the ship's captain informed Anton that he hoped to pick up a load of furs in Petropavlosk. From there he would sail south to China to trade for goods like tea, silk, silver, or gold. Impatient to finish the journey and finally reach Petropavlosk, Anton walked quickly across the wooden gangplank and boarded the ship, glad to leave Okhotsk behind. As he opened the door to the inner rooms of the vessel, he heard the unmistakable sound of horse hooves clopping across the lower gangplank and looked back to see Ilya paying for his fare to Petropavlosk in raw gold that he pulled from a thick leather pouch.

Chapter 6, PETROPAVLOSK BY THE SEA

Eighteen-year-old Nadia Anichkov was a woman who had the lithe look of a ballet dancer, and it was true that she performed at the top of her ballet class. In a town as small and as far away from the Bolshoi as anyplace in Russia, no one bothered to call her a Prima Ballerina though her arch-rival, the ambitious and resentful Katarina Vasilev, could barely spit out Nadia's name out of jealousy for her prowess on the floor. But Nadia's passions extended beyond the confines of a dance stage. It was the sheer joy she felt as she moved artfully through space. Off the wooden dance floor, she felt it in the forest, the mountains, and by the sea, though she confided those euphoric thoughts about movement through wild places with no one. While her family limited her to aristocratic pursuits like piano, dance, and horse jumping, her secret desire was to float barefoot through verdant forests like a Grecian Artemis. Fleet of feet, Artemis the huntress carried a bow and a quiver of arrows and chased quick running deer through the pines by the light of the moon over which she ruled. The Kamchatka peninsula offered all of these loves even if she was not allowed to openly embrace them. Where her primal feelings for wilderness came from, she did not know, but she had a suspicion.

Half-Indian children were not unusual in the fur-hunting region of Petropavlosk and Alaska where Russian women were vastly outnumbered by lonely Russian men. Baranov, the head of the Russian American Company, had three such children with a Kenaitze Indian woman on Kodiak Island while his Russian wife stayed behind in Irkutsk, Siberia. But Baranov was the son of a low-ranking merchant with no ties to aristocratic nobility. Thus, having illegitimate children with an indigenous woman had little effect on his already low standing in the social hierarchy of Russia.

But for general officers of noble birth, having an Indian concubine, or worse, having a mixed-race child with such a woman was a serious matter that could damage their social standing. And in Petropavlosk, one such rumor about a high ranking naval officer was still being repeated almost twenty years after it began, but no one was certain of the parties to the scandal.

As the story went, this officer had gone to a far-off post in Alaska leaving his wife behind in Petropavlosk. Soon after he arrived in Alaska, he took a young Indian girl as his concubine. This girl was the mixed-race daughter of a Russian trapper and an Indian woman from the Aleut tribe. Soon, the girl became pregnant by the officer and bore a beautiful blue-eyed daughter, but her mother died in childbirth leaving the baby orphaned.

When the officer's barren wife in Petropavlosk learned of the love-child she sailed to her husband's outpost in Alaska. A devout Catholic woman who descended from Venetian nobility, she forbade her husband to abandon the child to an uncertain fate at the mercy of her tribe. One year later, she and her husband took the child and sailed back to Petropavlosk, and she presented it to her friends as if it were her own. Peeking beneath the blankets, the women cackled about how exotic the child looked, unaware that the child's blood was mixed with that of her husband and his Russian-Aleut concubine. The mix synthesized her features in a way that was both curious and comely.

Over the years, many in Petropavlosk still wondered who that mixed-race girl was or whether the old story was even true. But by the age of eighteen, the faintly copper-skinned Nadia had concluded that she was likely that Aleut-Russian baby, though she never asked her mother if she was. She knew it through the soles of her feet and the joy she felt when she danced alone in the forest by starlight. And she liked it.

That June, Nadia and the entire class of five dance students burst out of the dance studio into the afternoon sun. Petropavlovsk was a small Pacific Coast settlement founded just forty years before Nadia's birth. It lay four thousand crow-fly miles from civilized St. Petersburg. But as Anton Niktovich had just experienced, it was a six-thousand-mile journey across indirect routes. Distant as it was from civilization, its upper-class inhabitants, mainly naval officers from St. Petersburg, made efforts to ensure that their children had a proper upbringing in culture and the arts including dance despite their isolation from civilized centers of Russia.

Nadia stepped into the sun, closed her eyes, and hungrily drew in the competing smells in one deep breath. There were aromas of the ocean, fish, seal droppings, pine, remnants of melting snow, and a fowl-smelling distant tannery. All of the odors swirled up the street and hugged the masts and rigging of the tall ships in the harbor. With her eyes still closed, she heard the harbor bell ringing out to herald a ship at full sail in the distance nearing Petropavlovsk. It was probably returning from *Alyeska*, the exciting fur-rich land across the Pacific, and the only reason that Petropavlosk existed at all. She opened her eyes again to see the billowing banners that were strung across the street announcing the Festival of St. John which would start later in the day.

To her left, within speaking distance, a man carrying a long canvas bag and a long rifle over his shoulder trudged head-down up the steep road from the harbor toward a row of cottages. Nadia stood alone at the gate of the dance studio as the other girls rushed out of the building led by Katerina who bumped into Nadia's shoulder as she passed. Nadia ignored the intentional affront and Katerina's hollow apology. The group of four then giggled their way up the hill together to the big houses where the naval officers lived and left Nadia behind. A crisp sea breeze tugged at Nadia's white dress and the long tufts of spring green grass that surrounded her feet. As the young man came closer, he glanced up. Like her, he had deep blue eyes set in a kind face browned by some kind of outdoor work that she could not divine by his clothing. He smiled at her. Startled, she frowned and looked away as if she had not seen him, then glanced back, then away again. His look remained steady. After he passed, he cast his eyes ahead and walked on. Nadia turned and walked down the hill toward the ships even though her house was in the other direction. She swiveled her head over her shoulder every few seconds to see which cottage he went to. Later, when she turned to go back up the hill to go home, she had no choice but to walk by the stranger's house.

His cottage was set on a rise apart from the other summer dwellings. The back of the house looked Southeast out over Avacha bay, and to the Pacific and Alyeska beyond. The front of the house faced Mt. Koryaksky and Avachinsky, two of several volcanoes ringing Petropavlosk that grumbled every few years.

Nadia knew he could not be just a seaman. They were forbidden to live this far into the town. Most seamen lived at-the-ready in the boarding houses down by the ships, and the upper-class townspeople frowned on them if they overstepped their bounds, even if they could afford it. *Why was he here*? she asked herself. A gull perched on his roof. As Nadia approached, the gull's head bobbed up and down screeing, "Hraaa, hraaa, hraaa." Its head bobbed faster and faster in time with its ever hastening scree. Then he lifted his wings to the breeze and wafted north off the roof toward the volcano without even the beat of a feather. His head turned to watch Nadia with one eye as she neared the white picket fence surrounding his house. Fresh geraniums poked through the picket throwing purple and lavender color along the walk while a single red rose cast a bluish shadow on the white clapboard of the house. A lace curtain blew in and out of the upstairs window with each opposing tug of wind.

Nadia slowed her pace as she approached the gate to the cottage. It was then that he appeared - muscular and shirtless in the window holding a silver razor high in one hand that glinted in the sun. His face was half-covered with shaving cream. Nadia, startled to see him in the window, quickly straightened herself, set her shoulders, lifted her skirt a few inches to keep from tripping as she picked up speed, and aimed for her home with her lips pulled flat against her reddening face before he could see her. As she bustled up the hill, she muttered and blustered unintelligible reproaches to herself until she reached her father's house whereupon she kicked the gate open and glowered down the hill toward the stranger's cottage.

The stranger stepped back from the window and leaned over the small mirror that hung above the porcelain sink. The mirror was wood-framed and painted with bright green enamel. Gold-leaf cruciforms danced in patterns around the frame. Afternoon sunlight streamed in from the window that faced the gate. Inside the room, the sun lit up faint flecks of lint that had sloughed off the curtains. A light breeze blowing off the Pacific blew the airborne bits of fabric back and forth in the room. He looked cross-eyed to notice a spot of shaving soap on his nose and wiped it off before resuming shaving with a chuckle. With his left hand, he touched the edge of his black sideburn and lifted it before striking it deftly with the razor he held in his right. His hands moved with the swiftness of a card player, and the accuracy of a swordsman. He repeated the maneuver with his left hand taking care to miss the protrusion of his cheekbones which stood out high on his face, and was especially careful to miss the dimple on his chin below his lower lip.

On the blue enamel dresser laid a half-opened journal. The first page lifted slightly in the breeze, then it dropped back flat. As he made the final stroke of his razor, the wind lifted the page to the third leaf and laid it open to show several studies in charcoal. One showed the Menshikov Palace where he had completed his studies as a First Cadet. Another showed a long rifle leaning against a tree in a forest.

When he was done shaving, his face was smooth and brown. He rinsed his razor, dried it, and placed it in a case. Then he took care of the brush, cup, and soap. On his way to the porch overlooking the town and the sea, he reached for the sketchbook, closed it, and then pulled the leather cover over the binding. On the lower right of the cover was embossed: ***The First Cadets of St. Petersburg, Anton Niktovich.***

Anton sat in the afternoon sun with the journal in his lap and mused on a thought for half an hour. Then he began to draw. As he sketched, he left large patches of white as he made marks and squiggles elsewhere on the page with the charcoal. A stranger looking over his shoulder would not have recognized anything at first: dark and light, light and dark, a tone of grey side-by-side with a dark black line. Then suddenly, a figure emerged from the sunlit page. It was a young woman standing rectilinear straight. She had a long shock of black hair that glistened and shined at the top. Shadows cast by her face, hair, and bosom cascaded down her white dress and collected in a dark mass by her feet. She wore black shoes, stood on fresh grass, and looked to be a dancer. At first, he drew the lips straight and firm, but he made the eyes flash with fire. Then he laughed and played with the mouth. He drew a faint smile upon her lips and forced her head to cock slightly to one side. Her eyes still flashed, but they laughed at the same time.

Twenty-five-year-old Anton had a one-week layover before he could board the ship that would take him from Petropavlosk toward the island the Tlingits called Sheet'-ká X'áat'l and the Russians called Sitka. When he was strolling up to his summer cottage through the town, he noted that the people were excited about

The Festival of St. John and the celebration of the summer solstice. He was familiar with the celebration because it was held all over Russia, even St. Petersburg. It was really two festivals with one overlaying the other.

One was a Christian festival that parents approved of. But the other was an older Pagan rite that they did not condone, yet could not seem to keep some of their more adventurous children from partaking. Centuries before, Russian priests had tried to Christianize the original pagan festival by melding it into the Festival for St. John. The one for St. John the Baptist took place at mid-day and involved dancing and other festivities at the harbor. The Pagan festival was called Ivan Kupala and began after dark. Kupala was held deep in the forest and involved mysterious rituals. For a man with a week to wait for his next voyage, it was fortuitous that he had arrived to Petropavlosk in time for the two festivals. He recalled that years earlier while confined within the walled palace and home of the First Cadets, he had managed to sneak out past the night-guard to attend Kupala. This was his chance to do it again. He spent the rest of the day settling into his cottage, sorting gear for his mission on Sitka, and sketching the volcanoes that circled the town. Because of the high latitude, the sun would not set until ten at night. And that was when the young people would filter one-by-one or two-by-two into the forest where Kupala would begin.

Nadia, the copper-skinned girl he had passed on his way to the cottage, and her pale adopted sister, Anna Maria were also thinking about joining the Kupala celebration. As Nadia mused on the thought of the pagan rite, her face took on a mischievous look. The idea of sneaking out of the house and venturing deep into the woods late at night seemed deliciously naughty. While she was too young and proper to have yet experienced Kupala, she knew it involved a ritual baptism in a cold lake, a search for a magical fern-flower, and a bonfire over which lovers would leap barefoot while holding hands. For the young aristocracy in Petropavlosk, Kupala was an excuse to sneak away and frolic in the forest long after bedtime. Especially delicious in her mind was the possibility of espying the strange man she had seen earlier in the day.

Chapter 7, IVAN KUPALA

Nadia and Anna Maria went to bed early that night, stretching and yawning in front of their oblivious parents to show them how tired and sleepy they were. Before retiring, Nadia busied herself by topping off her father's wine glass until his eyes became glassy. When his eyes glistened, it was a good sign that he would fall asleep in his chair and that his wife would soon be snoring in her bedroom. Then with a "Good night, Mama" and a "Good Night, Papa," Nadia and her sister Anna Maria pretended to retire to their beds. Instead, they propped up pillows to make it look like they were still sleeping under the covers. Nadia donned the traditional wreath of Kupala flowers she had secretly made earlier in the day. Then they plotted how to get from the second story of the house to the ground without waking their parents. They decided to exit their bedroom window via the porch roof and climb down one of the Sitka-spruce trees that surrounded the house. Nadia swung from a high branch down to lower branches until her toes brushed pine needles lying on the ground and she stepped down. Anna Maria grabbed the main trunk and shimmied down rubbing slivers of bark into her dress until she let go and tumbled the last five feet falling awkwardly on her face. After standing up she shook her head to rid herself of pine needles in her hair and dusted splinters off her dress but only succeeded in transferring them to her fingers.

"Eeew," was her response as she looked scornfully at her fingers and her dress. Soon it was dark.

In Petropavlosk, Kupala was held at a small-nameless lake that lay in a clearing of dense Taiga forest to the south of town. Starlight and a crescent moon lit the path worn by fishermen and hunters leading to the lake and beyond. Nadia liked the fact that the lake was nameless. In her view, by the time all lakes and ponds had names the "wild" in "wilderness" would have lost its meaning and succumbed to the will of man. As Nadia led the way, she felt the tread of the trail through her shoes. Her skill at feeling her way down the trail was keen enough that she could stay on the path even with her eyes closed. The smell of pine along with wild celery and wild onion filled her nostrils as she held out her arms to her side to feel the wildflowers and berry bushes scrape her fingers as she walked by. While Anna Maria snapped twigs, tripped, fell, and often cursed, Nadia stalked silently along after they entered the thick forest which hid the moon and stars. Now, every faint shadow began to look like a bear and Anna Maria inched closer to her sister and held on to her white dress to guide her.

"How do you know where we are going," Anna Maria complained.

"I don't know. I just do."

"You know Nadia, I think that Katerina is right - you are that little half Indian girl: the girl in the rumor. You walk trails like an Indian."

"Katerina told you that?"

"Yes, and the rest of the girls too."

"Well, you will have to ask momma or papa about that," she answered.

After a mile of walking, they reached a clearing where a freshly lit bonfire ten feet tall was sending flames and bright sparks and embers high into the dark purple sky and painting the faces of other young people from town with a glow of golden light.

There were only three venues to the Kupala ritual. First was the jump over the bonfire. That would take place later after the flames had died down. Then there was a hunt for a magical fern flower that no one ever seemed to find. Nadia knew it was just an excuse for girls to wander through the forest with boys. Ferns, she knew, do not flower, and she wanted no part of the fern flower hunt but knew that her sister would. And so would Katerina Vasilev, her rival at the dance studio. The third venue was a pagan ritual of baptism in the cold lake. For some reason, Nadia was fond of both cold and water. Each seemed pure in their own way.

Walking around the meadow surrounding the lake on sponge-like grass she reveled at the light of the quarter moon shimmering on the almost still waters. Picking up a flat stone, she hurled it onto the lake surface with a side-arm worthy of a boy and counted the skips. "Eight." Then she tried a heavier stone, but even though it was flatter than the first, it did not go as far and only skipped three times. As she picked up a bright white quartz stone and readied it, another stone slapped the water twenty-five feet to her left and skipped eleven times before sinking into the middle of the lake.

"Anna Maria, is that you? Nice rock skipping!"

"No," came a man's voice from the other side of a bush. "It's not Anna. I'm called Anton. Sorry if I startled you. It looked like fun so I thought I would join in. You're quite good with that. How did you learn to do it?"

"I don't know. I think I just always knew how to do it."

"Born with it eh," concluded Anton in reply.

"Yes, maybe."

Then, after an awkward silence and feeling ill-at-ease talking to a stranger she could not see, she asked if he was going to go on the search for the flowering fern.

"No, I don't think so. You know it really is a futile exercise." Showing off his botany with: "Ferns don't flower."

"They don't?" she quizzed, as if she did not know?

"No, but I think I will jump the bonfire a bit later, skip a few more rocks, and maybe even get baptized."

Feigning shock, she asked: “you’re not baptized?”

“By the Orthodox Church, yes - by Pagan Gods, no. Think I should?”

“It’s really cold in there you know?” she evaded.

“Cold and water are two of my favorite words.”

“Well then, maybe we should get baptized together?”

“Yes, why not,” he answered as he strode over in her direction and stood near her as they both faced the edge of the lake?

“Ready?”

“Yes.”

And with that, they strode into the sandy-bottomed lake making hardly a ripple as they pushed against the snow-melted water and went further and further out. Nadia’s gauze dress swirled behind her until they both stopped when the water was just over their waists.“

“Lovely isn’t it?” she asked in a relaxed voice as she listened to the roar of silence.

“Delicious as my father used to say,” he answered. “Now what?”

"I think we are supposed to submerge," she answered.

"All right then, ready?" Anton held out his hands and faced her.

"Ready," she answered.

Then they both went under holding hands. Each heard the bubbly silence of the cold water and each could see the dimly lit face of the other graced by the moon and stars through the crystal clear water. As they rose up from their immersion, drops of water from their hair and clothing rained back into the lake making a tinkling plopping sound and Nadia's wreath of flowers fell off and floated away without sinking. Exiting the waters Anton was struck by the beauty of Nadia as her white dress clung tightly to her skin. Without a towel, they wrung out their clothing as best they could and headed for the warmth of the bonfire.

"Cold and wet is good, but warming up afterwards is good too," said Anton. With the fern flower hunt holding no interest for either of them, there was nothing left to do now except leap the fire. A key part of Ivan Kupala was jumping over the flames while holding hands with a friend or lover, or even a sister. As this part of the ritual began, people lined up on either side of the pyre. Pairs of leapers would then run toward the fire holding hands and jump barefoot over the flames. If they landed on the other side while still holding hands, they would be friends or lovers forever. If they broke apart during their leap or after they landed, it was not a good sign for their future. Pair after pair leaped over the flames to the shrieks and laughter of the encouraging people lining the bonfire until finally, it was Nadia and Anton's turn.

Holding hands twenty feet away from the fire, Anton turned to Nadia: "Ready?"

"Yes," she answered with a determined wide-eyed grin, and they both ran toward the pyre holding hands with the glow of the fire on their faces.

As they reached the flames, they leapt high into the air. Nadia floated like a ballerina as the light from the fire lit up the white soles of her bare feet, and Anton bounded like a hurdler on a track race. When they landed on the other side, they tumbled askew into the soft meadow-grass almost losing their grip. But Nadia squeezed hard and would not let the grip fall away. Getting up, they brushed the pine needles off of themselves and looked sheepishly at each other.

"By the way, who are you?" she asked while laughing at her audacity for being in the company of a man she had not been properly introduced to.

"I am Anton Niktovich," he answered.

"No, I mean who ARE you?"

His answer started with a "Well." After droning on about his pedigree, ties to nobility, and the First Cadets, and his journey from St. Petersburg to Petropavlosk accompanied by a Cossack named Ilya, he informed Nadia of his mission and his imminent departure to the island of Sitka. The news of his travels relieved the pressure on their nascent and unexpected relationship. But she winced at the probable danger he would soon be facing, even as she envied the adventure of it. Both realized their chance meeting could not grow to be more than a budding friendship and perhaps result in a few letters between them to let the other know of new events in their lives.

Nadia informed Anton that she would be traveling soon on a trip from Petropavlosk from which she would probably not return. She was being sent to St. Petersburg within weeks. The weather that year had been unseasonably rainy in Siberia and would affect her travels. The frozen rivers that Anton crossed with a sledge in the bitterly cold winter travel-season were now running high. But the unusual rain was allowing a late-season departure by boat and foretold a more comfortable lazy passage on the long trip back to St. Petersburg.

She was eager to experience the perilous journey but was not pleased with its purpose. She was being forced by her mother to leave Petropavlosk and live with her aunt and learn all the proper things that an upper-class Russian woman should learn. Those things would probably include having been more circumspect about being baptized in a pagan ritual with a strange man she had just met. Her parents were especially concerned that Nadia had grown up in the provinces in complete ignorance of polite society. Thus, her mother, Justina Chelishchev had enrolled her at the finishing school at The Smolny Institute for Girls, and she encouraged her to continue with her ballet at a studio in St. Petersburg. After all, as her mother told Nadia many times, she had once been a popular ballerina herself. She had danced at the Teatro San Benedetto near her girlhood home in Venice, until she married Nadia's Russian father, Admiral Timur Ulan Anchkov who promised her a life of great adventure. On the day of her marriage in St. Marks Basilica, she could not have divined that her adventure would be a life of misery in a backwater place called Petropavlosk on the other side of the earth from civilization and surrounded by savages.

After Nadia's future graduation from the Institute for Girls in St. Petersburg, her mother hoped that she would join high-society and live with her aunt whose home sat on the banks of the Fontanka River, not far from the First Cadets. Of course, there was always the chance that Nadia might return to Petropavlosk. But even if she did return, it would not be for at least a year or two.

Thus, despite their successful hand-holding leap over the bonfire by the lake, it did not look as if their relationship could go much beyond a friendship they might build over the next few days. As the bonfire burned down to its embers, Nadia promised to show Anton around the tiny town the next day, and Anton agreed to show Nadia his beloved rifle, and maybe the sketch he made of her when he first saw her standing in front of the dance school that sunny morning. As they walked back along the unlit trail back to town under the dark cover of the trees, Anton spied movement twenty feet to his right. Stopping in his tracks, he reached for his knife at his belt. A shaft of moonlight briefly lit upon a bearded man in a wolf-skin hat half-hidden behind the trunk of a Sitka spruce before he vanished into the night like a ghost without a sound.

"Ilya," concluded Anton. "He is a strange man."

Anton's ship was scheduled for arrival at Petropavlosk to take him to the Tlingit's Island in four days. On the first of those days, she escorted Anton around the town. First, they went to the harbor and inspected the ships anchored at the docks. Then they went northeast toward the fur tanning factory. Though the odor coming from it made their walk unpleasant, Nadia wanted to show Anton the mix of Indians living around the outskirts of the town on the other side of the tannery. Aleuts, Koryaks, and Yakuts were among them. She did not know why, but they fascinated her with their primitiveness, their poverty, their filth, and their difference from civilized people. She wondered aloud how they had survived in this frigid wilderness for so long with the vacant look she saw in their eyes. Nadia scratched at her arms in sympathy with their dogs covered in fleas so thick that their fur seemed to be moving. She knew these Indians were a beaten people and that their very existence was scorned by their conquerors. They were a people whose hearts and dreams had been scraped from their souls. But she imagined that in the wild, there must have been a dignity about them that they had lost in defeat and in the loss of their land.

"There must have been, don't you think?" she asked.

But neither of them really knew. Then, she asked Anton an odd question.

"What would you think if I was part Indian?"

"You? I hardly think you look like an Indian. But if you were, I suppose I would say that you are a very pretty one."

"No, that's not what I meant. I mean, what would you think of me? You, Mr. Anton, son of noble birth, firmly ensconced in privilege, what would you think if one of those women we just saw was my grandmother?"

"My apology, I sense now that you are asking me a real question. And so, I will give you a serious answer. First of all, I don't think you are an Indian, so the question feels silly. But secondly, if the question is—would I consort with a woman whose grandmother was an Indian—would I do that? My candid answer is that since I have never been faced with the prospect, I have no idea. Are you telling me that you are an Indian?"

Nadia demurred. She and Anton spoke little more on that walk, and they were glad to be back at the docks late in the afternoon. Anton could not decide that the tension between them came from the sight of the poor Indians, or from Nadia's strange question. But he hoped tomorrow would go better.

The next day, Anton had her sit on a log in front of his house and then fetched his sketchbook. Handing it to Nadia, she marveled at the drawings. He had documented his entire journey across Russia and Siberia and even the voyage from Okhotsk to Petropavlosk, something she had never experienced herself. She especially liked the image of the man he called Ilya who sat tall on his horse ahead of Anton on the trail. The last two drawings she saw were of her. The first was from the day before. He had captured her in front of the dance studio while standing in the full sunlight. There were shadows at her feet. The second was of her as she stepped into the cold clear lake wearing her white gauze dress and her Kupala wreath made of wildflowers. She was turning back with a smile and with her hand outstretched toward his. She marveled at how he had captured her image by moonlight. And she knew he had captured the image not only on paper but in his memory, and it felt intimate, sensuous, and delicious.

"They're beautiful, and you are a gifted artist Mr. Niktovich," she said, quite pleased that he had put her image to paper.

Feeling his emotion rising, Anton went on to distract her with the mundane. He showed her his manly Kentucky long, and his pair of coat pistols: the same kind of weapons that women carried in their muffs on the long journey across Siberia to St. Petersburg. Holding the pistols up as an offering, he said:

"Take these. They will protect you on your trip."

"Oh, I mustn't." I've never even learned to shoot one of those things.

"Well then, there's no time to lose since I am to leave soon," he said as he grabbed his powder horn, side-bag, the pistols, and her hand and strode up the trail toward the lake where they were baptized during Kupala. Standing next to a large spruce, he took ten steps toward Nadia. With the second pistol still secured in his belt, he half-cocked the first pistol, opened the frizzen pan to check for powder, re-closed the frizzen, then pulled the hammer back to a full-cock. Then, he aimed and fired at the tree blasting bark away and scaring an eagle in a nearby tree and causing it to fly away over the lake in haste. Now standing close behind Nadia who faced the tree, he reached over her right shoulder and placed the second pistol in her right hand. Nadia felt his breath faintly on her neck and felt a quiver scamper down her spine.

"You are right-handed?" he asked.

"Yes."

"Good. Now, while you aim at the tree, pull the hammer back to a full-cock, with your left hand." Following his instructions, the pistol clicked into the firing position. Are you aiming at the tree?"

"Yes."

"Are you ready to fire?

"Yes."

"Then squeeze the trigger slowly and shoot. Do not pull the trigger, just squeeze."

Fearing the blast and the recoil of the pistol, Nadia slammed her eyes closed, jerked the trigger, missed the tree and the pistol flew out of her hand to the mossy ground below. After a moment of silence, Anton announced: "We will need to practice a little more."

By the end of the day, Nadia had learned to keep her eyes open as she aimed and fired, and she managed to hit the tree at least half of the time. Anton was also pleased that she never dropped the pistol again. He knew she would not have to be an expert shot to scare a highwayman into ending his assault. Just brandishing a pistol at a robber should be enough or so he hoped. But if it did not scare them, firing it would. And if that didn't work, she had a second pistol. As the afternoon shadows grew long, Anton carefully reloaded the pistols, placed them in a lacquered black box with some extra black powder and balls, and presented his gift to Nadia earning a curtsy and a "thank you kind sir" for his generosity.

Then, suddenly feeling guilty that he would be going unarmed among the Tlingits without them, she protested: "won't you be needing them when you get to Sitka."

"No, don't worry, I have two more pistols among my gear. I want you to have these with you on your journey. It will make me feel better knowing you have them."

"Will you write?" she asked.

"Yes, I will write. But you know the letters will take months, and that much will have happened between the mailing and the receiving."

"I will write anyway," she said.

"Then we have a pact between us," said Anton as he walked her back to her home.

Anton now had just one more day before his ship would arrive to carry him to Sitka and away from Nadia, perhaps forever. Even as they were saying their polite goodbyes, he felt a dread come over him at the thought of never seeing her again. Although they had only just met, parting was too soon and too final for a budding relationship that seemed so pregnant with promise.

Suddenly and without his will, an impromptu invitation welled up from his soul that would not be denied.

"Meet me at dawn - before sunrise at the lake?" he asked suddenly to his surprise.

Feigning offense at his impertinence, she asked "Whatever for? Dawn will be very early this time of year. And me, alone at night in the wilderness with a strange man?"

"Yes. Dawn. That will give us more time, and I'm hardly a stranger anymore."

"Time - time for what?"

"Time for me to see you one last time and sketch your image next to our lake so I can take part of you with me to Alyeska."

Flattered that he would want to draw her again, that he referred to the lake as theirs, and that he wanted a part of her with him on his journey she asked, "Dawn?" as if she needed to put it in her calendar.

"Yes, and wear your Kupala dress," he insisted boldly.

That night Nadia curled up on her side and went to sleep with a pillow between her legs biting her lower lip in anticipation of what she was not sure. But she felt a glow near her belly. After midnight she awoke every few hours to ensure she did not miss the breaking of dawn out her window. Finally, when the forest outside began to form black silhouettes against the bluish blackness of impending dawn, she excitedly but quietly exited her bed, donned her Kupala dress that he had insisted she wear, and slid out the window. Then she climbed down the tree next to the porch roof with ardor and purpose. Still almost inky dark, she ran barefoot hurriedly up the trail through the forest until she reached the clearing by the lake breathing hard. Stopping still, she heard nothing but her heart pounding against her lungs causing a faintly audible pant. Just then, a rock skipped ten times out to the middle and she held her breath waiting to hear Anton.

"Hello, my beautiful one."

"Hello, my friend," she answered as the tension in her shoulders eased and she filled her lungs again with needed air. "Hello, Anton."

Nadia turned her head slightly down and faintly askance with eyes wide open and fixed on Anton. Then she launched into a barefoot sashay across the soft green spongy growth beside the lake while swishing her gauze dress over to Anton who sat on a bright white granite rock lit by starlight with paper and pen beside him. When she reached the rock, she took a playful akimbo pose and held it under the heavenly light from above until Anton spoke.

"You are quite a sight young lady."

"Why thank you Mr. Niktovich. And what brings you out so early this morning" she teased?

"You. Just you Nadia," words that sent shivers down her spine.

In the dim light Anton discerned a mischievous smile as the brightening dawn backlit her dress betraying the outline of her legs thinly draped in white gauze.

"Dance for me?" he entreated in a tone that was both a request and a demand at the same time.

Taken aback for the moment, Nadia then bathed in the sweetness of his request even as she detected a trace of lasciviousness around its edges that she felt in her loins. At the same time, she felt honored, adored, and seen by Anton for asking her to dance by starlight in the wild by a lake surrounded by pine. *He sees me*, she thought. With that, she stepped away from his rock to get closer to the lake, took a starting pose, and then danced quietly to the lilting music of the spheres as Anton sketched and sketched. Intoxicated by her own movement as she floated over the meadow, she lost track of time until finally the sense of an ending tugged, and she took a final pose as a coup de grâce to the soft applause of Anton.

"Beautiful," he said softly.

Putting down his sketchpad, he went to her and they stood face to face for several moments before he pulled her toward him, and they kissed and then pulled back smiling again.

"Baptism?"

"Again?

"Yes."

With that Anton began to unbutton his shirt and Nadia reciprocated by pulling the pins from her hair and let it all fall to her shoulders. Crossing her arms in front of her, she grasped her dress near her waist and pulled it over her head tossing it to the ground showing Anton the full glory of her body. Anton in turn removed the rest of his clothing while holding his eyes on hers. Then they held hands and walked together into the ice-cold lake just as a sliver of the sun cracked into view above the Pacific. As they submerged into the glacial waters, a swirl of bubbles caught the rosy-fingered light of dawn and floated up toward the fading stars.

Chapter 8, THE EDUCATION OF NADIA

Nadia had been born and raised in the provincial outpost of Petropavlosk. Despite being the daughter of a high ranking naval officer with a noble pedigree, her exposure to the cultured ways of civilized Russians far to the west in Moscow or St. Petersburg was limited. Her mother had been plotting to change that for years, but had procrastinated on telling Nadia of her plans. One night over dinner a few weeks before Kupala, her mother abruptly blurted out what she had dithered on telling Nadia.

"Nadia, you will soon be sent to St. Petersburg to stay with my sister Maria and attend finishing school."

Rushing to get it all out quickly, she added: "I know you have never met her, but she knows all about you. We write often, and I tell her everything. She has no children of her own, so she has a special interest in you."

Shocked at the suddenness of her mother's announcement Nadia dropped her spoon into her bowl splashing Ukha soup all over the tablecloth and her father's white shirt. Eighteen years old and very independent, Nadia stood up from the dinner table, put her hands on her waist, and protested.

"How much more Russian do I need to be," she pouted. I've learned ballet, play the piano, have read all of the classics in Literature, and learned the history of the world."

Wistfully, her mother answered. "Books and learning will not get you a worthy husband. It might even drive men away. A man does not want his wife to be smarter than him. He would rather she knit while he is off to war."

"Isn't that true my husband?"

But he was still daubing at the Ukha soup staining his shirt and ignored his wife's attempt to help her frame a truth for Nadia.

"Maybe your ballet will count for something? But worse, there is a part of you that is a little bit unpolished—no wild about you Nadia," she said with a dash of motherly worry.

"And you know, noble and wild are contradictory terms," vaguely hinting that she knew of Nadia's infatuation with wild places and more.

"You are a beautiful girl in your own way, but you have edges in need of polishing, proper eligible men for you to meet, theaters, ballet, and even tea houses to visit if you are ever going to be part of polite society."

Then with a hint of a sneer aimed at her husband, she added: "You will see soon enough that Petropavlosk is a small dirty little place."

Nadia listened to her mother with a furrowed brow and tight fists, but, as her mother went on about the treacherous months-long journey to St. Petersburg that lay ahead, she grew naively excited. How thrilling it would be to book passage on a ship to Okhotsk, hire horses and a guide to cross the mountains to Yakutsk, and boat up the Lena River to Irkutsk and on to St. Petersburg on the Siberian Track. Her mother and father, having completed the trip themselves two-decades earlier, viewed it as an unpleasant trek that they never wanted to experience again. They were resigned to die in hardscrabble Petropavlosk. It was a trip so arduous that they expected Nadia would never want to ever return either. In fact, her mother secretly hoped she would never see her daughter again. But in return for losing her, she hoped that Nadia would rise in Russian Society with the help of her wealthy and socially connected sister, Maria, who lived alone as a widow on the other side of the long continent.

"Here is Maria's last letter to me. She mentions you. It came last week," she said tersely as she thrust it out toward Nadia above a bowl of dried apricots and shook it as if it were proof of something.

Dearest Sister Justina,

Oh, how to start. I am so excited about your proposal. In answer to your question, yes, of course, I will be most pleased to take Nadia into my home, enroll her in finishing school, and take care to introduce her to the proper people. We have a very good finishing school for girls that is very close-by. And as for ballet, the Big Stone Theatre which is dedicated to ballet is also just a few miles away. I am sure I can introduce her to the ballet company. There is a new ballerina there that is something of a rising star. I have met her myself and can introduce Nadia to her. They are almost the same age. Of course, as a ballerina yourself, you know that Nadia could never aspire to be an important ballerina this late. But at least she will have that polish to her background. Who knows, it might even help her to attract an upstanding man of stature?

Dearest sister, having Nadia as my niece is the closest I will ever be to having my own daughter. Through your kind and constant letters starting with the day she came into your lives from that primitive island I think I have learned to know her a little even if we have never met. And I have certainly been apprised of her affinity for the wilds of Petropavlosk. Perhaps she will learn to appreciate what St. Petersburg has to offer even if it lacks for wilderness. Tell her that we do have lovely parks with well-tended trees. I am looking forward with great pleasure to seeing her near the time of Christmas, God, and weather willing.

Your Loving Sister,
Maria

"What island is she talking about mother? asked Nadia after reading the letter.

"Oh," her mother stammered, "I'm sure she just meant Petropavlosk. Maria confuses easily and simply misread my letters describing Petropavlosk as a place that is almost surrounded by the sea: which we are, aren't we?"

"Yes, that is true…almost surrounded," answered Nadia flatly with a far off gaze on her face.

As the day neared for her departure, Nadia pretended to be afraid of the dangers along the trip while ingenuously relishing the idea of traveling such a long distance over rough territory alone. In her bedroom, she opened the weapons box and excitedly hefted the two pistols given to her by Anton before he sailed away to Sitka Island the week before. As she pointed the pistols menacingly at her image in the mirror, she delighted in the feeling of power and independence the pistols gave her. But her credulous hopes for a solitary trip across the continent, impractical and perilous as they might be, were dashed when her father told her that he had hired a man to accompany her and keep her safe. The man was to meet her on the dock next to the ship that would take them from Petropavlosk to the Yakutsk-Okhotsk trail.

The next day at the harbor, her father introduced her to an old Cossack man named Ilya, whose business it was to guide people across the wilderness. Though still pouting that her trip would not be a solo adventure, she managed to greet him cordially.

"Nice to meet you, Mr. Ilya, she said as she saw something familiar about him. Have we met before?"

"Nyet," he answered. Fierce looking, tall, and bristling with weapons, he spoke little. But when he did speak, Nadia noticed that his voice growled and formed only the most basic of words in Russian. To Nadia's eyes, he was a fine specimen of a man for his age and surely a skilled protector. As she shook his hand in greeting, the silver fur of his hat blew back and forth with a slight puff of wind.

"Ilya is an old acquaintance and loyal friend to Russia," said her father as he introduced them to each other. 'In his youth, he and his band of Cossacks tamed savages like the Yakuts, Koryaks, Itelmens, and Chukchis along the Lena River Valley, the Kamchatka Peninsula, and the shores of Lake Baikal. Ilya worked for the Russian Government as a scout. He knows every inch of the land between Okhotsk and Irkutsk. His instructions are to take you as far as Irkutsk where he will hire a carriage for you to travel overland via the Moscow Track to St. Petersburg. Now daughter, if Ilya gives you a command, you will be wise to obey it."

Nadia curtsied and said, "yes father," resigned to be chaperoned, but still excited at the prospect of a grand journey. *At least he's a tough old Cossack and not some smelly old fat man*, she thought. As she held that sentiment, she kissed her crying mother goodbye, gave an obligatory smile to her sister who was looking the other way and stepped across the gangplank to the ship followed by Ilya who lifted her trunk to his shoulder with one arm and carried the one-hundred pound trunk to her cabin. As they walked to her berth she asked him a question.

"Mr. Ilya, did you guide a man named Anton to Petropavlosk a few weeks ago?

"Da, I take across the Yakutsk-Okhotsk trail. "He good boy. Good heart. Good on horse and good with rifle, but talk too much and know little."

Ilya's terse assessment of Anton intrigued her. Having known Anton but for a few days, she also sensed that Ilya felt the goodness in him like she had. And the old man's frank comment that he was a "good boy," as he put it, was reassuring even if she did not understand what he meant by "knows little."

Uncomfortable with calling Ilya "Mr. Ilya," she asked: "Mr. Ilya, do you have a last name?"

"Nyet."

"Well then, what was your father's name?"

"Not know." Turning toward her, he donned a toothy grin and said: "Never met him."

Then with a wink, he said, "call me Kalnyshevsky, it is as good as any name."

"Well then, Ilya Kalnyshevsky it is."

After stowing her luggage, Ilya returned to the harbor, went to the livery, and fetched his horse. Then he secured him in the animal hold with food and water below the decks of an American merchant ship out of Boston that would take them to Okhotsk. Then he laid out his saddle, weapons, and trekking gear before he lay down on the soft hay strewn across the floor of the stable and took a nap as his long-maned horse named Kassandrov munched oats and stood watch. Eight days later, they arrived at Okhotsk.

Nadia disembarked the ship wearing trousers, knee boots, and a linen tunic. She had learned to wear men's clothing whenever she practiced horse jumping or trekked through the forest surrounding Petropavlovsk. The trousers protected the tender skin on her legs from the rubbing of the saddle and horse-hair and was far more practical than the more proper and customary riding dress for women. Once, when she was admonished by a proper woman in town for wearing trousers while riding her horse, she had a ready retort.

"If they were good enough for Joan of Arc, I suppose they are good enough for me."

Ilya had already ported the luggage and taken his horse to the livery to pick up a mount for Nadia and two pack horses. Ilya saw her walking across the sand toward him wearing men's clothing and with her long hair stuffed into a hat. She looked like a boy, so he looked twice to make sure it was her.

"Good porty," he said summarily, referring to the style of pants. "Good for ride horse."

It was early July and very warm for the coast, so Nadia wore no jacket.

"You wear coat?" asked Ilya who was astride Kassandrov and donning a string of garlic, citronella grass and mugwort to wrap around his neck.

"But why would I, it's so warm today?"

"Mosquitoes," he said tersely.

Nadia smiled condescendingly. "I'm not afraid of bugs," she said as she dowsed Cinnamon powder on her face, neck, and arms. It had always worked in Petropavlosk where the air was usually washed over by southerly breezes from across the bay in summer keeping mosquitos to a minor nuisance.

"You see soon," he snorted. "Ilya have medicine when you need."

"Thank you but I shan't need it," she assured confidently. "I don't like the smell."

"You like soon," he promised.

As they rode up the trail from the sea at Okhotsk into the mountains, ever-larger clouds of mosquitos came in waves across the landscape and descended on Nadia. The high-pitched whining of their wings ignored her cinnamon defense and attacked her neck and face. They even poked through her thin linen tunic to her tender skin. Ahead of her, she saw Ilya riding high in his saddle almost free of the pests and singing to himself in a language she could not understand, and she could hold out no longer.

"You say you have more citronella – mugwort?" asked a besieged Nadia as she swatted away the relentless beasts and struggled to avoid breathing them into her lungs.

"Da. You want?"

"I want."

Ilya stepped off Kassandrov, and put a smelly necklace around her neck and helped her put on her coat and gloves. When he was done, he readjusted her strong-smelling necklace, patted her on both shoulders like a grandpa, and grinned. "Now you ride like Cossack Missy," he proudly exclaimed. Her porty pants and her boots would protect the rest of her body, but she would itch everyplace else this night at camp and go to sleep with a face full of bumps.

"Better?" he asked.

"Da," was her answer as she heaved a sigh of relief from her buzzing tormentors. Thank you, Mr. Kalnyshevsky. You are kinder than you look."

"Da, Ilya very nice Cossack."

"By the way, where do you find Citronella?

"China."

"And mugwort?"

"Sayan Mountain – can see mountain from Irkutsk."

As they crested a pass above tree-line and started down a rocky valley cut by a fast-flowing stream they came to a flat spot surrounded by boulders.

"Camp here," said Ilya abruptly - my spot."

"Your spot?"

"Da. Anton and I stop here for camp. We talk."

"About?"

"Man talk."

Clicking her heels into the ribs of her horse, she rode up even with Ilya. "That's silly. Men are no different than women when they talk."

"Da. Missy right. All same. Like sour berry and sweet apple—both fruit."

"So, what did you men talk about?"

"Killing Indians," he said as he dismounted. "Missy, know how to make fire?"

"No"

"You killed Indians?" she asked incredulously.

"Da. When Ilya not know better—now he know better. "Missy, know how to raise tent?"

"No,"

"Missy and Anton good match," he grumbled.

Nadia watched carefully as Ilya unrolled the tent, set up the poles, pounded in the stakes, and set the guy lines. Then she noticed he had kindling stored in his pockets for a fire along with a few medium-sized branches he had picked up along the way stuffed into his saddlebags. Stacking the kindling loosely on the ground, he struck his steel and flint and started a small blaze, making it burn hotter by blowing into it. After it was started, he laid larger by larger branches on top until they burned as a pyre sufficient for dinner.

She good learner, like Anton - not have to show her again. Looking up with the glow of the fire on his face he asked:

"You know how cook?"

Presuming that she could not, Ilya cooked a humble dinner of wild onions he picked from the banks of the creek and dried venison stew after they settled into camp. Ilya laid his blanket outside, and Nadia lay on hers inside.

"Food always better outside," he asserted as he tossed an onion into his mouth?"

"You are going to sleep outside?"

"Da. Better outside."

Nadia smiled at his rustic sense of chivalry and then peppered him with questions about his life and where he lived. "You live in Irkutsk?"

"Da."

"What is it like?"

"Good enough place. Have many crazy people. Ilya feel good with crazy people. Sane people bore Ilya."

"Crazy people?"

"Da. Everything not same. One is Pole. Another is Koryak. One is Jew man. One man always think. Another always write. Friend play chess. Woman always read book. All crazy, all come from other place. Irkutsk all mixed up like salad, and dressing always different."

"And you Ilya. Do you read?"

"Da"

"Like what?"

Smiling, he answered with a strange sense of pride. "Ilya read sky, read trail, read stars, read trees, read water, read horse, read people, read future. And when Ilya not reading, he play chess with Jew man and Pole—sometimes Ilya win."

"You said you read the future?"

"A little bit maybe. Or maybe just dream," he answered as he glanced up to peer through her pupils and read the look in her eyes.

Chapter 9, SITKA, SUMMER 1800

Three weeks after saying goodbye to Nadia at the harbor in Petropavlosk, Anton arrived at Sitka and disembarked the ship to the land of the Tlingits. With him were two sailors and they rowed a longboat to shore and beached it near Baranov's contested fort. It was called Redoubt Saint Michael, and it was the only Russian foothold on Sitka Island. The three of them carried building and sawing tools, food, and supplies for the small cabin Anton intended to build there. The goal was to follow a Tlingit trail three miles northeast to a lake with no name where he hoped to engage the Tlingits and establish a dialogue in a setting that would be neutral and non-threatening to them. There on a foundation of granite, he and the two sailors set about building a shelter across from the shallow blue pond.

Opposite the site for the cabin was a well-worn trail used by the Tlingits to travel north from main villages on the Pacific side to deep fiords on the other side where rivers and streams drained into a bay and provided salmon-rich fishing grounds. The trail also provided Tlingits access to mountain goats. These animals were a source of food, but more importantly, they prized the mountain goats for their dense wool that the Tlingits used to make intricately woven blankets and other clothing to keep them warm in the arctic climate. Anton's cabin location would give a good view of the trail two hundred and fifty yards away, but it purposely did not encroach upon it.

For self-defense, Anton armed himself with his American made Kentucky long rifle and a pair of .50 caliber flintlock pistols. As Anton had demonstrated to Major General Kutuzov in St. Petersburg, his long rifle was accurate to two hundred twenty-five yards as he had proven more than once during his army training to the awe of his fellow Cadets. But if the Tlingits were to decide to rid themselves of Anton and deny him the protection of the laws of hospitality, neither his long rifle nor his pistols would be able to hold off an attack for long.

Upon their arrival at the lake, Anton and the two men accompanying him went about building the cabin using yellow cedar split into long planks. They used planks for both the floor and the walls. Then they stacked stones for a fireplace, and used mud covered logs to form the flue. Then, they covered the roof with bark. All in all, the cabin mimicked the houses Tlingits had been building for thousands of years on Sitka.

The bare spot of granite that Anton chose for his shelter had the advantage of a clear view to the other side of the lake where the trail cut through the woods, and the disadvantage of having no timber growing nearby for firewood. The only exception was a tall Sitka Spruce that had rooted through a crack in the granite and gathered just enough nutrients to survive on the otherwise barren rock. For firewood, he planned to cut timber on the other side of the lake and then float it across like a barge, propelling it through the water using poles against the shallow bottom. Soon he completed building the cabin. The only thing missing after he carved firing slots into each side of the structure and through the door was glass for a window to see through and keep the mosquitos out. From his cabin, he planned to make drawings of the surroundings. In the place of a glass window that he wanted, he mounted a solid wood shutter on the only opening in the cabin other than the door to keep out the cold. What the shutters and firing slots could not do was keep out the mosquitoes. They were everywhere. So, even in summer, he kept embers in the fireplace to smoke up the cabin to deter their entry. Mosquitos don't like smoke. The other benefit was that Anton smelled more like burnt pine than the infrequently washed man that he was.

Anton said goodbye to his companions who had helped build the shelter. He waved as they began their hike back down the mountain with muskets on their shoulders to the ship anchored below. He wished them good luck and hoped they would not encounter any Tlingits coming up the mountain. The cabin now completed, he began to settle in and develop household routines. From scraps of cedar left over from the build, he stacked them up to make sitting spots outside. He chopped the rest of the scraps into usable sizes for the fireplace and stacked it against the side of the cabin. And every time he ventured to the other side of the lake, he made sure to drag a usable spruce sapling back to add to his firewood supply. Two weeks later, he had yet to see even one Tlingit.

Then, the next morning he awoke to a thud against the door. Jumping out of bed naked, Anton went for the long rifle, but because the threat was so close, he picked up the two pistols instead. Naked and with guns in hand, he peered out the defensive slots. Seeing nothing, he slowly opened the door. An arrow had struck the door head high. Looking at the arrow near his head he remembered what a naval officer had said to him before he took on his mission:

"Son, the Tlingits don't like us. Don't expect them to welcome you into the territory. It's their territory."

Anton was keenly aware that two Russian expeditions using longboats launched from the ship Saint Paul fifty-nine years earlier on Chichagof Island just north of Sitka had never returned to their ship. And several Russians were also killed while building Fort St. Michael in the year before in 1799. But Anton was gambling that a solitary presence would not be viewed as a similar threat and that the custom of hospitality usually offered by indigenous peoples toward harmless strangers would prevail.

Over the next few weeks, he welcomed each morning by opening the door to see another Tlingit arrow. It had become routine, almost like a macabre good morning greeting between enemies at war, and he began to leave them in place as a sort of comment that he was not going to budge. Soon the door looked like a porcupine. Toward the end of summer, the days were becoming colder and colder.

Early in the morning, Anton felt a chill and was stoking a fire when he heard desperate yelling in the distance across the lake. Rushing over to the door, he peered through the rifle slot and saw a small figure standing along the shore on the opposite side. Confronting the lone figure was a nine-hundred pound male Brown Bear. Anton took out his long glass and pressed it against the slot. The small figure was a Tlingit boy.

The bear was not charging yet, but its ears were back, and it was bobbing its head from side to side low to the ground and snorting into the dirt. Anton took out his long rifle and poked it through the slot. The narrow channel formed a convenient rest for the rifle and increased the odds that the bullet would hit its target. Weeks before, Anton had sighted in the firing distance to the far shore by firing rounds into a tree across the lake. It was a standard military practice to sight in a target area on a battleground long before any bullets had to be fired in anger.

By good fortune, that same target tree was near where the boy was now facing off the massive bear. By sighting it in on that particular tree weeks before, he was certain of the elevation needed to hit the bear in a vital organ. The only question was the wind. Looking away from the sights, he looked for evidence of ripples on the water that would betray gusting that would deflect his bullet off course. The lake was still and mirrored clouds in the late-summer sky. Relieved, he went back to looking down the barrel through the sights as the boy continued to stand his ground, yell, and wave his arms above his head at the bear to make himself look larger.

Then, the monstrous ursine began to hop up and down on its front legs. Anton knew this was often a sign of aggression and that the animal was about to charge. There was no time left.

Anton took three deep breaths, exhaled, held his lungs almost empty, and then relaxed as the bear walked menacingly toward the boy. He sighted the rifle to a target midway up the bear's ribs just behind its left shoulder where his heart pumped his lifeblood. The bear was far away, but the target was large. He lined up the front sight until it fit precisely into the U shaped rear-sight. Then, to compensate for the pull of gravity tugging on the bullet over such a long distance, he raised the barrel slightly using only feel and experience, squeezed the trigger—then came the boom. White smoke from the gunpowder roared out and shrouded the cabin and the whole area in front of it.

When the smoke finally cleared, the boy had vanished, but the bear lay in a heap near the tree he had used to sight in the rifle. The next morning, he did not hear the customary thud of an arrow in the door. Nor did he hear it the next and the next. There were no more arrows in the door for the rest of the fading summer. In October, he left the cabin, hiked down the mountain to Fort. St. Michael, and returned to Petropavlosk for the winter and hoped the cabin would still be there when he returned the next spring. The only Tlingit he had seen in his first summer on Sitka was the boy across the lake.

Chapter 10, LETTERS

Nadia wrote her first letter to Anton after she arrived at her Aunt's house in St. Petersburg in December of 1800. But it did not arrive in Petropavlosk until the spring of 1801. Anton, in turn, wrote Nadia after he returned to Petropavlosk in October of 1800. but Nadia did not receive his letters until late winter of 1801. Though disjointed in time, both Anton's and Nadia's letters exuded a fondness for each other that ignored the immense distance that separated them in time and space.

Christmas 1800
My Dearest Anton,
I hope this letter finds you safe and well back in Petropavlosk and away from dangers on your first summer on Sitka. Thanks to Ilya, I am safely ensconced here in my Aunt's cozy home in St. Petersburg. But my long journey home was delayed shortly after our long trip on the Lena River. When we finally arrived in Irkutsk pouring rain turned the Siberian Track into impassable mud. Dear old Ilya, gruff as he is, is a kind old soul. He has a hostel on a bluff above the banks of

the Irkut River on eighty-one acres of land just outside of the town of Irkutsk. He said the land was granted by the government for his military service. It's rustic but quite beautiful. Fortunately for me, he had no guests when we arrived, so we had the whole of the place to ourselves.

The inn is run by a pretty young Koryak girl and her little sister. The older one is a gracious host and a very good cook. Somehow, she speaks perfect Russian even though Ilya can barely speak it himself. His native language is Balachka that is a language spoken in a place called Zaporizhia. Strangely, he says it is a land full of sorcerers, whatever that means. Ilya has a bookshelf full of books written in Russian that he cannot read, yet it is the first thing he showed me. I think he knows they contain powerful knowledge, so he treats them like talismans. He was guarded about his relationship with the girls, but he acts like their father or more likely their grandfather. He said nothing about a wife or consort. The girls run the business when he is off guiding patrons through the wilderness to Petropavlosk or to the Amur River which he says is a smuggling route to China. How romantic a life he has!

Irkutsk is a strange but wonderful town. I think I am in love with it despite its rough edges. Many of the people are exiles sent to Siberia no doubt for their political opinions or views on forbidden subjects. Ilya took me to town several times and all the people seem to know him, especially the eccentric ones. He has lively conversations with these exiles who all seem to be very bright. Some are artists, professors, and writers, but others are just displaced nobility. It is a strange mix of people to be banded together so far out in the wilderness. But Ilya fits in with them even with his bad Russian. I found his friends charming as well. Did you know they have a library, a small wooden theater, a tea house, and a bookstore? Imagine, in Siberia! And did I mention that all the houses are made of wood? Not a stone or masonry building to be seen though they build them with squared timber to look like they are built of stone!

Ilya kindly accompanied me all the way to St. Petersburg. When the freeze set in and the Track was finally passable, he insisted on escorting me on the road from Irkutsk to St. Petersburg saying it was too dangerous for a single woman to travel alone. That was despite the two pistols you gave me. When I showed him the pistols, he said something about "good for shooting mosquitoes." On the way, he told me of his plans to expand his inn which is set on a lovely spot with a magnificent view of the Irkut River and distant mountains he calls the Sayans. If I ever return to Petropavlosk, I hope he can accompany me again, and I will certainly stop for another stay at his Inn. Did he tell you anything about the two Koryak girls? Why didn't you tell me it was Ilya who escorted you along this same trail I took? We will have much to share about Ilya and his strange ways.

Auntie is trying to get me excited about finishing school and ballet lessons, but I am not interested. St. Petersburg is all about manners and social position. Auntie introduced me to several other young girls my age who are attending finishing school with me. We had tea with them at a tea-house. When I told them my father is a high-ranking naval officer, the first thing they wanted to know was what rank. I bit my tongue.

They also asked me how I came to get such "lovely" dark skin. Feeling condescension in the air, I told them my mother was from Venice, and also that summers are sunny and hot in Petropavlosk and everyone lies on the beach just like on Russian Holiday in the Crimea around the Black Sea. They believed me when I told them that all of us in Petropavlosk develop a copper tone to our skin. Then, when I told them about the pistols you gave me, they gasped, but, of course, they wanted to know all about you. So, I told them you were a Cossack, and they became silent.

But enough about me Anton. Tell me about your cabin. Did you build it? Have you met any Tlingits? Will you be going back to Sitka this Spring?

I miss you, Anton. Our chance meeting had too much promise to be over so soon.

Nadia

October 3, 1800

My Dear Nadia,

I hope my letter finds you safe and well in St. Petersburg, and that you had no need to fire your weapons in self-defense on your journey. The cabin I told you I would build on Sitka is finished. It lies above a small lake and an important Tlingit trail on the far shore. My side of the lake is solid granite except for a solitary Sitka Pine which grows out of a crack in the rock. The lack of forest on this side of the lake affords an expansive view of everything I need to see on the other side.

The Tlingits have been scarce, but they let me know that they are here by firing an arrow at my door each morning at sunrise. But they have not threatened me other than that. So far, I have only seen one Tlingit, a boy on the other side of the lake. He was about to be attacked by a large bear. Fortunately, I was able to kill the bear with my rifle before it could harm the child.

I am drawing a lot. In my next letter, I will send you a sketch of the cabin. Mother Russia is such a large country. But I am further away from you than just the breadth of Russia. I am another thousand miles from its eastern shore in a foreign land. By the time this letter reaches you, I may already be on my second visit to Sitka. This time I will arrive in spring and have all of summer and fall to do my work. I hope your schooling goes well. But one day, if you tire of all the manners and courtliness of St. Petersburg, I would welcome you back to Petropavlosk. If you write to me before Christmas, perhaps it will reach me before I leave again for Sitka in Spring of 1801. If not then, perhaps it will be waiting for me when I return to Petropavlosk next fall. We would have the whole winter together.

May I also say that I remember our baptism in the lake with great fondness, and still ponder the significance of our leap over the fire holding hands and not letting go?

With warm feelings for you my friend,

Anton

Chapter 11, PLACER GOLD AND ROE DEER

In the spring of 1801, Ilya stepped into his pantry at the rear of his hostel. Lifting a lantern high over his head, he kneeled down to a heavy door mounted to the floor. He lifted the access open and peered down into the wood-lined shaft cut deep into the permafrost where he stored his supply of meat and other perishables.

Climbing down the ladder to the bottom, he counted the frozen packages that remained and confirmed that his meat supply had dwindled over the winter. It was time to restock. Ilya included fish, fowl, and eggs in his diet, but venison was his meat of choice, and he preferred to harvest his own. *Why*? he asked himself, *should I let some other man enjoy my hunt.* And

Ilya was particular about deer meat. He wasn't satisfied with just any venison; it had to be venison from Roe Deer. But Roes were becoming scarce in and around Irkutsk where he had built his hostel because they had been over-hunted to feed the ever-increasing assortment of travelers moving along the Siberian Track and passing through Irkutsk. The developing town now acted as a hub to other distant locations like Okhotsk and Petropavlosk to the north, Vladivostok, Korea, and Japan to the East. Legal trade involving Russian furs, Chinese tea and vodka, and other goods prospered in a town called Kyakhta to the south of Irkutsk on the Mongolian border. A brisk black-market also existed along the lengthy Amur River which separated Russia from both Mongolia and China.

Irkutsk and its surrounds had also become a repository for criminals and political exiles like the writer Alexandr N. Radishchev who had offended Catherine the Great by questioning the impoverished status of the serfs. Other political undesirables included a large group of Poles who in the 1770s rebelled against Russian oppression in their land. They were members of a group called the Bar Confederation and were destined for work-camps and isolated villages near Yakutsk to the north of Irkutsk. Many exiles were simply thinkers who were being punished for their dangerous thoughts. Ilya, though uneducated, enjoyed engaging with them on all manner of topics and played chess with them, a game at which he excelled. These exiles had slowly transformed Irkutsk into a sort of intellectual community of thinkers, artists, and writers. Bookstores were beginning to pop up alongside tea-houses, and Ilya's hostel was part of the trend.

The number of travelers flowing through Irkutsk was good for his business and for expanding his thinking, but bad for the once plentiful Roe Deer in the area. Due to the scarcity, and Ilya's penchant for Roe Deer in particular, a trek to more fertile hunting grounds was in-order. But there was another reason as well. Though he loved his Koryak girls, he was anxious to get away from their incessant chattering and be free for a time to roam the wilds like the Cossack that he was. Thus, he set his goal on a nearby mountain range where he was sure to be alone with his thoughts, and where he could live like a Cossack again even for just a month.

In preparation for his hunt, Ilya hired a young Yakut woman to watch over the two Koryak girls he had saved from a massacre years before. The Yakut would help the girls run the hostel in his absence in the slow season of spring and summer. After safely securing the hostel and taking care of his girls, he packed his weapons and provisions and ventured out on a four-week hunting trip in late spring up the Irkut River. The snowmelt had just begun, so the current was still tame, but the water levels had become deep enough to float his eighteen-foot dugout canoe made by an old Yakut friend who lived on the eastern shore of Lake Baikal. Standing on the gravelly edge of the river in shallow water with a pole beside the canoe, he turned and waved to the girls and the Yakut woman. Then he shoved off into the water poling the dugout against the flow toward the Irkut's source high in the Sayan Mountains near the Mongolian border. Out on the river, Ilya was relieved that it was still flowing gently and figured it would stay that way until he neared the steeper elevations near the Sayans.

Even though the Irkut was wide and the flow still gentle, the sturdy fifty-year-old Cossack still strained to pole and paddle his craft upstream against the current. But Ilya knew that all the work he would put in going upstream would pay off with a return trip floating effortlessly like a log on the current all the way back to Irkutsk. Hopefully, he would return with a load of fresh-game covered with ice-cold snow. Few people ever went up the Irkut River. It was hard work to go against the flow even in early spring, and it led to little except Lake Ilchir, which lay just across the border into Mongolia. Ilya knew he would not likely see another human for a month or more.

His goal was to travel eighty miles upstream. To keep a good pace, he hugged the sides of the river where the flow was either not as swift or formed reverse eddies that helped his forward progress. When the current was too strong for paddling or poling, he pulled his craft with a rope using a technique called cordelling as he walked along the riverbank. When the opportunity arose, he would also take side-branches of the river if they were flowing slower and then reconnect with the main channel further upstream. Along the way, he spied all sorts of creatures from mule deer that sported fangs, owls that fished the river, Lynx, Brown Bears, a lone Tundra Wolf loping along the riverbank, and he even caught a glimpse of a Caspian Tiger gliding through a stand of Sitka Spruce. He hoped he would not see another tiger for the rest of his trip, but he was also curious why the wolf was alone and not in a pack as they usually were. After twenty hard days of poling, cordelling, paddling, and musing to himself, he reached the Kyngyrga River. It tumbled swiftly down the Sayan Mountains onto a flat plain which then emptied as a tributary into the Irkut. From that intersection, he left the Irkut and paddled north up the Kyngyrga as it flowed slowly across the flatland below the mountains. But as

Ilya neared the foothills and the elevation rose, the flow of the Kyngyrga began to speed up. Finally, paddling further against the strengthening current became futile, and he stowed his dugout on the riverbank, donned his pack and weapons, and took off on foot while following the Kyngyrga into the high elevations where he knew he would find his coveted Roe Deer.

Along with his pack and frame on his back, he carried a sturdy old .65 caliber Swedish Snaphaunce hunting musket with copper inlays on its stock. An eight-inch hunting knife in a leather scabbard secured by his belt was at his side. Two .50 caliber pistols were stowed in his pack. After a day of hard climbing, he made camp beside the river two thousand feet above the place where he left his canoe. As he sat on a smooth rock beside a small fire, he drank his evening tea and marveled at the stars twinkling through the mist rising from the rushing river. The hollow sound of boulders crashing into each other under the snowmelt frenzied water filled the air and shook the ground. After finishing his evening tea and stowing his gear, he crawled into his shelter, lay on his back, and pulled his blankets up to his chin. Then he fell asleep rocked by the roar of wilderness and the glow of the moon and stars painting the roof of his tent in a ghostly blue.

The next morning, he awoke at dawn, made tea, studied the steep canyon and the river flowing down it, and planned his hunt. When he saw a rare black sable on the other side of the river, he thought of reaching for his rifle, then stopped. Such sable pelts were very valuable, more valuable than gold. But Ilya had long ago pledged he would only kill for self-defense or for food, not for fur. He trudged up the mountain through the canyon, after a breakfast of fresh-caught Grayling. He had his musket at his side and left his tent and other gear behind at his base camp. Soon he reached his first sight of some melting slush. He was pleased to see it since he would need it to keep the venison cold. The spring weather was cool enough, and it was still freezing at night, but he would still need snow to keep his meat fresh and cold all the way back to his hostel. Within the hour, he began walking through snow. After an hour more, the snow became deep, and he had to stop frequently to rest. His chest heaving due to exertion and altitude, he sat on an exposed rock to catch his breath. To his right, he noticed an anomaly in the landscape. It was a landslide dam that formed where a slurry of wet rock and sand had ended after a landslide broke loose from the mountain somewhere above.

Curious, he climbed the dam to look over the other side. There he saw a pond of water contained by the landslide debris. Beneath the clear shallow water, he saw bright objects. Most were small pieces of white quartz, but others had a softer glint. Looking closer, he saw nuggets of gold lying just beneath the water's surface. He looked up the canyon to see if he could locate the scar of the landslide that had carried the quartz and gold to its resting place in the pond, but he did not see it. It was obvious that a large vein of gold lay somewhere ahead.

Had Ilya been a prospector, he would have dropped his plans for Roe Deer and run up the canyon frantically looking for the mother lode. But Ilya had never caught the madness of gold fever. He had found gold before on occasion and had a pile of nuggets stashed in his underground permafrost vault below his pantry. The pond had plenty of gold just lying there for the pickings and he had no urge to scurry up the canyon to find the vein it came from. He resolved he would load his pack with as many nuggets as he could carry on the way back, but only after he had finished this day's hunt.

An hour later, after climbing another five-hundred-feet up the canyon, he saw his first Roe. It was noon, and the Roe stood on a hillside one hundred and fifty feet on the other side of the Kyngyrga happily eating fresh grass. The wind coming down the canyon blew over the rump of the deer toward Ilya, so it was never warned of Ilya's presence by his scent on the wind. The roar of the river also masked the sound of Ilya stepping through the shoulder-high vegetation growing along the banks. Randomly, the Roe would lift its head and turn its ears in all directions to check for threats, but it never detected Ilya who was now crawling slowly through the brush with his weapon. When Ilya reached a granite rock near the edge of the river, he sank slowly to his knees, raised his musket with steady deliberation, and rested it on the rock with purpose to steady the barrel. Then he cocked the hammer, took several breaths, emptied his lungs, aimed, and fired. The bullet roared out across the river, echoed through the canyon, tore through the Roe's heart, and knocked him on his side. Instinct made his legs kick the air aimlessly as if running sideways until his life ebbed out. Then, he was still. Leaving his musket behind, Ilya jumped from boulder to boulder over the rushing water and crossed the river. When he reached the Roe, he kneeled, pulled out his knife, and dressed him. He left the offal on the ground for the ravens. When he finished gutting him, he lashed the seventy-pound hollowed-out carcass onto the back of his pack, donned the load, and headed back toward camp. On the way back, he picked up the two pounds of gold he had placed in a pile by the pond and poured them into a leather pouch and stuffed it into the hollow carcass of the Roe. A hundred feet from his tent he dropped his pack, removed the gold, and hoisted the carcass with a rope slung over a large branch of a spruce tree high enough that a bear could not get to it. He hung it there to age for two days before he would pull it down and butcher it into steaks. The aging insured the meat would have good flavor. After the two days passed, he laid the carcass on a grassy spot by the river, sliced the meat into thin portions, salted them, and then laid each piece out on a cloth laid over a lattice of spruce branches to dry in the air and sun for several days. Just as he had done with the carcass, he hoisted the lattice high into a tree to protect the salted meat from predators. As the last step, he would brine the meat for three more weeks back at the hostel and store it in his permafrost bunker.

Ilya would treat the last kill of his hunt differently. The last kill would be quickly followed by a swift return to the hostel. Drying and salting would not be necessary. Instead, he would quarter it, tamp it dry, wrap it in waterproof oilcloth and then submerge it in a bed of snow in the dugout where it would stay refrigerated for the trip back. Then he would rush it down the rising river which by then would be raging from snowmelt. Back at the hostel, he would carry the fresh quarters down the shaft in his pantry to the permafrost to freeze it while it was still fresh. The steaks from those quarters would belong to Ilya and Ilya alone. The dried salted meat would be for the guests.

That night Ilya saved one thick steak from his first kill that he did not cut into a thin strip for drying and cooked it over his campfire. It was the best venison he had ever eaten, but then, *food always tastes better in the wild*, he mused. The only thing he missed with his dinner was his vodka. Vodka was heavy - too heavy to carry overland on such a long trip. Tea was dry until he needed it, so it was very light in weight until steeped in boiling water. *Tea will do, for now*, he concluded as he contemplated his next day and toyed with the gold nuggets he had placed into the large leather pouch. He smiled and gloried in an irony. *I trade Russian gold for Chinese tea and vodka from Mongolian friend. He know black-market in China. Make good deal for gold. Then China trade Ilya's gold back to Russia for higher price. Ha!*

In the far reaches of Eastern Siberia people mainly traded goods for goods. Alexandr Baranov, the man who had recruited Anton to reconnoiter the Tlingits on Sitka knew that well. Years before becoming head of the Russian American Company to exploit the fur trade in Alaska, he was a successful merchant in Irkutsk trading baubles and goods for furs from the Chukchi Indians on the Chukchi Peninsula. In the parlance of Eastern Siberia, furs were called soft gold. With furs, you could barter for anything.

Ilya placed a modest value on gold. The main currency in Irkutsk wasn't gold or even rubles it was blocks of tea, Chinese vodka, or animal furs which eastern Siberians used as barter for almost everything else. Ilya liked tea and vodka because unlike Rubles or gold, tea and vodka could also be drunk, and tea could even be eaten if needed. And unlike furs where an animal had to be slaughtered just for its skin and the rest of its body left to rot, tea and vodka did not involve killing. Any rubles that customers from the west paid him for his guide work or for stays at his hostel he quickly converted to tea or vodka and did almost the same with gold. Nevertheless, on every visit he made to the Sayans, he collected another bag of nuggets until the entire floor of his cold storage was lined with it. He had heard from British foreigners that gold was very valuable in their country. *Maybe in their country, maybe in St. Petersburg, but not so much where Ilya live: not yet.*

But another reason Ilya preferred tea and vodka over gold was that it was against Russian law to own it or trade it to foreigners. Under the law of the land, all the gold in the realm belonged to the Emperor in St. Petersburg. Ilya recalled an old conversation he had with his black-market friend Altan the Mongolian.

"You know Ilya, Russia punish you for having gold?"

"Da," he answered, "Peter send Ilya to Siberia to punish him for own gold. Ha!"

"Peter," queried his friend?

"Da," the man who live in the palace at St. Petersburg and own all gold in Russia."

"Ah. You mean Emperor in St. Petersburg."

"Da, but Ilya say Peter. It Ilya's joke. You get?"

Altan laughed then offered his own joke in return. "Altan like gold."

Ilya looked at him askance waiting for the funny part.

"You know what name *Altan* mean in Mongolian?"

"Nyet."

"Gold. Haha. Altan mean gold." You get? Gold like gold."

Ilya turned away waving his hand and gave a grumbling response to his friend. "Joke must be funny to be joke."

Ilya tidied his camp, reloaded his musket, checked his pistols, and lay flat on his back in the tent planning his hunt for the next day. Ilya always slept on his back like a corpse with his hand clasped on his chest. The moon was almost full that night and lit the fabric of his canvas tent with a blue glow. No breeze came down the canyon, and the roaring river masked almost all other sounds. But near midnight, he thought he might have heard the faint sound of a branch snap near the tent.

Fully awake in seconds, he reached quietly for the musket. Getting to his knees, he crawled to the entrance flap of his tent and pointed the musket outside. Then he looked to see what might be creeping about. Squinting through the dimness, he saw a bear twenty yards out sniffing the air in the moonlight with steam coming from its nostrils in the cold. Ilya was confident that the meat of the Roe drying on the lattice was hung too high in the spruce a hundred feet away for the bear to reach. But then he noticed in disgust his uncleaned plate of juicy venison by the fire and cursed himself under his breath for not cleaning it before going to bed. The bear had caught the scent of the bloody remains of meat on the plate. But it also smelled the threatening scent of a man inside the tent and was wary. Ilya slowly cocked the musket and got into firing position. At the same time, he reached back into his pack for the two pistols, which he cocked and laid by his side.

In the dark, he could not tell what kind of bear it was but both Black Bears and Brown Bears in this region were aggressive. So, Ilya prepared himself mentally for an attack. In the dim light, he could see that it was not especially large: only about five hundred pounds. Still, he would need to hit it in the heart to stop him cold, and he pondered whether to wait until it got closer to the tent or attacked, or fire preemptively as soon as the bear presented his side to him.

Uneasy about the human the bear smelled in the tent, the bear started pacing back and forth aggressively as it got close to the coveted blood of the venison on the plate. Ilya could not wait. He fired when the bear presented his broadside.

He did not miss the heart but as is sometimes the case with enraged bears it did not drop immediately as he hoped. Instead, it charged across the twenty yards fueled by anger and adrenaline toward the tent. Ilya reached for the first pistol, a .50 caliber flintlock, and fired directly at the center of his chest. When the round struck, the bear shuddered and slowed momentarily from the shock but then kept coming and was now growling menacingly. Ilya reached for the second pistol and fired again at his chest when it was just ten feet away. This time the bear stumbled. Blood and saliva poured from its mouth as it roared. Yet it still came forward even if on legs that shook until it found Ilya standing outside the tent with his knife drawn. Ilya plunged the ten-inch blade deep into the bear's carotid and when he pulled it out to strike the bear again a stream of blood splattered Ilya's face just before the bear finally collapsed into the embers of the campfire. *Bear meat*, thought Ilya. *Good for guests.*

Ilya checked to make sure the bear was dead and then left it lying face down outside the tent. The night air had fallen below freezing, and there was no need to gut the bear in the dark. And there was no longer a need to clean the plate of venison that had attracted the bear. No predator would dare come near with the scent of bear so close to the plate. At dawn in dim light, he rose and dressed the bear, cut the oily meat into thin strips, salted it, laid it on a cloth over a lattice of boughs, and hoisted it into the same spruce where the venison from the previous kill was still hanging out to cure. By now, the sun was lighting the trees and the area around the camp. When he returned from hoisting the bear meat up into the spruce, he noticed wolf prints rounding his tent and the unwashed plate of venison had been licked clean. Somehow it had felt safe enough to brave the human and the bear for a meal.

Having now secured several hundred pounds of meat, he went out for his last hunt of Roe deer. It did not take long. He found it within an hour and dressed it out and carried the carcass back to camp only stopping to pick up a little more gold from the pond along the way. After aging the Roe for two days, he quartered it, wrapped it in waterproof oil-cloth, filled his pack with snow and Roe, and hiked back to his canoe where he packed it near the bow. The rest of the day found him making several trips back and forth for the dried and salted Roe meat from the first kill, which by now was fully-cured. Then he loaded the bulging bag of placer gold. The bear meat was not fully-cured yet, so he left it on the lattice and rigged it to the canoe to continue drying on the trip back down the Irkut. Then he packed extra snow in the stern to help balance out the load.

That night he camped without a tent beside the ladened canoe while guarding the meat. He launched the dugout into the Kayunga at sunrise, and paddled toward its intersection with the Irkut River, which was now swollen with snowmelt and flowing rapidly. After almost a month in the Sayans, summer was now at hand. In little more than a week of lazy paddling due east on the swiftly flowing Irkut, he arrived at the riverbank below his hostel. As he pulled the bow of the heavily loaded dugout on to shore, he heard the giddy shrieks of his girls as they ran down the steep hill toward the river and Ilya. The Yakut woman stood high on the bank with the sun behind her shiny black hair and waved. Ilya shielded the sun from his eyes as he looked up toward the woman and paused, before smiling and giving her a salute back.

Chapter 12, SITKA, SUMMER 1801

While Ilya was on his spring hunt near Irkutsk for Roe Deer, Anton was returning to Sitka from Petropavlosk in the spring of 1801 to continue in the second year of his mission. As he offloaded from a longboat at Redoubt Saint Michael on Sitka, he pushed his way through several filthy Russian trappers. The men were drunkenly cavorting with Tlingit women, pouring liquor down the women's throats with one hand and wrestling them close to their stained buckskin with the other. He also noticed two Tlingit men several feet away with angry faces that glared at the way the Russians were treating their women with such disrespect. The burly Russians, for their part, glowered back at the Tlingits and taunted them to do something about it. Seeing the filthy trappers abusing the Tlingit women and threatening the Tlingit men reminded Anton of Gregor Ivanov, the bully he took down in the hallway at the First Cadets. But he thought better of intervening this time. He had a mission, so he held his tongue but could not withhold his own disgusted glare at them in concert with the Tlingit men.

To bring supplies up the mountain from the harbor, he carried a large backpack supported by a wooden frame that spread the ninety-pound load evenly across his back. He would need to do this several times to get enough supplies to last until fall at the cabin. It was only a bit more than three miles, but it was all uphill. The trail had been made easier by centuries of Tlingit footsteps following the path from the sea to mountain camps where they sought their mountain goat meat and wool. The footpath also led over the mountains from the main Tlingit villages south of Fort St. Michaels to Katlian Bay to the north where salmon ran up the Katlian River all summer and herring laid their roe in the shallows in April. In that month, Tlingit women waded into the sea and collected herring roe in baskets.

While breathing heavily and putting one foot slowly in front of the other up the steep trail with his heavy load, Anton heard the sound of a rock being dislodged by someone coming down the mountain toward him. Anton quickly moved his hand closer to his knife. Looking up from under the brim of his hat, he saw it was a Tlingit man. Anton stopped and stood as tall as possible while the weight of his pack forced him toward a stoop and assessed the threat. He guessed the man was thirty years of age, but his face was weathered, so it was hard to tell. The man wore a simple hat woven from goat wool, a long brown leather tunic, leather trousers, and moccasins. His hair fell almost to his waist, and he carried a walking stick in his right hand. A leather pouch hung over his shoulder. Anton and the man stood ten feet apart for several seconds until the man stepped aside and gestured for Anton to walk by. Both relieved and surprised at the Tlingit's offer for him to pass peacefully, Anton lowered his hand away from his knife and trudged on. But he glanced behind him several times until he was closer to the lake.

As he approached the cabin, he was relieved to see that it was still standing and had survived the harsh arctic winter and the ire of Tlingits. The arrows he had left in the door from the previous year were still deeply embedded with their barbed tips of whale-bone. He decided he would keep them there for luck. Trudging across the smooth granite toward his humble shelter, he was astounded to see a twenty-five feet tall pole carved in front of the cabin where the solitary spruce that grew out of the crack in the granite once stood. On inspection, he determined that the Tlingits had carved it on the rooted tree in its upright position rather than cut it down and re-erect it in the almost solid rock. He knew enough about the ways of the Tlingits by now to know that this was a method rarely used. Saplings stacked below the totem suggested that they had been used for scaffolding to give the carvers access to the height of the tree. He also saw fresh-cut firewood piled on top of last year's stock. Anton removed the heavy pack outside and put his hand on one of his pistols before he went through the door, which was ajar. Upon inspection, he noted that nothing had been taken and took his hand from the pistol. Lying atop his crude table inside was a rattle with carved figures that mimicked the heads carved into the totem. At its top was the head of a Raven. Below that was the head of a bear, then there was a human face painted in bright white and below that near the rattle beads was the head of a Tlingit boy. Hanging from the firing slot on the door was a necklace made of bear claws. Each claw was over two inches long. Only Brown Bear claws reached that length.

The next morning, he awoke to a rustling outside. Pulling on his trousers, he pushed a pistol into his belt at his spine and peered through the slot to see a pretty young girl with short-cropped black hair and an odd-looking old man standing with an old woman. Anton, feigning confidence, placed the pistol on the table by the door and stepped out among them while raising one hand in salutation and showing a brave smile to his visitors. The old woman dressed modestly with a robe made of goat wool to keep her warm. She had a copper ring through her nose and a large wooden labret inserted into her lower lip. The girl wore robes of eider duck feathers and marmot skin. Her short black hair shimmered in the June sun.

The old man wore a columnar headdress that was twelve inches tall with feathers standing straight up around the top of the column, which made it even taller. Slices of rabbit pelts were attached to each side and hung like long dog ears down the side of his face. In the center of the columnar hat was a carved symbol of an animal that morphed into several other animals that Anton could not decipher. In his right hand was a fierce ceremonial rattle. From the base of its sturdy round handle, it morphed into the shape of an animal figure. Then it morphed again into a long-beaked bird with a lethal point to its bill. In his left hand was a walking stick, which also had many animal heads carved into it. Around his shoulders was a stiff ceremonial blanket made of goat wool with multi-colored images of the heads of eagles, bears, ravens, wolves, and whales. By his dress and manner, Anton knew he was a shaman. When he chanced to look deeply into his eyes he was roiled by the piercing power of his gaze. These were eyes he had seen before. They were Ilya's eyes – seer's eyes.

The old woman spoke in broken Russian and explained that she had learned the language from a captured Russian seaman when she was a young girl. The wooden labret in her lower lip distorted her speech so Anton leaned forward and tilted his ear to hear her better. Pointing at the old man she said:

"Stoonook, war shaman of Kiks.ádi clan."

Anton raised his hand to his heart and gave a slight bow and looked at the shaman. "Stoonook," he said pointing at the shaman's chest. Then pointing to his own chest, he said "Anton."

Stoonook looked at the old woman and asked something in Tlingit. After her reply, he repeated: "Anton," and the woman confirmed by nodding.

Then Anton pointed again to himself and said: "Anton," to the old woman and then pointed at her.

"Ahhh, me "Puyuk."

"Puyuk?" repeated Anton while pointing at her.

"Yes, I Puyuk." Then she said: "You save son of Stoonook from bear. You may stay now forever as friend of Tlingit."

With that, Stoonook gave a stiff perfunctory bow, turned, and walked away toward the shore of the lake with the young girl walking behind him. But he left the old woman behind and she announced summarily.

"I teach you."

What she would teach him Anton did not yet know. But he did know what he wanted to learn. It started with learning how to speak the strange tongue of the Tlingits with all of its clicks, guttural growls, and changes in tone. Next, he wanted to understand their customs, how they saw their world, and how they viewed the Russians. Were they happy with their deal to trade with them, or were they sorry they had allowed them to build the fort on Tlingit land?

Anton suspected that Stoonook was a clever man. Perhaps he had his own plan to use Anton to learn about the Russians. How strong was the Russian force should the Tlingit decide to eject them someday? Were they trustworthy, or did they lie? These were the things Stoonook wanted to learn from Anton. And if Anton was also there to learn about the Tlingit, so be it.

Whatever Stoonook might be plotting did not change the fact that Anton could not have had better luck. By fulfilling Stoonook's offer to teach Anton about the Tlingit, he would be helping Anton perform the mission that had already assigned to him: gain their trust, learn their ways, gage their strength, and smooth over conflicts if needed. Whether Stoonook had divined Anton's role to reconnoiter the Tlingits, he could only speculate. But having peered into the deep gazing and all-knowing eyes of the shaman, Anton suspected that Stoonook was no fool and understood Anton as an agent of the Russians. For the time being, he could afford to tolerate one witless stranger who had built a cabin in a foolish place on top of a rock by a lake that had no fish. Besides, he had saved his son from the bear. He owed him at least the gift of time and maybe more.

Puyuk went quickly about cleaning up the cabin, gathering wood, and washing the blankets. She also prepared fresh venison that she had brought with her in a deerskin pouch packed with snow. Then, in the mid-summer of 1881, the old woman began the education of Anton in the ways of the Tlingit. Between lessons, Anton made sketches. One showed Puyuk standing in front of his cabin with the arrows still stuck on his door behind her. Another depicted Stoonook, Puyuk, and the young girl with the short black hair. Still another showed Anton and Puyuk cooling their bare feet in the lake that had no name.

Chapter 13, THE EDUCATION OF ANTON

Each morning, Anton now awoke to the sound of his door opening along with the chatter of Puyuk instead of the sound of an arrow hitting his door. She had already been up since before dawn for the long walk up the trail from the village several miles away, one of several Tlingit villages, fishing camps, or goat hunting camps in the area. Her teaching method was simple. Starting with the ashes in the fireplace, she picked some up and rubbed it between her fingers and then said "gan eetí," the Tlingit word for ashes. Then picking up firewood, she said gán," Anton smiled when he saw the relationship: "gán" for firewood, and "gan eetí" for burnt firewood. Moving around the cabin, she named the window and required Anton to repeat the Tlingit word for window: "ýaawaaçéi." When it came to two objects that were the same, she would point to one of them and give its name. Then she would touch both and gave the plural for the two objects. Soon Anton knew enough common nouns in the Tlingit language that the old woman began weaving in verbs. First, she would point to an object like a chair and name it: "káayaçijeit." Then she wove in the verb for hit and her name. Puyuk hit chair," which in Tlingit was: "Puyuk át ayawashát káayaçijeit." she said as she pantomimed the action by pointing to herself, then hitting the chair with her fist.

Belatedly curious about the young girl who had accompanied Stoonook and Puyuk to their first meeting, he asked who she was and why she had accompanied Stoonook in broken Tlingit.

"She slave of Stoonook, answered Puyuk in a matter of fact way. " He have many slaves. Her name is "Aluki."

"Slave?" asked Anton to be sure he understood.

"Of course, Tlingit have many slaves. All people have slaves. Aluki is Aleut. Mother and father die in raid by Tlingit last year."

The news that Tlingits held slaves and warred with other tribes pierced his naiveté, and he pondered its relevance. While he often referred to Indians glibly as savages, he did so with a dash of the notion of "noble savages." It was an idea he had read about in an English book by a man named Dryden when Anton was a student at the First Cadets. *What could be noble, natural, or innocent about keeping slaves and inflicting war on your neighbors*?" he asked himself.

Then he remembered what Ilya had said about Indian babies impaled on the lances of blood-lusting Cossacks as they decimated the tribes in northeastern Siberia at the behest of Imperial Russia decades before. It had taken time, but even Ilya the staunch Cossack, could stomach it no longer and abandoned his comrades and the warrior culture he was born into. Ilya had finally seen the cruelty for what it was, and his wrenching belly would no longer allow him to distance himself from it by calling them savages. Anton resolved that if he ever saw Ilya again, he would ask him more questions about his Koryak girls and the night of the massacre. But now the word slave and Puyuk's nonchalant acceptance of it addled him.

He wondered, by comparison, were Russian serfs a sort of slave? *I suppose so,* he conceded? *They own nothing, work for nothing, and barely survive each winter while toiling to enrich their masters until the day they die in rags. Yes, like slaves.*

Meanwhile, Puyuk moved on to teach the practical things she believed a helpless man like Anton who had never had to survive on his own in the wilderness needed to learn. *Even a Tlingit boy knows more than this poor wretch of a man*, she worried.

In her mind, a man like Anton needed to learn how to use the bark from cedar to start a fire in a rainstorm. He also needed to know other skills like how to make a bow and arrow in the Tlingit fashion, and which wood to use to make them with. She taught him how to tell direction when the sun was behind the clouds by finding moss on a tree. When the sun was out, she taught him how to place a pole in the ground and then mark the spot with a rock where the shadow of the tip of the pole lay on the ground. That marked west. Then in half an hour, she showed him how to mark a second spot with another rock to mark where the shadow had moved. That spot marked east. Then She told Anton to place his left foot on west and his right on east. When he did that, he would be facing north. Then, she named north, east, south, and west in Tlingit as she pointed in each direction. When she got to south the old woman stood behind him and slapped him as if slapping a horse to show him which direction his rear was facing. Anton jumped in surprise then they both laughed at her playfulness.

As he put the finishing touches on the bow and arrows that he had made under the guidance of Puyuk, he thought of sending his creation to Nadia in St. Petersburg. How thrilling that would be to her friends at finishing school, he imagined. He also remembered that Nadia had always talked about a Greek Goddess named Artemis who carried a bow, hunted deer, and danced her way through the forest. But Puyuk pulled him away from his daydreams.

"Moss mostly grows on the north side," she said.

Then, sitting side-by-side on moist sand at the lake one night, Puyuk taught Anton the stars in the constellations that guided the Tlingits without the sun on the sea and overland as the lake water lapped rhythmically at their feet. Every day he learned something new about the ways of the wild. And as the days passed, Anton was falling ever deeper in love with the Tlingit wilderness and the Tlingits themselves. He thrilled each day to learn essential things about living in the wild that his upbringing in St. Petersburg never considered important for the son of a wealthy noble who, god forbid, would ever need to use such skills.

As he learned more and more of the language, Puyuk began to tell him stories in Tlingit. One story was about a boy who was lost in the forest and shivering under a driving rain. The boy saw an open space in the woods fill with fog, and then quickly recede back into the forest. That was a sign that good weather would follow the next day and gave him hope he would survive the storm. She told him that another method Tlingits used to predict the weather was to study the clouds over the mountains. One cloud formation meant clear skies coming, another meant rain, and still, another meant snow. Then she told a story of a strange friendship between a beaver and a porcupine. Another regaled a love affair between a frog and a beautiful woman.

When Anton was curious about something, he asked his own questions, and he asked about the pole beside the cabin.

"Totem protects Anton. Tells story of Tlingit friend. Raven is for our clan. We belong to the Kiks.ádi. Great bear spirit is next. White man below the bear. Below white man is boy, son of Stoonook. You save boy from bear. You friend now forever always."

As she told the story of the totem, Anton sat beside her listening and looking up at the details of the totem as she explained each one. Then, without any warning, Puyuk suddenly stopped and stood up. He had become inured to sudden changes in attitudes and topics in dealing with Puyuk, and he suspected it was just part of the Tlingit way. As he waited for Puyuk to change the subject, she announced summarily that Stoonook and the

Kiks leader, Skautlelt would expect Anton to attend a Potlach at the main village six miles south of Fort St. Michaels as a guest tomorrow. It was an order, not an invitation.

"Potlach," queried Anton?

"Yes," you come in two days. I go with you. Long walk."

"What is a Potlatch?"

"Potlatch mean give gift. This a special Potlatch. Last year you give gift of son to Stoonook. Stoonook give gift of pole. This Potlatch celebrate making of pole, give gifts, eat, drink, tell stories, and tell about Russians."

Immediately startled at the mention of Russians, Anton became apprehensive. What could he honestly say about the Russians without jeopardizing his mission to befriend and learn from the Tlingit? He had long suspected that Baranov had purposefully hidden important details about his motive for a foothold on Sitka. But all Anton knew for certain was that Baranov had negotiated for a small plot of land with the Tlingits, and he needed Anton to help with a negotiated presence of the Russian America Company on Tlingit soil. But was that all that Baranov wanted? Or did he want more than what he promised the Tlingits in return for the land: that promise being equal status with the Russians, fair trade, and respect for the Tlingits' sovereignty over the land? But now Anton questioned: *were his promises just a ruse to solidify that foothold and to push a broader plan to take over all of Sitka and adjacent fur rich lands?*

Baranov had not said that. But Anton had heard that he had already done that to other *savages* in the Aleutians. Village by village, he would press the fur hunting men into work gangs and hold their women and children hostage to force the men into supporting Russian greed for furs. Why would he not do the same with the Tlingits after getting his Trojan Horse onto Tlingit land?

Anton might have excused himself for his failure to acknowledge the obvious. After all, he did not yet know this for a fact. Or, he might simply have wished away the truth of such a thought so that it did not interfere in his great adventure. But in his heart, he suspected that was exactly what Baranov had in mind. And Anton worried that he had allowed himself to become a mere pawn on one side or the other of a deadly chessboard. Whether he was white or black did not matter. In the game of chess, pawns are always expendable after their usefulness has expired.

Before meeting Puyuk and Stoonook and learning about the people and the land of Sitka, his thoughts about helping Baranov never went beyond the idea that the assignment was nothing more than a chance for derring-do among *savages* which appealed to his fancy. Thus, he lent a blind eye to what was obvious. But now that he had spent time with Puyuk, and learned more about the Tlingits, he was beginning to grow fond of the people and the land. Certainly, they could be savage, he thought, but that did not make them *savage*s. In one way, it just made them like Russians who seemed intent on robbing them of their land, or like Cossacks who did the Russian's bidding by annihilating tribes that stood in Russia's way as they expanded into eastern

Siberia and then on to Alyeska. These were disturbing thoughts that Anton feared he was long overdue to ponder. Among the children of nobles like him, it seemed, there was no lesson offered on empathy except the empathy reserved by nobles for other nobles. No one else seemed to have a right to it. It was as if everyone else in the world were branded with fungible labels like *savages*, *peasants*, *slaves*, or *serfs* that could be discounted, and their suffering too unworthy for a noble to consider.

Wrong, he thought as he remembered the gratitude and generosity of Stoonook at the door of his cabin after he saved his son from the bear.

Wrong, he concluded as he remembered the hospitality and knowledge shared by Puyuk. The belated insights tore through his mind like a flood. *So, this was what my chess playing friend Alek was trying to tell me at the Academy*. But his conclusions also startled him and shook the ground of his identity in a way he did not anticipate from the simple act of concurring with a thought. If it was no longer valid for him to ignore the suffering of lessers, that very thought contained a seed of insurrection against his own kind and against the viability of his privileged status in the Russian hierarchy. He wondered what Nadia, daughter of Russian and Venetian nobility would think of his irreverent thoughts. Then he remembered what she said on his first day with her in Petropavlosk when they saw the bedraggled group of Indians huddled with their flea-ridden dogs by the tanning factory:

"There must have been a dignity about them that they had lost in defeat and in the loss of their land. There must have been, don't you think?" she had asked.

His sudden self-awareness of the suffering of others would forever deny him the comfort of believing his privileged status could be valid based simply by the accidental virtue of his noble birth. Worse, he could not take the thought back. It frightened him enough that he tried to push the musings back into his mind, and tried as best he could to obscure it by going back to thinking like a Russian noble about a familiar subject, but in the end, he was unpersuaded.

THE POTLATCH, FALL 1881

Two days later Anton heard Puyuk call outside the door.

"Anton come out now. Long walk."

Puyuk had already hiked three miles down the mountain from a temporary goat hunting camp to Anton's cabin. From there they would hike three miles further down to the Russian fort at Redoubt Saint Michael, then six more miles south to the main village called Shee-Atika, the village of Stoonook and the Kiks.ádi chief Skautlelt and their war chief Kotlian. Anton struggled to muzzle his excitement at the prospect of meeting with the clan leaders at the Tlingit ritual called a Potlatch. Anton was still donning his trousers inside the cabin when he heard Puyuk repeat her call, this time with an edge of annoyance:

"Anton come now! Long walk!"

As he pulled up his pants, he could see Puyuk through the rifle slit in the door with her feet set firmly on the ground. She had one hand set curtly on her hip as the other worked her walking stick to tamp the ground around her feet impatiently. She wore a ceremonial dress covered with animal symbols for the Potlatch. Before he left the cabin, he put both pistols in his belt. Since an ugly encounter with some Russian trappers at the fort weeks earlier, Anton decided it would be prudent to carry them any time he went near there just in case they might run into others of their ilk of which there seemed to be more and more. Finally, Anton exited the cabin and joined Puyuk and they were quickly on their way. She made no comment about the pistols and led the way down the mountain toward Fort. St. Michaels. She had only one lesson for Anton on the walk.

"You watch what Puyuk do at Potlatch. Anton not say nothing. If Stoonook give gift, only say thank."

Thank?

"Say Tlingit words: Gunalchéesh hó hó. Much thank you."

"Do I give a gift back?"

"Never give gift back. Never. Only take gift."

"What if I don't want the gift?"

"Anton want even if not want. Anton say Gunalchéesh hó hó and take gift."

Anton detected a tone of urgency in Puyuk's voice as she gave instructions. The tone was to take her words seriously or else face consequences of a dangerous kind he could not envision. But he determined it would be best to follow her edict. Three miles down the trail they neared Ft. St. Michaels and began to see refuse. Piles of offal from skinned sea otters swarmed with flies, and a heavy smell of human feces reeked through the ripe forest floor. Nearing the fort he saw female Aleuts clinging to smelly trappers offering their bodies for a drink of their Russian vodka. The same Russians he had seen weeks earlier were there groping the women again.

Puyuk looked directly at them and said: lichán awé wé eex̱!

The Russians did not know what she said, but from her tart tone, it was clearly an affront. The largest of the three shed his drunken woman who slumped to the ground. Then he stood up to flaunt his size and shook his long red hair that hung down to his shoulders as a threat and took a step toward Puyuk who stood firm against his intimidation. But when the Russian took a second step toward Puyuk he faced two pistols which Anton quickly pulled from his belt and pointed at his bounteous belly. The Russian paused. But it wasn't just the pistols that stopped him. Most at the fort knew Anton worked for Baranov himself, and if they wanted to sell furs to the Russian American Company, they knew it was best not to cross Anton.

All the Russian could do was utter a future threat: "I know who you are puppy. And I know the kennel you live in. We'll meet again when no one is looking. Maybe find your squaw there too. When I do, I'll put you both on a short leash and take you on a long walk," he menaced.

Anton tipped his hat with one of his pistols as he walked backwards down the trail still holding his weapons as the Russian slid back down against the wall of the fort and put his drunken arms back around his Aleut woman. Anton hesitated to face forward down the trail until he and Puyuk were safely away. Then he placed his pistols back into his belt and asked Puyuk what she had said to the Russians to rile them up so much that he had to draw his weapons.

"Puyuk say truth. Puyuk say "*pigs always stink.*"

And with that Anton laughed for half a mile. He thought of slapping her on the back as he chortled but then thought better of it. He never appreciated Puyuk more than on that day. The next six miles hugged the flatlands by the Pacific on their right and they walked to the murmur of small waves rippling over rocks and seaweed. Two hours later they crested a small rise and saw the main village of the Kiks.ádi clan lined up along the shore facing the sea. Many Tlingit canoes dotted the bay as they were arriving from other villages and clans along the coast. The houses were lit by the afternoon sun. They were made of planked cedar much like the cabin Anton had built except these houses were much larger. He guessed some were over a hundred feet long. Each was windowless and rectangular and had animal images painted on the side that faced the sea. Totem poles like the one that Stoonook had carved from the lone tree by his cabin picketed the shoreline in front of the buildings. Some were painted in bright colors; others were not painted at all. Each told a story about the village, its people, its folklore, myth, and gods. As they neared the ceremonial house where the Potlach would be held, they began to encounter Tlingits from other villages and clans as they gathered around the entrance. Strangely to Anton, the entrance to the lodge was an oval hole with no door so small that everyone had to stoop to enter. Several of the Tlingits outside the entrance looked at Anton with a look of disgust. Since the building of the fort, many Tlingits had gone from tolerating Russians to despising their presence. A few even attacked trappers or harassed the walls of the fort with their arrows. But they also knew that Anton's companion Puyuk was close to Stoonook the fearsome war shaman of the powerful Kiks.ádi clan so they held their tongue.

Puyuk gestured to Anton that it was time for them to go through the oval opening into the ceremonial house. As he went through the portal, he noticed that the only light entering the expansive room was coming from an opening in the ceiling above a fire-pit in the center of the room which was sunken two feet lower than the main floor. The opening allowed the smoke from the fire to exit the room. The exhaust hole was covered by a small roof of its own that kept out the rain, and sitting benches surrounded the rectangular perimeter of the building and the sunken fire-place in the center. The smell of raw cedar and burning wood pervaded the space. Surrounding the area near the far wall were benches where local dignitaries had taken their place. Behind them were paintings on the wall depicting mythical animals important to the identity of the Kiks.ádi clan, especially the trickster Raven and the Frog.

Dignitaries arriving by canoe from distant villages were dressed in elaborate ceremonial costumes including tall wide-brimmed woven hats adorned with rabbit fur. Puyuk did her best to explain the confusing spectacle to Anton. Many of the hats, she told him, depicted the Raven which symbolized the group of clans that the Kiks.ádi belonged to. Many wore elaborate Chilkat blankets worn as shawls depicting animals, vines, flowers, and geometric patterns. They also wore Moccasins adorned with similar images. Some of the men and women had rings in their noses and paint on their faces. A few of the women had tattoos on their arms. As the long-house filled up, the guests sat in order of their rank and eagerly anticipated the entrance of the host so that the dancing, speaking, and feasting could begin.

The sponsor of this Potlatch was Stoonook, and Anton knew that part of the ceremony was to tell the story of Anton saving Stoonook's son from the bear and to tell the story of the Totem Stoonook gave in return.

But accompanying the war shaman Stoonook was Skautlelt a chief of the Kiks.ádi clan and the clan's war chief Katlian. It was Skautlelt who had bargained with Baranov for the land for Fort St. Michael. From Puyuk he learned that many of the other clans were unhappy with the deal Skautlelt made and resented the gifts that Baranov had showered on him in return for granting permission for a Russian presence on Sitka. But Anton suspected that it would be Katlian, the war chief who would be asking him questions about Russian intentions. If relations between the Russians and the Tlingits were to go bad, it would be the military leader of the clan, Katlian, who would have to take action.

Anton sat nervously in anticipation of the queries, not yet knowing how candid he should be with the Tlingits about Russian intentions since he was still just guessing what they were. As he watched the smoke from the fire in the center of the room rise up to the square vent hole in the roof, Stoonook entered through the oval door followed by Skautlelt and Katlian. They went to the back of the room which was decorated with Tlingit animal symbols and took their places. Then, with a nod from Stoonook, dancers began circling the center of the room around the fire. The women were almost stationary, only moving their feet and swaying gently to the drums. The men, however, were lively and animated, some gesticulating wildly with feathers extending from their fingers.

The dances regaled ancient stories such as the origins of the clans, how the earth came into being, where mosquitos came from, the story of how the raven saved the frog from a flood, and the story of the beaver and the porcupine.

Eating followed the dancing. After the feast of salmon, halibut, shellfish, seaweed, berries, and roots the crowd became quiet and the pace of events slowed down. Puyuk tugged on Anton's arm and pointed to the doorway. Puzzled, Anton hesitated, but Puyuk pulled again and had an urgent look on her face so he followed her through the oval doorway. Once outside he turned to face Puyuk and ask her what was happening when he sensed a large presence behind him. As he turned, he saw the fearsome war chief named Katlian. He had been waiting for him. While Anton's skill with the Tlingit language was passable, he wanted to be careful with his words, so he asked Puyuk to translate as Katlian greeted him.

"I am Katlian, war chief of the Kiks.ádi. It is good to meet you Russian."

"I am Anton. It is good to meet you. And yes, I am Russian.

"Did you know that Katlian does not like Russians? Katlian does not trust Russians. Katlian think all Russians lie. Do you lie Russian?"

"No. I do not lie."

"We will see in your answer to my simple question. Katlian think Russians want all of Sitka. Katlian think Russians want us to be their slaves under chiefs from Russia. Katlian think Baranov lie. What do you think Russian?"

Anton knew that truth was his only choice because Katlian had already gleaned the truth by seeing what the Russians did, not by believing what they said or had not said. All Katlian wanted now was confirmation from a Russian that his own conclusions were correct.

Anton decided to tell the truth as he believed it to be, but disguised his answer as a question for which there was only one answer. That way he would show Skautlelt that he was not a traitor to his own people, but also, that he would not lie.

"Does Katlian know the Aleut?" asked Anton.

"Katlian knows the Aleut. We have many Aleut slaves. Aleut makes good slave."

"Does Katlian know that the Russians hold the wives and children of the Aleut hostage to force Aleut men to work for the Russians?"

"Katlian has heard of this."

"Then my answer to your question is this. Why would the Russians treat the Tlingit any different than the Aleut which they treat like slaves?"

Katlian looked deep into Anton's eyes before he gave his answer. "Katlian finally meet first Russian that speaks truth, even if he speaks truth in circles."

"Why are you here Russian?"

"I am a scout."

Hearing that Anton was a scout, his brow furrowed in a flash of anger. Then he held out his left-hand in Tlingit fashion and pulled out a knife with his right. Seeing the knife, Anton began to step back, but Puyuk blocked his path. Then, Katlian simply gave him a firm handshake with his left, looked Anton yet-to-eye and then put the knife back in its scabbard.

"You good scout Russian?"

"I try."

Relief flooded Anton's worried face. Then, without another word, Katlian turned and went back through the oval portal into the smoky long-house. Anton looked to Puyuk for an answer about the knife.

Quietly she said, "I tell later."

Then, they followed Katlian through the oval door and returned to their places in the long-house.

Stoonook seeing his guest of honor back in the lodge then began to tell the tale of a Russian named Anton who saved his son from a bear with a long rifle by a fishless lake and how he gave Anton the Totem by the cabin. He went on to describe the totem and the story it told of his son's encounter with the bear and Anton's gift of life to his son. By telling that story he bestowed honor on Anton and by so doing gave him a place among the clan of the Kiks.ádi., "always and forever." he said.

Then he announced with a smile: "Now Stoonook give good gift to Anton."

Anton uttered a "but" in Russian to which Stoonook halted his speech and frowned. Puyuk immediately poked her finger as deep into Anton's side to stop him from saying anything more. Anton glowered in pain at Puyuk. But Puyuk reminded him by whispering in angry tones what she had told him on the trail.

"You watch what Puyuk do. Anton not say nothing. If Stoonook give gift, only say Gunalchéesh hó hó. Much thank you. You remember now?"

"Yes," he said still wincing from the pain in his side.

Stoonook paused until he had recaptured Anton's attention, relaxed his brow, and then went on. Stoonook then made a gesture to someone on his right who escorted a young girl to the center of the stage. It was Aluki, the same young Aleut slave he had seen when Stoonook and Puyuk came to his cabin for the first time earlier in the summer. Her hair was still cut short in the manner of Tlingit slaves.

Stoonook continued with his gift-giving ceremony by saying "Aluki make good slave for Anton. Aluki now belong to Anton."

"Gunalchéesh hó hó," replied Anton dutifully while suddenly wondering what would become of the rest of his life now that he was burdened with a girl too young to marry, too old to adopt, and not the woman he wanted. Nadia was who he wanted, and owning Aluki would destroy any chance he had with her. Unaware of the reason for Anton's consternation, Puyuk sat beside him and displayed the widest grin he had ever seen on her face. Then she erupted in a titter which she muzzled with both hands over her lips. Anton had his own grin to manage with his teeth clamped shut to keep dangerous words from escaping his teeth's barrier. Stoonook saw the grim toothy smile on Anton's face and mused to himself that *Russians have a strange way of showing they are happy.*

Giving away Aluki was a generous gift and it enhanced the reputation of Stoonook in the eyes of the clan. That was its purpose. What Anton did not know was that if he had objected to the gift, even for a good reason, Stoonook would have had no choice but to kill Aluki to save face. Tlingits often killed slaves at Potlucks just to show how wealthy they were: so wealthy they could destroy their own valuables and even lives with impunity. But Puyuk knew. And that was why she buried her finger so deeply into Anton's ribs. It was to save Aluki.

But now Anton's mind raced over the unexpected addition of Aluki in his life. And he wondered how he could weave the story of her into his next letter to Nadia let alone weave Aluki into his life at all. He hoped Puyuk would agree, at least, to take care of Aluki when he left Sitka and returned to Petropavlosk for the winter. And what, he worried, would happen on his return to Sitka the following spring? Could he avoid taking Aluki into his cabin as his slave, his daughter, his woman? He was too young to adopt her. And he had no intention of marrying her or spending the rest of his life with the Tlingits on Sitka. These questions prowled his mind the rest of the day as the ceremonies went on into the night.

The potlatch finally ended long after dark. It was not safe to walk the trail at night past the fort with its unsavory characters, so Anton stayed in the village and slept fitfully as a guest in the house of Stoonook. Aluki slept with one eye on her new master and wondered about her own fate as she lay by the side of Puyuk, her putative grandmother ever since her capture during the Tlingit raid on her village that killed her parents.

The next day the three of them would walk the trail back up the mountain to the cabin. After their long walk and some dried venison, he gave Puyuk and Aluki his bed. But before Aluki went to sleep, he gave her the small totem, and rattle Stoonook had left for him after he killed the bear and saved his son. The little totem mimicked the large one carved into the lone spruce beside the cabin. At its top was the head of a Raven. Below that was the head of a bear, then there was a human face painted in bright white, and below that near the rattle beads, was the head of a Tlingit boy.

Though exhausted, Anton pulled out his sketch paper and began to draw everything he could remember about the Potlatch. First, he drew the faces of Katlian, Skautlelt, and Stoonook. Then he captured the village with the canoes as they arrived and the totems facing the sea. He sketched the interior of the lodge where the Potlatch was held. He also drew the ceremonial costumes of the dancers as they swayed in front of the fire while smoke rose up to the hole at the top of the lodge.

As he lay down on the floor to sleep, he saw Aluki asleep in her bed clutching a doll and went back to his sketch paper to capture it forever. The last thing he saw before falling asleep was a small fire flickering in the fireplace casting a dancing light on the slumbering inhabitants as heavy rain began to beat down on the thick cedar roof.

Chapter 14, CHRISTMAS IN ST. PETERSBURG, 1800

Almost six months had passed since Nadia watched Anton's ship leave the harbor for Sitka in the summer of 1800 to begin what he called his adventure among the Tlingits. She watched his ship until the sails faded ten miles away and turned east toward Alyeska. A week after Anton sailed out from Petropavlosk, Nadia departed on her own journey west to St. Petersburg to live with her Aunt Maria.

There she would attend finishing school at The Smolny Institute for Girls, continue with her ballet lessons, and usher herself into civilized society with the help of her aunt. After the long overland passage escorted by Ilya, the kind old Cossack, and a layover at his hostel in the little town of Irkutsk during bad weather, she arrived safely in St. Petersburg just before Christmas without incident.

Nadia exited the Tarantass carriage in a light Christmas snowfall in front of the neo-classical Evmentev House, a new luxury apartment building near the First Cadets in St. Petersburg. Ilya lifted Nadia's heavy trunk over his right shoulder and looked up at the massive white Corinthian columns.

"Big house," he gruffed.

"Oh, Ilya, Auntie doesn't own the whole house, only a part of it."

"Green Big house," he said again as he entered the door into a large open rotunda that rose forty feet supported by Greek columns standing in a circle.

The building had three stories, and her aunt was on the third floor. After climbing the stairs, Ilya knocked at 321. Nadia had sent a letter ahead as they neared St. Petersburg, so her aunt was expecting them. Aunt Maria, a short portly woman, opened the door expecting to see a petite-sized niece, but Ilya took up the whole doorway with his size and rough-hewn clothing, and she stepped back in alarm.

"It's all-right, Aunt Maria, Nadia comforted. "Ilya is my friend. He brought me safely all the way from Petropavlosk."

Just as she finished her saying "friend," one of the pistols Anton gave her fell out of her muff and crashed to the floor near Maria's feet. Then with a thud,

Ilya set the trunk on the imported French Parquet floor of the foyer and held out his hand to Maria. She managed a timid smile that looked almost like a frown and then took a small step forward and touched his hand.

"Ilya," he said.

Maria treated his hand like the paw of a wild animal and was ready to snatch it back to safety if necessary.

"Maria," Pleased to meet you," she said as she stepped back.

"Big house," answered Ilya.

In the silence that followed, Ilya held his large hat in his hands and fidgeted. He was uncomfortable being in such structured surroundings. In his mind, his work was complete, and it was time to go. Lacking the most basic of social skills and needing to bolt, he put on his great hat and turned around to make a clumsy exit when Nadia called out his name, and he stopped short of the door. Then he removed his hat again and turned wide-eyed to see Nadia rushing toward him with outstretched arms to give him a big bear-hug. "Oomph," he exclaimed when she ran full force into his chest and threw both arms around his neck and put her soft cheeks against the ragged beard of the man that had been stalwartly by her side for six months.

"I will miss you Ilya," she said as tears began to flow, knowing deep down that with his departure, her last connection to the wilds of Siberia would go with him.

"Da, Ilya miss too." You marry that Anton boy?"

Surprised that he would blurt out such a question in front of Maria without warning, she answered partly to maintain composure and not be embarrassed in front of her aunt:

"I barely know him Ilya. And I'll probably never see him again. He is far away."

"Ilya think in Russia we are all far away."

"Yes, and Anton is even more than far away. He is on another continent."

"Da. Ilya understand. You right. Anton good boy, but you find another boy in town of St. Peter quick. Just as good maybe."

Then after a pause, "Ilya go now. Ilya miss home. Tomorrow Ilya miss Nadia."

Then he put his large weathered hands on both of her small shoulders, lowered his head toward her face, and said with great sadness in his deep blue eyes: "Dasvidaniya."

"Yes, until we meet again," said Nadia as she held back more tears.

With that, Ilya left and began his long journey back to his girls, his hostel, and his beloved woods.

Aunt Maria had been a confused spectator to the entire conversation between Ilya and Nadia. She was now wondering who this man Anton was and worried that Nadia was already entangled. Nadia sensed her aunt needed some reassurance.

"The boy Ilya mentioned by Ilya is a nice young man from St. Petersburg. He went to school at a place called the First Cadets."

"Oh, my," said Maria who seemed relieved and impressed. "A very prestigious school for noble young men. It's in the Menshikov Palace just across the Neva River," as she gleefully pointed north in great relief at the news.

"Yes, but you see now he is on an assignment in Alaska. I only knew him for a few pleasant days last summer, and it is very unlikely that I will ever see him again. For all I know, he'll marry an Indian squaw and never come back. Ilya was just being a silly old curmudgeon when he asked if I was going to marry Anton. He likes Anton. And as you saw, he likes me too."

Blushing, Maria exclaimed with disgust: "Squaw? You mean this young man of noble birth might take a savage for a wife?"

"No, I don't think he would really do that, but some men who go there do marry such women."

"Disgusting to think of what men do to satisfy their base desires, is it not."

Then, acquiescing to the easy way out of the conversation, Nadia replied: "Yes, so disgusting. I so agree with you Auntie," she said in a mock huff as she recalled how she felt a warm flush when she first saw Anton walking up the street above the harbor.

"Well now, it's time I showed you to your room," she said in a singsong voice. "You must be exhausted from your long journey with Ira."

"It's Ilya, Auntie."

"Well yes, Ilya"

Maria walked with Nadia down a long hallway painted mint green with white accents in the color scheme of the Winter Palace, and then stopped at the room she had prepared for Nadia. As she opened the door Nadia saw that it was spacious with a wide view overlooking the Fontanka River below with promenades on both embankments and the Semonovsky Bridge which crossed over it. Snow had piled up on the windowsills leaving the kind of chill in a room that you feel below your knees during winter even with the deep green malachite copper fireplace in the corner of the room burning bright.

"Don't worry about your luggage. I will have one of my servants bring it to your room later. I allowed all of them a few hours off to be with their families. Christmas is coming soon you know. But they will be back shortly."

"Oh, Auntie. The room is beautiful. Thank you so very much!"

"Think nothing of it my dear. Rest up now. We have a lot of catching up to do you and I, and after we do that, we will be very busy."

"Busy?"

"Yes. I will introduce you to the headmaster of the school, Yuri Ivanov. Then I will take you by the Big Stone Theatre. There is someone there that I want you to meet."

"Well, that sounds tantalizing. Who might that be?"

"Her name is Eugenia Ivanovna Kolosova: A ballerina."

"Is she famous?"

"Not yet, but soon. Bring your proper dress in case she asks you to go through a few steps with her, won't you?"

"How exciting," she said as she suddenly worried about her legs which had barely been used on the long trip!"

"Oh, and I almost forgot. Your schoolmate from Petropavlosk will also be there. You must know her. She says she was the Prima Ballerina of her dance studio there. She will also be attending your finishing school with you. Won't that be nice?"

"Katarina Vasilev?"

"Yes, that's it. She says she knows you well. Too bad you could not have traveled together on your long journeys from Petropavlosk. "

"Yes. What a shame," answered Nadia mechanically: "what a shame."

While excited about going to see the Big Stone Theatre and the ballerina Eugenia Kolosova, she worried that Katerina had likely bundled her simmering hatred and jealousy toward Nadia all the way from Petropavlosk to St. Petersburg. It caused a sudden wave of nausea in the pit of her stomach. In Petropavlosk Nadia could simply ignore Katerina's resentment of her because it was clear to everyone there that Nadia was the best dancer in the small studio no matter how Katerina boasted. But in St. Petersburg, both of them would be starting afresh as they entered high society, competed in dance, and Katerina would be sure to use her political venom to define Nadia as less worthy than her. And as Maria had said, Katerina had preemptively convinced her that she was the *Prima Ballerina of Petropavlosk*, which to Nadia was a silly claim to an empty title since there were only five students of dance in the tiny frontier Siberian town. Nadia's only comfort was that the dance floor would soon be a fair witness to her talents and put Katerina's silly claim of being a Prima Ballerina to rest. But on the social side, that was another matter.

Who knows, Nadia worried, *what a resentful person like Katerina might do to try to sully her name here, a city full of people born to privilege who valued title, pomp, and circumstance above all else?*

Nadia knew too well that St. Petersburg was a world apart from Siberian Petropavlosk where a harsh wilderness worked to temper the sting and rigor of rank and title. By necessity, those on the frontier valued duty and merit over birthright. But there was no such tempering in St. Petersburg where pedigree was the sine qua non of social status. Nadia already felt herself longing for the rugged simplicity of Petropavlosk, and but for her love of dance, she might have already decided to leave when spring arrived.

After three days of rest, Maria came into Nadia's bedroom while she was still asleep and sat on the edge of the bed watching her slumber and waited for her to awaken. Soon Nadia stirred, rubbed her eyes, and squinted to see her aunt.

"Good morning Auntie," she said as she sat up and stretched her arms out to her sides accompanied by a wide yawn.

"Good morning my dear. What do you think about beginning to catch-up? What do you say?"

Though she preferred more time to wake up more slowly, she complied. "Of course, Auntie. Where shall we start?"

"Let's start with you."

"Well, I think mother has told you all of the events in my short life. What else can I tell you?"

"Tell me what you like."

"Starting with chocolate," she laughed?

"Yes, starting with chocolate. What kind of chocolate do you like Nadia?"

"Bird-cherry-chocolate-cake, of course," answered Nadia quickly. "It's my very favorite."

"Oh my," bumbled Maria, "I don't think I have ever had that, though I must have tried every other kind, light, dark, mixed in coffee."

"Well, bird-cherries grow on the bird-cherry tree in eastern Siberia. The berries are picked wild, dried, then they are mixed with flour, nuts, honey, and very bitter chocolate. Then it is baked into a cake. I have it every birthday, but it has to come all the way from Irkutsk to Petropavlosk and only when it is winter to preserve it, so it is very expensive."

"Well, one is never too old to learn a new thing." And what do you like to do besides eating Bird-Cake?"

Laughing, she corrected Maria who was always getting things wrong: "Bird-cherry Chocolate-Cake Auntie."

"Oh, yes, that cake. But what I meant was what else did you like to do in Petropavlosk?

"Dance. I dearly love dance."

"Why?"

Nadia hesitated to give a full answer but then decided to lay it bare.

"Because it lets me move through space, light on my feet like a bird, or maybe like a young goddess running through her forest haunt or by the light of the moon skipping over water in an ice-cold lake in a trance."

Taken with Nadia's complete candor, all Maria could say was "oh my, that is so-so poetic!"

"Yes, that is how it feels to me."

"You are lucky to have such passion. Not many ever have it in life," she said as she shifted her gaze out the window in a moment of reflection.

"So, my passionate one, what else stirs your soul?"

"It's all the same Auntie. It starts with moving through space, maybe even through time. Horses. I love horses because they fly lightly across the land with their manes and tails tugged by the wind. Perhaps I should not tell you this, but in Petropavlosk I used to run along the deer trails for miles through the forest barefoot with my hair let down like a horse. And I can run like the wind."

"Yes, your mother told me about that."

"She knew?"

"Yes Nadia, your mother is not a stupid woman." And what do you know about your birth?"

Surprised at the seeming serious shift in conversation, she asked: "my birth?"

"Yes, what do you know about it?"

"Auntie, I do not understand your question, but I can answer thus. I was born like everyone else. Why do you ask?"

"Because I think you already suspect that there is something secret about your birth that you should know.

"And what is it that I should know?"

Maria smiled but did not answer. Instead, she told her this: "one day I will tell you a story I have never told to anyone. It is a story about a young girl who was born in Venice to a noble family just like you. And just like you, this girl had a secret."

"Did something bad happen to her because of the secret?"

"In time, my dear, in time," she said as she patted her knees which were still under blankets. And with that mysterious ending, their first catch-up conversation ended.

But Nadia still had an urgent question. "Auntie, where might I find the throne?"

"Throne?"

"Yes, Auntie. I have to, you know, go."

"Go?"

Exasperated, Nadia blurted out the word "dermo."

"Oh that. Under your bed is the bedpan."

"Bedpan?"

"Yes, of course. That is where they are always put. You do your business in there and then, well, then a servant takes it away, yes?"

Nadia pretended she knew what Auntie was talking about. "Oh, thank you. I must have overlooked where you kept it.?

In Petropavlosk you used a throne. Some called it an outhouse. Nadia's throne, which she shared with her family, was a wooden board with a hole in it that you sat on and did your business and it dropped into a pit dug down to the permafrost where you could dig no further. The throne was enclosed within a small shack built outside the house. Even in the harsh winter, Nadia had to brave the snow to get to her throne. Since Petropavlosk always had a breeze from the sea, the air stayed fresh there. Nadia was not so sure that would be the same with a full chamber pot sitting inside her room in St. Petersburg. While she was certain Auntie would have objected to her outhouse in Petropavlosk as crude and uncivilized, she was equally sure that the chamber pot was no improvement.

Maria busied herself with an agenda. She had arranged that over the next week she and Nadia would visit the Smolny Institute, then the Big Stone Theatre where they would meet the ballerina Kolosova during her practice session. Maria was a wealthy childless dowager. She had little else to do in life except to dote on philanthropic causes. One of those was her role as a patron of the arts and her past generosity to the theater made her request to see the ballerina unwise to refuse.

A week after she arrived in St. Petersburg on a bright Tuesday morning, Nadia and Maria had an early breakfast of boiled egg, toast with jam, and tea, served by a servant named Olga at a small table near a window that overlooked the Fontanka river. Then they boarded a carriage that followed the road alongside the Fontanka two miles northeast until it emptied into the Neva River. From there they followed the Neva for two more miles east to the Smolny Institute for Girls which was across from the Smolny Cathedral and convent. Maria had sent a servant ahead the day before with a message to let the headmaster know they would be arriving at precisely nine o'clock. She expected them to be prepared. Standing in front of the neo-classical building with its rolled ionic columns, the headmaster of the institute, Yuri Ivanov, met them on the snow-covered steps holding a studded cane. It was a sunny but chilly day that followed a light dusting of snow late in the night.

Yuri Ivanov welcomed Maria and Nadia into a spacious office that looked south over the Neva and seated them in diminutive leather chairs set in front of Ivanov's immense oak desk replete with carvings of wild creatures running in all directions. To Nadia's eye, the wild images seemed foreign in such a structured environment. After they sat down, Ivanov took his place behind his desk, sat on a silk pillow, and held a pen pensively between his two hands while resting his elbows upon the glass top of his desk. He wore a red velvet frock coat over a tan vest and a frilly white cravat at his neck beneath a high stiff pointed collar. His breeches went just below his knees to a pair of bronze buckles that secured the tops of white stockings that stretched down to a pair of French shoes with elevated heels. His curly white wig extended to a ponytail tied by a gold ribbon. It was all very Parisian, and Nadia struggled not to stare over the elevated desk at him from the modest height of her chair.

Maria spoke first in a voice and tone that Nadia had not heard before. It was a studied voice, stiff and nasal with higher and lower notes issued for effect. It was the language of aristocracy and it was the first time Nadia had heard it from her. She remarked to herself at how easily Maria adopted it when the social situation demanded it and then was able to revert to her normal voice when they were alone together.

"My dear Headmaster. We so desire to have a tour of your splendid school for girls, and look forward to meeting some of your students so that my wonderful niece, Nadia here, can chance to meet a few of her future classmates."

"Of course, madam. All has been arranged. Please, now permit me to inquire as to Nadia's application for admittance. Nadia my dear..."

"Yes, sir."

"I have come to understand you are from the provinces?"

"Petropavlosk."

"Yes. Precisely, the provinces. Perhaps I should say, the frontier," he smiled while looking over the rim of his glasses that he wore low on his nose.

"And I understand that you are the daughter of his lordship Timur Ulan Anichkov, and his wife Justina who are both of noble birth?"

"Sir, I have never heard my father called "lord." He is an Admiral in the Imperial Navy."

"Yes, of course, I only mean to establish that your parents are of noble birth which is, above all, a requirement for all girls who aspire to attend the Institute. You understand, of course?" he asked while exhibiting a courtly smile at both Nadia and her aunt.

Interjecting curtly in the same aristocratic tone that Nadia heard before, Maria throttled his questioning: "Mr. Ivanov, Nadia's mother Justina and I descend from the Renier family two of whom were among the last Doges in Venice. Anichkov, as everyone knows is an old noble family dating back three centuries in Russia. These are duplicative questions that I answered before this meeting and are settled matters. Don't you agree Mr. Ivanov," purposely ignoring his title as she delivered a rebuke to his line of inquiry?"

"Yes, yes of course," said Ivanov fidgeting and dropping his pen sending it clattering on the glass top of his desk. "Let's start our tour, by all means, shall we?"

Ivanov stood up quickly while straightening his velvet coat before rounding his desk to assist Maria from her chair. Nadia noticed he walked more like a girl than a man. While still holding Maria's fingers loosely in the high pose of a minuet, he escorted them both to the door and turned right down the cream-colored hallway toward several classrooms where teaching was in progress.

As they passed the doors and the blackboards inside, Nadia saw that the students were going through formal education in mathematics, reading, and writing. Some classes had students who were very young while other rooms held classes with students near her own age. She would be attending a different section of the institute reserved for those who had already received their basic education. Her school would be for finishing, which meant, learning the kinds of things an aristocratic woman should know. There would be no academic subjects at all: only how to speak the language that Maria had been using when she spoke with Ivanov, how to manage servants, entertain, and all the other cues, manners, and mannerisms that signaled status and rank. Nadia's hard-won grasp of history, knowledge of the major authors of the world, understanding of philosophy and art would count for nothing here. Only her skill at ballet would be considered of any importance on her aristocratic resume which the finishing school intended to expand.

At the end of the hallway was a closed door. Nadia could hear a woman with an aristocratically toned voice instructing students on a topic Nadia could not divine. When Ivanov opened the door, Nadia saw a dozen young women walking in a circle with the instructor coaxing their backs, chins, and shoulders with a conductor's baton into the proper posture for ladylike walking. The lesson of the day was to look straight ahead without expression, but as they rounded the room, their eyes were distracted toward Nadia in the doorway. One of the students was Katerina Vasilev, her unpleasant dance rival from Petropavlosk. When she saw Nadia, the bland look on her face turned to a confident smirk before she tripped and fell into the girl in front of her, and both tumbled to the ground. "Clumsy, clumsy," chided the teacher who hovered over them with her baton until they could get to their feet. Nadia suppressed a chuckle but was unable to hide the thinnest suggestion of a smile.

"Let us retire to the tea-room, shan't we?" asked Ivanov after the room settled down. "We will be joined by this class soon for tea and you can all get acquainted."

The tea-room was, in fact, a tea-room, but it was also a classroom, where under the eye of the teacher, the young ladies went through the rituals of having tea served by a servant. Nadia saw the servant and immediately said hello and introduced herself. "Hello, I'm Nadia." The servant was both alarmed and flattered to be noticed and looked to the headmaster and then back at Nadia before solving the awkwardness by curtsying to Nadia. "No need to introduce yourself to the servants," offered Ivanov. It was her first lesson.

At the top of the hour, the headmistress led her class into the tea-room, walked past Maria and Nadia, and then circled a large round table, took their assigned places, and sat down. Maria gestured for Nadia to sit in the only empty chair. The ten o'clock tea, unlike the afternoon tea was a relaxed time when the young ladies could be girls again at least for a few minutes. Ivanov asked each young lady to introduce herself to Nadia. After the introductions, it was not long before giggles and chatter broke out and they began peppering Nadia with questions.

"Katerina says you took ballet lessons with her in Petropavlosk?"

"Yes. We danced together in the same studio for many years."

"And she was the Prima Ballerina of Petropavlosk? It must have been thrilling to be dancing under her lead?"

Nadia hesitated before she answered. "Yes, all four of us were fortunate to be dancers in her troupe of five," she answered while looking directly at Katerina.

"Five?"

"Petropavlosk is a small place."

Katerina's face turned to an ugly scowl noticed by the headmistress who was still in the room. It was now clear to the students that Katerina's inflated claim to the title of Prima Ballerina had suppressed some important context. Katerina's boast was now laid bare in the eyes of the class which now understood her to be the proverbial big fish in the proverbial small pond that was Petropavlosk. As Katerina continued with her menacing scowl, the headmistress called her out and the class suddenly hunched their shoulders and went silent.

"Miss Vasilev, there is no scowling in this institute."

Soon Katerina asked the headmistress to be excused to use the toilet. "I don't feel well," she offered.

And with that, the room began chattering again with Nadia the center of girlish attention.

Three days later on a Friday, Nadia and Maria took another carriage north crisscrossing rivers until they reached the Big Stone Theatre. By the crow, it was only a mile away but by road, it was three miles due to the winding rivers.

Distant from the world's center for ballet in Paris, the Big Stone Theatre in St. Petersburg might have been expected to have been modest. By comparison, the Salle de la rue de Richelieu could hold two thousand three hundred in the audience. But modest did not describe The Big Stone Theater with its scale and imposing neoclassical design.

As the carriage pulled up to the front entrance, Nadia's eyes opened wide and followed the eight white columns rising up to the ornate Corinthian carvings at the top. It was mid-morning, long before the theater would open for the evening when carriages would be parked by the hundreds outside. But Maria had arranged for Nadia to enter and possibly even touch the stage, peruse the dressing rooms, and meet the budding twenty-year-old star Eugenia Ivanovna Kolosova as she went through her last practice routines on the stage where she would perform. The doorman who had been told of their appointment opened the door and welcomed them in.

Inside they faced a grand staircase and its landing. The steps led to four levels each with hallways lined with doors leading to the many private balconies that surrounded the main hall and the stage. Nadia and Maria bypassed the stairs and proceeded through the doors of the main hall stage. Ahead of the rows of seats on their right and left was the dimly lit stage. There a small figure was moving quietly to an unheard melody. The only sound was the dry sound of silk strapped feet stepping and sliding across sanded wood and the staccato sound of cushioned toes landing *en pointe.* Nadia stood motionless with a faint glow of gas lamps lighting her face. She did not want to break the spell. She just wanted to keep watching the figure float over the stage. But Maria cleared her throat and the dancer stopped and shielded her eyes to look over the dim lights of the stage to the back of the hall where Nadia and Maria stood.

"Hello," said the figure in the form of a question?

"Hello," answered Maria. "It's Maria. I'm here with my niece Nadia. Can we come in?"

"Of course, she answered," and guided them up hidden stairs near the orchestra pit to the stage. "I practice here instead of the studio some days. My feet need to know exactly where to step, and what the limits the stage presents. I don't want to step in the orchestra. It's a long way down," she laughed.

Kolosova had short spiked hair cut boyish for her role as the virgin huntress Diana in the ballet *Diana and Actaeon.* Kolosova noticed Nadia looking at her hair and costume and explained.

"The story is about Diana, the Roman version of Artemis, whose moonlit bath in a cool mountain lake is interrupted by a young man who spies her naked and must pay the price with his life when he is turned into a deer and devoured by his own hunting dogs. Sad, but severe isn't it?"

Then she broke the ice further with small talk:

"Your aunt tells me you want to be a ballerina?"

Blushing a little, Nadia answered, "No, not quite.

You see, it's just that I love to dance and feel myself moving through space. Running through a forest is a sort of dance. Running down a dry creek bed boulder to boulder is a kind of dance. Ballet is just another dance to me, and I do love it. But I have no plan to be a ballerina. But for the joy it gives me, I might share the joy and teach it to others. I have even thought of having my own studio someday."

"Oh, tut-tut," announced Maria who felt the need to correct her. "A person of your stature should not work for a living."

"Papa does."

"Kolosova continued with Nadia's thought. "Well, isn't love of movement a good start?"

As Kolosova talked, Nadia noticed that she had none of the aristocratic tone that she had heard from Maria and Ivanov. Its absence allowed her to relax.

"I love to move too," Kolosova observed. You know, being a ballerina isn't just about fame and fortune. It is really about a love of movement, so you are right. And for all its fanfare dance is really just about holding a pose, shifting to another pose, and telling a story with your body as you move." Then, after a pause, she added: "But, I confess, I also love the stage, the lights, and being seen by the audience. So, it's Ballet for me, not that I wouldn't want to run barefoot through the woods like you," she laughed.

Nadia liked Kolosova and was happy to meet someone so suited to their work. But in talking with Kolosova, Nadia realized how little she cared about the trappings that were part of dance: the stage, the lights, the costume, the adulation, and being seen. Her joy was only in the predicate of dance: movement itself of which dance was only one form. The thought freed her to find her joy even in the dark or under a dimly lit moon. Talking with Kolosova made her understand the difference.

"Would you like to go backstage?" Kolosova asked.

"Oh yes, very much."

Behind the stage was a maze of rooms, ropes, pulleys, and lamps. The dressing room was a mélange of tufted chairs and stools, dressers, hand mirrors, wall mirrors, paper notices pinned to the wall, and gas lamps. It was empty now, but Nadia could imagine the bustle of many dancers crowded together each vying for mirrors, checking their reflected images from all vantages and angles, and talking all the while. Nadia anticipated it would have a sweet smell like perfume. But it really smelled like upholstery, mildewed carpet, body-odor, stale sweat, and lamp-soot.

"Now that you have seen where the real things happen backstage, why don't you show me a little bit of your dancing?"

Nadia beamed in response and nodded yes. Maria had brought a bag with Nadia's costume for a ballet she had performed at the studio in Petropavlosk.

"I'm afraid you will find this a little dated," said Nadia. "We learned it at the studio because it was so important to the history of dance. It's called *Le Maître à danser*. It's seventy- five-years old."

"Yes," but it is still fresh enough," Kolosova assured. Come back to the stage when you are dressed. We will be waiting."

Nadia donned the costume, took a last look in the tall mirror, curtsied to herself, and went to the stage. When Nadia took the stage, she wondered where Maria and Kolosova had gone. Then she spied them beyond the stage lights which were blinding her vision. They were sitting in the audience seats. Quietly closing her eyes, Nadia took her position and held a pose as she rehearsed in her mind the steps, positions, and movements of the dance as she had practiced it in Petropavlosk. Then she imagined the music and began to dance and felt her silk-slippered feet glide over the stage floor making much the same sandy sounds Kolosova's feet had made the hour before. At the end of her piece, she bowed and heard someone in the darkened audience exhale.

After a pause, Kolosova asked flatly: "You don't think about your steps, do you?"

Nadia was still bathed in light on the stage and answered: "No. I just know. It's really no different than the forest at night. My feet find their way in the dark, and I never fall. When I dance on the rocks in a dry riverbed, I never know where my next step will go. It just goes where it must. It used to frighten me that my feet always knew where to land even if my mind did not. But now, I think, it's just who I am."

"It would be late for you to start now, but you would make a great ballerina. Your natural skills would serve you well."

"You are very kind. And I will treasure this meeting with you Eugenia Ivanovna Kolosova."

"That sounded almost like a goodbye," said a concerned Kolosova. "Are you leaving?"

Still standing alone bathed in the lights of the stage, Nadia smiled warmly at Kolosova, and thanked her for her generosity, but did not answer her question directly. Soon she heard Maria fumbling nervously with her bag in the dark as if she had lost something important deep in its recesses. Nadia and Maria then walked out of the theater without talking. When they arrived back at Maria's home, Nadia went to her room, closed the door, and began to write her first letter to Anton on December 20th, 1800.

Chapter 15, THE BETRAYAL

Nadia disliked everything about the Smolny Institute for Girls except for Annika Turgenev. Each of them was peculiar in their own way which led to a friendship among odd-fellows. Among the things the girls shared was a joy of running. Whenever they could leave the confines of the Institute behind, they ran along the embankments that lined the rivers crisscrossing St. Petersburg. Occasionally they would loop around the Smolny Cathedral next to the Institute. But for a longer run, they could go all the way to the Menshikov Palace along the Neva River where Anton had attended the First Cadets. Sometimes they raced in friendly competition. Other times they ran at an easy pace and talked. Still other times, they ran alone. Nadia was always calmer after she ran and felt at peace from the run and from being away from the school even though the other girls ridiculed them for it and called it unladylike.

Another thing they had in common was Eastern Siberia. Except for Katerina Vasilev, the Prima Ballerina of Petropavlosk, all the other girls were from urban Moscow or St. Petersburg. Not only were they not from a major city, but they were also from *the provinces* as well as Mr. Ivanov the headmaster liked to say while looking down his nose at Nadia. Nadia learned that Annika's family had come from an exotic line of wealthy merchants that originated in Mongolia but in later years had settled in Ulan-Ude on the Russian Mongolian border near Irkutsk. Her father, like most Mongolians, had slanted eyes and Annika had them too even though her mother had descended from the original settlers of Ulan-Ude: Ukrainian Cossacks who were sent there to suppress the natives.

One sunny day in late spring of 1801 they were sharing a path while running at a slow trot when they came upon a flat rock in a grassy field that seemed perfect for sitting and taking a rest. Still panting, they began to have a little talk.

"You say Irkutsk is near Ulan-Ude? I have a friend in Irkutsk," Nadia announced. "Have you ever visited there?

"Oh yes. My father has taken all of us there many times, usually in winter on a sledge crossing frozen Lake Baikal on our way west. We always go to the theater. It is small and made of wood, and the actors are all volunteers, but the plays are interesting and tell us things about the world. Before we return to Ulan-Ude, we visit an odd little bookstore there run by a hospitable old Jewish man and bring back books to read. When you come from a place like Ulan-Ude, it is sometimes good to get to learn about what is beyond Ulan-Ude," she laughed.

Nadia wanted to keep the subject on Irkutsk, but she was polite instead and asked: "What is it like in Ulan-Ude?"

Annika excitedly explained: "Ulan-Ude is like two places at once. Some buildings look Chinese or Mongolian. Others look just like those in St Petersburg. Often, we see Buddhists walking about wearing saffron robes. At their monasteries, they have large bells which they ring with a log slung from ropes. You will never see that in St. Petersburg," she laughed.

Nadia tried to imagine such a bell and its sound but could not. As she was trying to imagine it, Annika was musing on her own thoughts which included some youthful insecurities she was shy about. Unknown to Nadia, Annika feared that her new friend might think lesser of her for not looking as European as the others at school and wondered how Nadia felt about having darker skin color which set her apart too. It was part of their shared oddness. So, without malice, she formed a question in her mind she hoped would lead to a longer conversation:

"Katerina told us that your Indian grandmother gave you your pretty copper skin and your Russian father gave you your blue eyes. Is that true?

"I believe it is," she answered.

Nadia did not return to the finishing school that day. Instead, she walked briskly and alone back to Auntie's house and barged through the door.

"Auntie!"

Chapter 16, SECRETS

Nadia found Maria sitting by the fire in the main room humming a song to herself as she knitted a sweater for her niece.

"Auntie"

"Yes, my dear."

"Did my father have an affair with an Indian woman?"

"From your question I think you already know the answer. But yes, my dear, he did."

"Was she my real mother?"

"Not quite. She died in childbirth, and your mother, my sister, raised you as if you were her own."

"But I don't look Indian except for my skin."

"Your Indian mother was born to an Indian woman and a Russian trapper on an island in the Pacific near Alaska. She was a half-breed, and very beautiful. Your father fell in love with her while he was away on that island. They carried on in a relationship while your mother, my sister, stayed behind at Petropavlosk."

"Why am I just being told this now?

"Because it was not my place to tell you, and your mother was desperate to keep it a secret. She was afraid it would ruin your chance at rising in society."

"But you did tell me."

"Not until you already knew it was true. But there is more I have to divulge, and now it is time to tell you that too. Pausing for a full minute, she finally blurted out: Your mother and I are half Jewish."

Perplexed at this surprising news, Nadia reflected on what all of this might mean to her in St. Petersburg. She knew that Jews were a society apart and very few were allowed permanent residency in Russia proper, and certainly not a residency in St. Petersburg. Instead, they were forced to reside in areas called the Pale of Settlement: Belarus, Poland, Lithuania, and Moldova. Being Jewish was synonymous with being un-noble, and in all her life she had never knowingly met a Jew. While the news of her Indian blood was enough in its own right to ruin her future as a noblewoman in St.

Petersburg, it was not a surprise. It only confirmed what she had suspected for a long time. But being part Jewish was not something she expected, and it utterly guaranteed her ouster from the ranks of the Russian elite. Her mother's dream for Nadia to rise in noble society was now inexorably shattered.

Yet despite the finality of the news, Nadia's reaction was more of a release than of shock. It made her more curious than devastated. She questioned why her mother never told her the truth about her birth-mother, curious about how it happened, and curious about where the liaison had occurred with the Jewish man.

"Tell me more Auntie?" she asked as Maria continued with her knitting.

"Well then. Brace yourself."

"Long ago and even today, Venetians have some strange habits: habits that I hesitate to tell a young girl like you. As I said to you on the first day I met you for the first time, I made a comment about men and their base desires and about the horrible urges that cause men to assert themselves even upon savages. But I left out an important fact: women can also have such desires even if they do not admit to them, and go about satisfying themselves even if in less obvious ways. Venetians found a way to ensure that such desires could be satisfied in secret bouts of lust between nobles, between nobles and servants, and even nobles and Jews. The way in Venice, they say, is with a mask. Nadia, you look confused."

"I am confused. What might a mask have to do with my grandfather being Jewish?"

"Patience my dear, it will be explained soon."

"You see in Venice, it is permissible, even advantageous to hide your business, your identity, and your purpose by wearing a traditional mask. They are used at Carnival, Balls, and large gatherings, but they are also used during daily business where one desires their activities be done secretively. Which leads us to lust for the sake of lust."

"Auntie," exclaimed Nadia feigning embarrassment while her eyes opened wide eager to hear more.

"As I was saying, the word is lust. My mother who of course is your grandmother was married to a nobleman named Renier. Your grandfather was a fine gentleman, but he was unable to perform his essential duties to his wife as a man due to an accident. Thus, your grandmother had womanly desires that he could neither satisfy nor deny. So, she took to sating that desire. First, with the approval of her husband, she began to take dance lessons in the afternoons. Since the classes were focused on preparing for Carnival, she and all the adult students wore masks for each session. The masks also made it easier to be social and intermingle with strange men while incognito. Shy women could be flirty behind their masks. Shy men could be entertaining conversationalists.

Your grandmother's mask was sleek and golden. It covered her forehead and nose leaving only her ruby lips and her flashing eyes exposed. After her weekly lesson, she would walk along the canals while still wearing her mask toward the quiet Jewish Ghetto on the north side of Venice where there would be less chance for her to be recognized. A tall dark man at the dance studio began walking with her. He would go as far as the Ghetto and then he would excuse himself and disappear down a small alley. Then one day, after she had secretly rented a small apartment overlooking the Rio de Ghetto Canal, she invited him up to her room and he eagerly accepted her invitation. Ostensibly, it was only for tea, but we are not fools, nor were they. From that day forward, she saw him on the third Tuesday of every month, at four in the afternoon, for three years, at her place near the Ghetto.

In that time, your grandmother became pregnant twice with your mother and me. Your impotent grandfather simply stayed mum when his fellows congratulated him on his virility upon the births of his daughters. Then, one day after three years of meeting secretly, and by tacit agreement always wearing their masks, your grandmother and her lover decided to reveal themselves and made love one last time. And with that unmasking, your grandmother confirmed what she already suspected: her lover was a Jew and her children, therefore, were half-Jewish. Only her husband's impetus to keep his impotence a secret kept the secret of her lust safe—until now."

"Auntie, why are you telling me this? Why not keep the secret."

"Because it is only fair that you know who you are and what the consequences are if you stay. In this city, everyone is judged by their pedigree. You might still have a chance at success here if you battle the rumor of your Indian blood, and hide the secret of your Jewish grandfather. But you will never survive both revelations, and even the rumor of them without proof will taint your fortunes here forever. It is better for you to know now than after you have dedicated yourself to finding your place in St. Petersburg. Now, at least, you know enough to make your choice. Risk everything by staying here, or risk everything by not staying here."

Nadia furrowed her brow trying to digest the revelations and what they meant to her. Then she realized that Auntie faced the same predicament that she was now facing due to her mixed-blood heritage. Soon she had a question.

"Auntie: Why did you stay?

"Because I was too frightened to lose the privilege that the Renier pedigree gave me, too accustomed to being rich to risk my wealth, and too alone after my husband died to leave my familiar surroundings. I was, in short, a coward. And lest that sound like a brave confession, know this. I would be a coward again—a highly respected and ostensibly noble coward I might add. But as for you, well, tell me more about this adventurous Anton fellow who lives among *savages*.

Chapter 16, LETTERS

June 1801
St. Petersburg
Dear Anton,
Thank you for the letter you wrote to me in February of last year. I so looked forward to it, and

when it arrived, I was so happy, not only to hear that you were safe, but that you wrote at all. I was so pleased. We are good friends, aren't we?

Your cabin on the granite rock above the lake sounds lovely. The killing of the bear sounded dangerous, but you did a gallant deed by saving the boy. I look forward to seeing your sketches of the cabin with the lone tree beside it. And I am so happy that the Tlingits have stopped shooting their arrows at your door. Please be careful with your life Anton, you are dear to me.

Anton, I have some bad news. I care little for how it affects me, but greatly about how you may feel toward me after you hear it.

Anton, two family secrets have met the light of day to the detriment of my future in St. Petersburg. The first is that my mother is not my mother. My real mother was half-Russian and half Indian - Aleut I think. I had suspected as much since there had long been a rumor about an illegitimate love child brought back to Petropavlosk by a naval officer and his wife who passed the child off as their own. I never challenged it in Petropavlosk to anyone who suggested it might be me because it didn't matter so much there. It is, after all, the *frontier* as my stuffy headmaster constantly reminds. But unlike Petropavlosk where societal rank meant little to anyone, pedigree is everything in St. Petersburg. Any life I thought I might have had or what my mother wished me to have here is now impossible.

Second, I am also part Jewish. It seems my maternal grandmother had an affair and both mother and Auntie are children of that liaison.

It matters little how or why these family secrets were finally revealed to me. But suffice to say, that Auntie confirmed these truths. Mother knew of course but never told me. I think she hoped that by my move to

St. Petersburg her own secrets would die, and I would live the life she thought she would have with my father when they married in Venice. She is a disappointed woman, and this news of my unmasking will not be a comfort to her.

Yet, I am surprised to tell you that I do not care. St. Petersburg is beautiful, gilded, and civilized but cruel to those relegated to the margins of the upper crust of nobility. Life at those margins is now my dismal destiny if I stay. I never liked it here. I know I should feel wounded at my fall from social grace, but I am not. In fact, I am pleased with it. It liberates me and explains so much about my natural self. And I embrace it.

So now my esteemed, adventurous, and still very noble friend, I do hope that this will not affect our friendship. Like you, I remember our baptism in the lake. It was more than girlish fun for me, and hope it was more than a young man's dalliance with a frontier girl. I would jump over that fire again with you if I could but beware, I won't let go if we do.

Christmas of 1802 will find me in Irkutsk at the hostel of Ilya. He cannot read or write, but the eldest of his adopted Koryak girls can. She said that Ilya would welcome me back, though I do not think those were his exact words. Since I have been forsaken by St. Petersburg society, and since I have no interest in returning to mother and father in Petropavlosk, I have decided to adventure my way to Irkutsk. Like me, it seems to have an assorted blend of many odd things, and my prospects there are enticing. Auntie is a very wealthy woman and kinder than I ever suspected. She will be financing my adventure there, and I have a plan for a business. So please write to me at Ilya's hostel in Irkutsk. I will be there by Christmas this year or January 1802.

Your Kupala friend,

Christmas, 1801,
Petropavlosk
My dearest Nadia,

I received your letter of last June with the news you would be leaving St. Petersburg for Irkutsk to arrive around New Year 1802. You may have already arrived there as I write. Your departure from St. Petersburg will be a loss to that city. They have very few Russian, Indian, Jewish girls who dance ballet as well as you. But to your concern, you will find me far more attracted to your mixed bloodline than any pallid damsel with a pure pedigree from St. Petersburg. By the time you receive this letter, you will probably already be at Ilya's hostel with his Koryak girls. Please give Ilya my greetings.

Much has happened since my previous letter. My last summer on Sitka in 1801 was eventful and enlightening, but also delivered burdens that I cannot now discuss beyond telling you this. I am finished being complicit with Baranov and his plan to take over Tlingit land. I have come to respect the Tlingit and their ways. They are not a perfect people, but I find that I admire them above my fellow Russians. They see themselves as of the land while we see the land as something to take, dig up, or harvest. As a result of my wavering allegiances, I confess to you that the adventurous young man you met in Petropavlosk is now a confused man. I am neither Russian nor Tlingit. In that sense, I am like you—a half-breed of sorts. As such, I am adverse and unwelcome among the familiar ranks of my birthright.

And now, I am a spy on my Island hosts who have been good to me. Perhaps I belong in America where birthright is, as yet, unknown. Or perhaps, like you, I belong in a place like Irkutsk where, as you say, many are exiles, punished on high for their thoughts or actions, strangers in their own land, scolders of their own race, who belong to no place other than in the vastness of Siberia.

But enough of my philosophy: I will depart on my last mission in a few months. I need to tidy up some delicate business with the Tlingits, then I will resign my post and return on the next available ship: to where I have not yet decided. By the time this letter reaches you, I will be on Sitka Island for the last time.

Should we ever meet again, I hope it will be summer on Kupala near a cold lake deep in a wilderness of trees on a moonlit night. Will you dance for me?

Your loving friend,

Anton

Ps Enclosed is a sketch of the cabin.

REPORT

March 15, 1802

To His Excellency Alexandr Baranov

Your Excellency,

This is my sixth report on the Island of Sitka. As I noted in my report dated October 1801, I was summoned to a Potlatch ceremony at the main village by Stoonook, the War shaman of the Kiks.ádi. I was the guest of honor, and the Potlatch was in recognition of my saving the life of his son from an attacking bear with my long rifle. It was also to sacrament the totem Stoonook had carved into a tree next to my shelter. He also gave me a small replica of the totem and a necklace of bear claws from the bear I shot. My killing of the bear has endeared me to the Tlingit. They no longer threaten me and consider me their friend.

Most importantly for this report, in attendance at the Potlatch were Kotlian, their war chief, and Skautlelt the regional chief from whom you gained agreement for the land upon which the fort Redoubt St. Michael now sits. Puyuk, my confidant, and teacher accompanied me and guided me on the protocols of the Potlatch.

During a lull in the long ceremony, I went outside the house to get some fresh air and was met by Kotlian who asked disturbing questions about our true motives for our presence on Sitka. He suspects that you plan to take over the Tlingit lands on Sitka just as he said you did with the Aleuts. I, of course, said that I had not been told of any such plan; however, I must ask. Do we have such plans?

Of minor note to the Russian America Company, I was given the gift of a slave girl captured during a Tlingit raid on an Aleut village. Her name is Aluki. Her parents were killed, and Puyuk advised in no uncertain terms that I must accept her—but I cannot. When I return to Sitka this spring, I plan to work with Puyuk to resolve how I can return this young slave girl in safety back among the Kiks.ádi.

On an alarming note, I have observed Russians abusing Tlingit women. The Tlingit men appear quite angry at their conduct and fights have broken out. I had to intervene between three drunken Russians when Puyuk swore at them for abusing some Tlingit women in her presence. In return, they threatened her with harm. I fear this is escalating the kind of tensions that were implicit in Kotlian's interrogation of me for our motives for being here.

Finally, the Russians are despoiling the area around the fort with refuse, fecal matter, and offal from the skinning of Otters and other creatures. This is not sustainable and awkward since the Tlingit villages are far more sanitary than our own. The spread of disease seems imminent if these conditions are allowed to continue.

In closing, I also must inform you that I plan to resign from my position after this summer's visit to Sitka. My reasons are personal and not suited to a public report. I would deliver this news personally in great detail if Kodiak were not so far away from Sitka, but alas, it is a long voyage from here. Suffice to say I am no longer able to support the mission and will return to Petropavlosk this fall, and from there I have not yet decided on a destination although, I know it will not be St. Petersburg. Thank you for the opportunity to serve you on this mission.

Your humble servant,
Lt. Anton Niktovich

Chapter 17, SITKA, SPRING 1802

Anton departed Sitka in the fall of 1801 to winter in Petropavlosk, but he left Aluki behind in the care of Puyuk at the main Tlingit village. His question of what to do with the slave girl, Aluki, his unwanted gift from Stoonook at the Potlatch, was still unresolved. Whatever his decision about her fate, it had to assure her safety.

The fact that Aluki was gifted as property raised possibilities thought Anton. As property, he would have the right to free her and return her to her home village on an Aleutian Island. The problem with that was that her parents died in the raid that enslaved her. So, who in her village might take her in? He was not confident that she would be accepted back as an orphan by her people amid a Russian siege and when Aleut women were being distributed among Russian hunters to keep them happy in their beds far away from their wives at home. The second problem was that that the Russians were rumored to be seizing whole villages of Aleuts and forcing the men to hunt as slaves for them while holding their wives and children captive should they refuse. Anton concluded that the risk of freeing Aluki back to her village only to have her become a sex-slave of a Russian otter-hunter was unacceptable. Alternatively, he thought he might be able to gift her to Puyuk who was already acting like a grandmother to her. But that would leave her still a slave. What would happen to a slave if Puyuk died of old age? And how would Stoonook respond to seeing his gift to Anton walking in the village with Puyuk as her new owner? Still, that was a possibility so long as the arrangement would not embarrass Stoonook and Puyuk would agree to it. Anton would talk to Puyuk about that when he reached Sitka. He knew that if there was no good solution for Aluki, that his life would be changed forever.

On May 1st, he left Petropavlosk and set sail for Sitka and arrived on June 12th, 1802 expecting it to be his last trip to the land of the Tlingits. After hoisting his loaded backpack stuffed with eighty pounds of provisions, slung his rifle over his shoulder, and stuffed his pistols into his belt, he stepped off the longboat into shallow water and trudged toward the fort to the sound of sea water squishing out from his boots. Several Russian trappers in bloodstained buckskin outfits were lingering at the main gate along with Tlingit, Kodiak, and Aleut women sitting or sprawled on the ground. It was early afternoon and the fort seemed to be buzzing with voices from inside the walls. When the main gate opened to let in a load of supplies, Anton spied a full host of Aleut hunters from distant islands working their catch of furs. They had been forced into labor by the Russians who held their families as a ransom for their work. But he saw only a few Russians inside the gate, and security seemed dangerously lax given the hostile visages displayed by Tlingit men lingering at the edge of the forest.

Hiking up the hill toward his cabin, he noticed more trash and offal torn from otter bodies littering the way further up the mountain that he had seen the year before. Moose flies feasting on the otter guts buzzed and occasionally attacked Anton's neck with their fierce mandible bite until he got higher on the mountain and closer to the lake and his cabin on the granite rock. As he neared his shelter, he passed three Russians who had camped alongside the trail. Anton said hello but got little response from them. Based on their armaments, Anton surmised they were hunting for provisions for the fort but noted that they were drunk, and he gave them little chance of a successful hunt in their condition.

Soon he saw the tip of Stoonook's totem over the trees and he was at the cabin in minutes. Poking open the door, he peered inside before entering. All seemed to be in order, given the long winter that followed his departure in September of the previous year. It was apparent that someone, probably Aluki or maybe Puyuk, had cleaned the cabin and added to the store of firewood in his absence.

This year I will leave in August, he thought. *After I settle my Aluki problem and Baranov is confronted I will have no further business here. I'll be free to do I know not what.*

After stowing his provisions and gear, he leaned his Kentucky long rifle against the wall close to the bed and laid out his two pistols on the table by the door. A light rain was falling, and it was cool enough to warrant a small fire, which he stoked in the fireplace. As the sweet smoke of spruce filled the cabin and surroundings, the mosquitoes quieted and gave Anton some peace. Though he rarely smoked or drank, he prepared a pipe with tobacco and sat by the fire scratching his lengthening beard and hair and pondering once more what to do about Aluki, about Baranov, and what he would do next with his life. Then he reached over into his pack and pulled out a bottle of Chinese vodka and drank until he passed out on the floor.

Near sunrise, there were heavy footsteps and grumbling voices near the door. Quickly rubbing sleep from his eyes, Anton got to his feet and looked through the slot and saw the same three Russians he had seen on the trail the day before. As he donned his trousers, there was a loud pounding at the door. Sensing danger, he stuffed a pistol into the back of his trousers.

"You in there? Hey, you in there? Come on out!

Anton cracked the door showing only his face. "What do you want?"

"Food is what we want. We're starving back at the fort. We've been hunting but haven't found much more than a squirrel. What's this totem thing you got here?" "You some kind of Tlingit?"

"You'd find more game if you drank less."

"What'd you say?

Anton answered with one hand behind his back on the pistol. "I said you would find more game if you drank less and hunted more."

"And just who the hell are you to be telling us how to hunt."

"The name is Anton Niktovich, on assignment for Alexandr Baranov, your boss."

A long silence ensued until Anton finally heard a reply.

"I remember you. You're the cadet pup he sent to spy on the savages. You got any supplies to give out or not."

"My supplies are none of your business, and I'm a scout not a spy. You want supplies, go out and find them in the woods."

Responding with nothing more than an unintelligible growl, they grudgingly backed away. Anton's eyes surveilled them as they went cursing and stumbling toward the trail on the other side of the lake. *Damn*, he thought. As they retreated, he punished himself for not quickly recognizing who they were when he ran into them at their drunken camp the day before on his way to the cabin. These were the same Russians he had encountered at the fort the year earlier when Puyuk told them that they stunk like pigs as they ogled drunken Tlingit women. They had threatened Puyuk for her insults and called him "puppy" when he defended her just as they had called him a "pup" the moment before. He closed the door when they reached the trail. But they left their smell behind.

Yes, that was them. The same ones who said they would find him alone someday.

After breakfast, he packed up all of his weapons and left for the main village to see Puyuk and Aluki while keeping an eye out for the intruders. Three hours later, at ten o'clock in the morning, he found Puyuk near her lodge. They greeted like old friends: happy to see each other after the long winter. Aluki was nearby but stood aloof - guarded and frightened. The return of Anton only heralded another threat of change to her life over which she had no control. Still unsure of her future, she edged nearer but clung by the side of Puyuk and gave cursory bows to her disinclined master who smiled back and tried to be as reassuring as he could.

Poor thing: She can't decide if I'm her father, her lover, her older brother, or her slave.

"Puyuk. We must talk. I am not wise in the subtle ways of the Tlingit. I know I have received a great gift from Stoonook in Aluki. I know too that I cannot refuse this gift. You have told me that. But I cannot keep Aluki. I cannot take her back to Russia —I cannot."

In response, Puyuk told Anton of his powers over Aluki: "Slave is property. Tlingit can always give property, kill property, lend property, free slave who are property. Then, with a knowing twinkle in her eye, she asked him:

"You want kill Aluki?"

Irritated, Anton replied tersely: "No, I do not want to kill Aluki. Nor do I want to leave Aluki behind as a slave. I want her to be free, and I want her to be safe. Tell me Puyuk. How can I do that?"

"You are right Anton; you could not shame Stoonook by refusing his gift at the Potlatch. But you may give her back to Stoonook at another potlatch. It is honorable."

"But she would still be a slave, Yes? And Stoonook could do anything he wanted with her?"

"Yes, Aluki is property."

"Puyuk is kind to Aluki. Will Puyuk take Aluki?"

"Puyuk is old. If Anton give gift of Aluki to Puyuk, Aluki still a slave, and she will die a slave."

Frustrated by her confining responses, he pleaded. "Puyuk is wise in the way of the Tlingit. Show me the way."

"Not hard, Anton. You see. I fix and all be happy." With that, she began telling him a story. "Anton," asked Puyuk, "did I ever tell you story of old woman and cub?"

Anton gave her a puzzled look. *What,* he asked himself*, could a story about a bear cub have anything to do with solving his Aluki problem?*

Puyuk noticed his puzzlement and gave him an order only a grandmother could give to a grown man: "Sit Anton. Listen!"

Anton begrudgingly took a seat on the ground beside her lodge, which was named aptly for the story she was about to tell. It was called The Brown Bear Lodge. Anton crossed his legs among the fallen spruce needles dampened from a light rain and listened while

Aluki played with the small totem and rattle Stoonook had left with Anton the year before. Anton, in turn, had given it to Aluki before he had left for the winter. It had become her favorite toy. Puyuk stayed standing but swayed and gesticulated in all directions as she spoke in her storytelling voice.

"Once there was a great Brown Bear who roamed the forest near a village with her cub. One sunny day in summer, a hunter spied the mother bear in a clearing and shot her with an arrow through her heart. As she lay dying, the cub lay next to her body and would not leave even when the hunter skinned the mother and took its meat back to the village. When he went away, the cub still lay there and would not leave the place where its mother died and shrieked the way all cubs shriek when separated from their mothers. An old woman nearby with a broken leg was limping alone through the forest with a walking stick. She was weak from old age and hunger and expected to die soon, but then she heard the wail of the cub. When she came to a small clearing, she saw the blood and offal on the ground she knew what had happened and felt sorry for the crying cub and adopted it. In gratitude, the cub went out and found food to bring back to the old woman. Soon the woman's leg healed, and she was strong again. Then she went back to the village with the cub walking beside her like a loyal puppy. As she neared her lodge the cub changed its shape into a beautiful young girl. And forevermore, the young girl became part of the Brown Bear Lodge in the old woman's clan."

As Puyuk told her story, Anton watched Aluki's lips begin to form a smile. She understood. It was the first time he had seen her happy. At the end of the tale-telling, Aluki dropped the totem rattle and ran over to hug Puyuk and while still in her arms she turned to Anton and smiled again before burying her face back in Puyuk's bosom. *Like a grandmother with her grandchild*, he thought. Anton nodded and took a deep breath as he looked up to the sky and noticed a cloud that looked much like a dancer twirling on the wind – *Nadia,* he thought, *I'm free.*

"She will have all the rights of a clan member?" he asked.

"Yes. Puyuk will host a potlatch for Aluki's adoption when the days grow short. Aluki's clan will be the Kiks.ádi clan, the clan of Stoonook, Skautlelt, Katlian, and Puyuk. She will live under the roof of the Brown Bear Lodge - this lodge - my lodge. It will be law. You stay here tonight and go to cabin tomorrow at dawn. We bring small feast for Anton at noon. We sit by the lake with feet in the water and share happiness together.

Lying on the plank floor of the Brown Bear Lodge, Anton was relieved about Aluki, but the night was restive. He dimly heard unintelligible murmurs and agitated voices coming from the main lodge in the distance. The leaders of the clan seemed to be meeting late into the night. He also heard hurried footsteps scurrying from lodge to lodge and the sound of dry wood clinking together in the night. *Wind chimes,* he wondered? The whole village seemed awake. The annoying bustle continued almost until dawn. When the sun finally rose, a groggy Anton picked up his weapons and set off toward the cabin looking forward to seeing Puyuk and Aluki walking up the trail with a festive lunch and then sitting by the lake for the last time with both of them. But as he left the door of the lodge, he found Puyuk standing outside waiting for him.

"Anton take high trail this morning."

Querulous, Anton objected. "Why the high trail. It may be shorter but it's much steeper?"

Puyuk crossed her arms over her chest. "Today Anton take high trail."

"But..."

"High trail Anton. High trail today!"

The high trail led directly from the village over a steep section that eventually dropped back down to the main trail a mile up the hill from the fort. The main trail he usually took left from the fort and rose gently up a valley and had always been Anton's preferred route. But Anton had learned that when Puyuk insisted on something, she had a good reason for it even if she did not give her reason immediately. Instead of arguing, he acquiesced to her demand and waved just as Aluki exited the door and ran up beside Puyuk.

"Aáa tláa," said Anton in his best Tlingit for "Yes Mother."

Since there was not a word for good-bye in Tlingit, he put his hand on his heart and gave a slight bow. Puyuk and Aluki did the same. Fifty feet up the high trail he turned and waved again. Having risen above the village, he looked back from the distance and saw several men gathered near the main lodge. Two of them were wearing war helmets and body armor.

Anton cursed as the trail grew steep, slippery, and muddy in a light rain. The trail was not used often so it was not maintained. When a rock or boulder loosened by rain or melting snow would tumble down during the winter and come to rest on the trail, or when a tree blew down across it blocking the way, no one cared to take the time to clear it away. Anton was forced to go around many boulders in his path and straddle some large trees lying in his way which pressed splinters into his breeches. Finally, he reached the ridge where the trail descended back down to the main trail and intersected it a mile above the fort. *I hope Puyuk had a good reason for this* he cursed as he reached for breath from the exertion and turned right at the intersection. *Two more miles to go.*

As Anton neared the cabin the hair on his neck stood up and his instinct signaled that something was amiss. Pulling one of his pistols, he left the long rifle slung over his back and the second pistol at the ready at his spine and walked stealthily toward the cabin door which was ajar. He cocked the pistol before going closer. At the door, he held the pistol in one hand and slowly opened the door with the other. Things were on the floor – disheveled. Pushing the door to full-open, he saw no one inside. The bed was overturned, and all his provisions were gone—dried meat, hardtack bread, flint and steel, hatchet, spyglass. No Tlingit had ever taken a thing from him. It had to be the Russians.

Still fully-armed, he retreated from the door. *But which direction had they gone*, he pondered. If they had gone back to the fort, he should have seen them on his way up unless they saw him first and stepped off the trail to let him by; or, they had already passed the intersection at the high trail. It did not make sense that they would go the opposite direction past the cabin. The only thing in that direction was a Tlingit fishing camp on the bay and a Tlingit goat hunting camp high on the mountain. *No*, he thought. Their mission was to secure provisions for the fort. And now they had provisions in-hand—Anton's provisions. *No, they would not go toward the bay or the goat hunting camp. They would head toward the fort. But where were they? Think Anton. What are the possibilities? One, they are already at the fort. Two, they were already past the intersection at the high trail so I missed them on the way up the main trail. Three: they went off the trail to drink again and I passed them without knowing.*

Puyuk and Aluki were not due for another hour or two, so they were not likely to be close yet, but Anton did not know if they would follow the admonition Puyuk gave to Anton to take the high trail, or if they would simply go by the fort to the main trail up to the cabin. Of the possibilities, Anton could only eliminate one—the Russians would not have gone past the cabin toward the bay and the goat camp; they went toward the fort. All Anton knew now was that he needed to scout the trail all the way to the intersection. If the trail was safe from there, Puyuk and Aluki would have little chance of running into them if they took the high trail. *But did they take it?*

Unknown to Anton, the three Russians were halfway down the mountain toward the fort and had not yet reached the intersection with the high trail. They had decided to step off the trail and take a few snorts to celebrate their thievery. After imbibing, they would press on to the intersection and past it to the fort. But the few snorts turned into many. Laughing and cavorting the big one slapped the large bag of Anton's provisions while holding it like a woman. "That puppy is a dumb dog leaving all his supplies unguarded. Hah, hah, and harrumph," they laughed and cavorted until they all fell to the ground. "Dumb little doggy. Ha Ha!" Soon they were singing bawdy Russian songs, and they were still singing them when they saw Puyuk and Aluki staring at them twenty feet away on the trail.

Puyuk put her hands on her hips and uttered "lichán awé wé eex̱" at drunken men: the same words she had insulted them with the year before at the fort.

Though they did not understand her words they did understand her tone. At first, they did nothing more than turn to each other and giggle in the manner of drunks when nothing really funny has happened, but they laugh anyway. Puyuk was about to leave when they shouted. "What's in those packs you two are carrying grandma – Provisions they snickered?" At that, they all laughed as they lay among Anton's stolen goods.

Puyuk repeated her insult: "lichán awé wé eex̱!"

"I don't like the sound of your voice woman," said the big one. "Come over here and say that to my face. And bring your granddaughter with you. Kinda pretty isn't she?"

Higher up the trail, Anton hastened his pace in the direction of the fort – not so fast that he would miss the Russians if they had stepped off the trail for a drink, but quick enough to reach Puyuk and Aluki and escort them to the cabin. Half an hour had passed, and still, he had not seen Puyuk. *They must have left the village late,* he thought. Besides, he was almost halfway to the fort, and he had not caught up with the Russians either. *They're probably already at the fort celebrating over the provisions they stole,* he thought.

Just as he made that conclusion, he heard a distant scream and halted his movement while pricking his ears toward the sound. Hearing nothing more for ten seconds, he moved forward as quietly as possible to capture any more sounds ahead. Suddenly he heard a rush of air: whoosh-whoosh-whoosh as an eagle pumped its wings and flew low above the trees heading toward the cabin. *Just the scream of an eagle*, he thought as the tension in his shoulders went slack with relief. But after taking three steps, he heard it again, two hundred yards ahead.

Wanting to run toward the scream, he did the opposite and crept slowly down the mountain. Five minutes later, he heard a faint rustling of foliage to his right and then the sound of slurred speech from a drunken man in the bushes twenty feet away. Glancing down near his boots, he saw Aluki's totem lying in the mud. Quickly dropping down to a crouch, he quietly slunk further down the trail past the muddy totem and the drunks. After thirty feet, he reversed his direction and headed back toward the spot where the totem lay. As he did, he pulled out one of his pistols, cocked it, and held it hidden behind his back. Then he picked up a normal pace while casually singing a Russian folk-song loud enough to announce his nonchalant presence as he came up the trail: ostensibly from the fort.

"Ho the trail," boomed a drunk.

"Hey comrade from the fort, come take a drink with us," roared another one. "Come on over through the trees to our camp. Sing your song over here. We have provisions. Eat – drink."

Shrouded by boughs of spruce, he peered between the branches. Barely visible, Anton could see all three men sitting cross-legged on the ground in a clearing. But several feet away, he saw four naked feet and bare legs askew and motionless sticking out from under a huckleberry bush. Biting down on a finger, he feared the worst as he dropped down to hide behind a boulder. Barely controlling his quivering voice, he called out:

"Thank you, comrades, but I'm on my way to the bay on the other side. I must meet some comrades there. Have a drink for me."

After Anton trudged on, the big one turned to his mates. "To hell with him if he doesn't want to drink with us. More for us,"

Anton pressed on up the hill as if he were on his way to the bay. When he reached Aluki's muddy totem, he picked it up and put it into his belt. Now his prudent tactic of sneaking past the Russians toward the fort when he first heard them off the trail and then turning around back up the trail feinting that he had just left the fort was paying off.

Good, they think I am one of them.

If there was going to be trouble, he reasoned he needed a position above them not below them and not beside them when the fight began. So, the drunks, upon hearing a man loudly singing a Russian song coming up the trail, were disarmed and confident that it was just a comrade from the fort. Soon they were back to drinking and gloating near the strewn bodies of Puyuk and Aluki whose pale skin was motionless. Their wide-eyes stared lifelessly through the branches at the sky even as small birds busily picked huckleberries above their faces. *Nature is not cruel, it simply doesn't care.*

Anton knew where a large rock protruded out. It lay two-hundred-ten yards up the hill and just off the trail. From there, he could look down on the Russians in their small clearing below. Hidden by hanging branches of spruce, Anton could lay flat on the rock and be nearly invisible. After preparing his long rifle and cocking it, he yelled out to the men below.

At more than two-hundred yards away, his voice was distant and muffled. The Russians sitting in the clearing barely heard him. But one of the men heard his distant voice in mid-swig from his bottle and choked on his vodka. The big one also heard Anton and stood up to look all around like a bear on his hind-feet.

"Where are the women," shouted Anton?"

"You mean those two Indian whores," boomed the big one. "They're right here sleeping. That you puppy? Come on down and we'll wake them up for you. Oh, and thanks for the food."

"Last time I saw you, you had ivory buttons on your buckskin shirt. Point to the one above your bellybutton?" asked Anton.

Yes, please point to it. Do it and I'll blow it off!

Confused, the big one looked down.

"You mean this one?" as he pointed to the third button down and looked up in the direction of the voice with the smile of a child who had just pleased his father.

He was still smiling when a bullet blew off the end of his pointing finger, passed through his navel, blew through his liver, severed his large intestine, broke three bones in his spine, tumbled out of his back, and hit a tree behind him sending bark in all directions. He fell in a heap upon the ground: still alive, but unable to move his legs after the bullet tore through the nerve bundle in his back. Blood spattered out his mouth every time he coughed as he lay paralyzed with his face in the mud.

One down.

When they saw the big man fall, his two comrades ran for their muskets, but only vaguely understood the direction that the shot came from, since Anton was hidden so far away in the spruce. Anton was still re-loading when one of the men fired a wild-shot in his general direction, which whizzed harmlessly through the trees. The shooter stood up to re-load and was pouring powder into his charger from his powder horn when Anton's round went between his eyes and left a misty plume of blood and brain spewing out behind his head.

Two down.

The third one was the smallest of the three and whimpered as he sat in a fetal squat and hugged his musket as if it could give him safety and comfort. As the second man was still falling to the ground, the small one looked over at the leader who was coughing splatters of blood. The big man was now unable to feel anything from his belly button on down. At the brutal sight of his dead and dying brethren, the little one hurled his weapon to the ground and ran down the hill toward the safety of the fort. But he tripped over Aluki's body and fell. Looking back at the open eyes and lifeless bodies of Aluki and Puyuk, he gasped at the reckoning that seemed to be raining down upon him, and he got up and ran again. Anton assiduously trained his rifle on his moving target and adjusted for distance as he tracked him while running between the mesmerizing vertical lines of spruce. When the small one reached a grassy clearing surrounded by ferns, he was two hundred and fifty yards away. Anton led his aim to where he thought his target would be a second later and fired. It took some time for the bullet to traverse the distance and thread between the stands of spruce. Then the bullet tore through the small man's heart before he had the chance to hear the sound of the shot and was dead before his face skidded across the rain-soaked needles of spruce and his mouth filled with mud. It wasn't until his body stopped sliding that the forest finally erupted with the roar of Anton's rifle.

All down.

Anton left his long gun behind on the rock and carried one pistol in this belt at his back and strode down the trail toward the Russians. The other pistol was cocked in his left-hand. In his right, he gripped his knife. He walked deliberately down the trail to where the large one lay coughing near the bodies of Puyuk and Aluki, who lay under the huckleberry bush. As the man labored for breath, he rolled his eyes up toward Anton, who stood over his trembling body. When Anton started to kneel by the man, he hesitated as he heard a strange tinkling of wood tapping on wood behind him. It was the same sound he had heard the night before in the village as he fitfully tried to sleep in the Brown Bear Lodge of Puyuk. Looking over his shoulder, Anton saw a group of Tlingits. They wore armor made of inch wide planks of wood strung together with animal sinew hanging from their necks to their knees. The pendant planks of spruce knocked together to make a hollow sound like wooden wind chimes on a stormy night. The warriors were armed with muskets, spears, bows and arrows, hatchets, and hammers and had fearsome helmets with carved animals on their heads to frighten their enemies and even stop Russian bullets and swords. The day of the Tlingit had come. They were attacking the fort to rid the Russians of their land, and that was why Puyuk made Anton take the high trail avoiding the fort that morning at dawn. She knew.

As the warriors marched past the bloody scene with Anton hovering menacingly over the big one, several of the Tlingits paused as Anton kneeled and drew his blade under the skin of his scalp and cut while the paralyzed man wailed in pain. When Anton held the bloody scalp above his head in triumph and revenge, the Tlingits whooped with approval as blood dripped down his upraised arm and the big man's long red hair blew back and forth in the wind. Then Anton leaned down to look at the man eye-to-eye and slowly drew his knife across the man's throat. A thick stream of blood spurted out when the blade reached the jugular and splattered Anton's face. Still eye-to-eye, the man's eyes bulged in disbelief until they faded into a distant stare that saw nothing. There was no gloating or taunting over the other two dead men. They had died on the impact of Anton's bullets. But he scalped them nonetheless. It was the least he could do for Aluki, whose naked body lay with her eyes open to the sky, and her throat slit alongside Puyuk who died the same unjust death. Anton tried to console himself: *At least Aluki died free.*

But the words were hollow. Dead was what she was now. Exhausted from his blood lust and the loss of Puyuk and Aluki, Anton laid himself down among the litter of dead and fell into a deep sleep. He did not know how long he slept, but when he woke, he rubbed his eyes and shook his head as if to wake from a dream. Then he stood up and walked over to Aluki's body and dragged her out by her ankles from under the huckleberry bush. Kneeling down, he slipped his arms under her naked body and lifted her into his arms and carried her back up the trail to the cabin crying the whole way. Then he returned for Puyuk and then a third time for his rifle which he had left on the rock. Lying among the dead Russians, he found his pack from the cabin. They had thrown some provisions into it to carry them down the mountain. At the bottom of the pack, he found his wrinkled sketches. *I can press them flat.*

He dumped the provisions out and left those for the dead Russians. They were tainted and he wanted none of them. Then he donned the pack with his sketches onto his shoulders, picked up his rifle, and trudged back to the cabin.

After he laid Aluki and Puyuk side-by-side on the bed, Anton sat with them and drank vodka from the half-empty bottle that the big man was holding when the bullet tore through him. Between drinks, he spoke to Puyuk in Tlingit and thanked her for her lessons. As he sketched them in his bed, he apologized to Aluki for not being able to save her. Then after sitting with them for an hour, he stood up in the stillness of the cabin and checked for anything he might need. At the door, he saw Stoonook's bear claw necklace hanging from a nail. He lifted it and donned it over his head to his neck. The bow and arrow Puyuk had shown him how to make in Tlingit fashion leaned against the other wall. He lifted the bow over his head and shoulder and picked up the quiver of arrows. Then he laid out his army uniform on the bed next to Puyuk and Aluki and lit the cabin afire from the inside and walked out.

For a reason that drinking too much vodka could not explain, he danced and swayed around the fire as his necklace rattled and held Aluki's totem as the cabin crumbled to the ground in ashes. *Gan eeti,* he thought as he remembered Puyuk teaching him the word for ashes—*Gan eeti*. The big totem carved from the lone spruce was stained with soot, but it remained standing and bore silent witness to the tragedy.

Yes, father. Even a scout must take a side. But not Russia's side, not the Polish side, and not the Tlingit side. The right side father.

Some at the fort saw the distant plume of smoke on the mountain and wondered what it might mean.

Chapter 18, DESTRUCTION OF THE FORT, JUNE, 1802

Tlingits were streaming down the mountain from all directions toward the fort. Some came from the fishing camp by the bay and the goat hunting camp higher up on the mountain. Many saw Anton's burning cabin on their way down from there. A few saw Anton, scalping the Russians as they passed by on their way to battle. But their main business was to destroy the fort, and all vestiges of the Russian presence on Sitka. Many more would soon converge on the fort from the main village along with more distant settlements and other clans. The coordinated attack designed by the war chief Katlian would come from warriors on foot and by fighters in canoes in a pincer move. When all were in position, the attack began with arrows slung from land and war canoes at sea led by Katlian. Hundreds of high arching arrows were loosed almost straight up into the sky and then rained down inside the walls of the fort. Many who were out in the open were killed or wounded in the first volley. Katlian always kept spies inside and knew almost exactly how many were living at the fort—twenty-nine Russians, two hundred Aleuts in forced labor for the Russians, three British deserters from the Hudson Bay Company, and some Kodiak women. As the arrows began to fall, a young Russian Lieutenant ran toward the front gates which were still wide open.

"Close the God Damn gates you fools," barked the Lieutenant in command of the sentries as he ran brandishing the air with a sword. But before he could get to the gate, a falling arrow went through his clavicle and ruptured his heart in mid-stride. He died before he hit the ground with blood gushing out his mouth from his torn aorta. Others nearby were hit in the top of their heads by the falling shafts tipped with carved bone, hammered copper, or flaked stone arrowheads.

Two Aleut sentries were able to reach the double-doored gate and managed to push them closed then lock it with a sturdy log placed horizontally into the brackets just as more arrows began to fall straight down from the sky. Most arrows sounded like cruel rain pattering when they hit the dirt. Others hitting the wood siding on the houses buzzed until they were still. The seaborne group of Tlingits led by Katlian continued their arrow attack on the other side of the fort. Soon it was under siege from all sides by hundreds of Tlingits.

Amid the chaos, an affable young clerk wearing glasses who assisted Baranov rushed up the stairs to the walkway along the parapet. As he ran, other men took positions and began firing their muskets at Tlingits climbing up the walls. The clerk thought he saw movement on a hill by the outbuildings outside the walls of the fort and adjusted his glasses. There he saw Skautlelt, the chief of the Kiks.ádi clan. Beside him was Stoonook, the war shaman. Both were urging warriors to scale the vertical logs of the fort.

After the attackers climbed to the top of the walls, they dropped down onto the walkway. Then they leaped to the roofs of the buildings below them inside the fort and spread out rooftop-to-rooftop. In the chaos, the clerk turned in time to see one warrior standing on the roof of Baranov's personal house reloading his British musket while a Russian who lay on the ground below him was writhing in pain from a bullet wound.

From their rooftop positions, they rained down bullets, arrows, and spears on anyone out in the open below. Soon they would leap to the ground using knives and clubs and dug into cellars to find hidden survivors. The young man stayed low and ran along the walkway to the other side of the fort nearest to the sea as he dodged wounded and dead defenders. Below the wall, he saw the war chief Katlian driving his flotilla of canoes toward shore to disembark his warriors to the land and join the fighting, which was now hand-to-hand.

Then he saw three warriors lift the locking log at the front gate letting the Tlingits pour in through the open doors. The clerk craved the courage to shoot himself. But instead of taking his life when he had the chance, he watched a wall of Tlingits close in on him as he weakly pointed his pistol at the horde. He was the last Russian alive in the fort. For a moment it became quiet except for a few wails from dying men. Then suddenly, twenty arrows were loosed into his body and he fell from the walkway to the ground to the sound of the wooden shafts snapping when his arrow riddled body hit the dirt. Seeing the officer die, a warrior standing by Stoonook boasted:

"It is a great victory over the ill-mannered Russians, is it not?"

Stoonook looked back at the warrior and lamented, "No, all we have done is awaken the beast. In one year or two, they will be back. They will have bigger guns and bigger ships."

Three miles up the hill Anton sat in his bloody clothing by his lake with his barefoot feet in the water just as he often did with Puyuk when she had something to teach him. Embers from the cabin still smoldered. When he looked in the direction of the fort, he saw billowing black smoke rising high into the mid-June sky which had cleared and become sunny for the moment. And out to sea, he saw the faint silhouette of a large ship probably sailing toward the smoke and fire, unaware of what had befallen the fort. Then, shifting his mind from the tragedy, he pondered what he had to do next to live out the day.

He knew that the hot blood of the Tlingit warriors still rampaging at the fort would likely be boiling for the rest of the day. In their current state of murderous frenzy, they might mistake Anton for just one more Russian and kill him reflexively.

Better to hike up the trail and descend to the bay on the other side. There's safety there – I think. There's that small fishing village – probably heard of me through Stoonook and Puyuk. Can't risk the fort. No. They would tear me apart.

He had few belongings to gather, nothing to prepare, and no food. Most of his possessions had burned with the cabin. What he would take were his weapons, the bloody clothing on his body, his pack containing his sketches, the bear claw necklace around his neck, three bloody scalps, the bow and arrows, and Aluki's totem in his belt. His feet were still cooling in the lake when he stood up and hopped across the warming granite to a seat sized boulder and dried his feet. Then he donned his stockings and his boots and set off up the trail away from the fort. The path would lead up a steep rise and then drop down to the bay below and the isolated fishing village where Anton had never before set foot.

A pile of granite stones were piled three feet high and marked the spot of the trail junction. From there the path went up the mountain to a goat hunting encampment or went down an intersecting trail down to the sea. Far below Anton could see the wide bay and the river flowing into it from the east. Where the river flowed into the sea, a small Tlingit village was visible from three miles away from where Anton stood by the pile of stones. After he descended the trail and neared the village, he paused to check his weapons. Three dogs scampered toward him and splashed across the rivulets sounding a barking alarm to the village but wagging their tails and giving off a confusing message to Anton. He unslung his rifle, not to shoot them, but to use it like a stick to keep them at bay. As he crept nearer to the lodges with the dogs still barking and trailing behind him, two old men stepped out with their bows nocked and ready to loose while their thin arms trembled from the strain of keeping their bows taut and from their fear of the rifle-toting Russian dressed in bloody clothes.

Huddled behind them were several women and some children. Anton guessed that all the young men were fighting at the fort and the old men were the only defenders. To show he meant no harm, he laid his rifle at his feet then he held Aluki's totem high above his head in his right hand. Soon the old men were smiling at each other and nodding as they lowered the bows. They knew the story of Stoonook and the Russian who saved his boy from the bear. As Anton took a deep breath of relief, the women and children came out and surrounded him with giggles. He was in safe hands.

When he told the women he was hungry, they cooked a salmon filet over a fire for their famished guest and served it to him on a plate carved from alder and covered the fish with wild onions and sourdock from the riverbank. As Anton was wolfing down the lightly cooked flesh of the salmon, children at the shore began to jump up and down and shriek excitedly as they pointed out into the bay. It was a large ship flying a British flag. Anton dropped his plate to the ground spilling the fish into the dirt and ran to the shoreline. To get the attention of those on board, Anton fired his rifle into the air and waved. Through his long-glass, Captain

Barber of the Unicorn saw Anton and ordered a long-boat to go ashore with ten armed men aboard to investigate. The landing party soon learned that Anton was Russian and worked for Baranov. As the seamen took him into the longboat and rowed him back out to the Unicorn, Anton turned and waved good-bye to the villagers.

He could not have had better luck regarding his rescue nor his goal of seeing Baranov. Captain Barber happened to be sailing by when the attack commenced and had managed to secure many valuable pelts in the confusion from outbuildings around the fort. He also rescued two Russians who were outside the walls hunting for game when the Tlingit's attacked. Then he rescued twenty Aleuts who had been out in their baidarkas fishing. Many of the others in and around the fort were killed or missing. The Unicorn now looked for survivors north of the burning fort and his seamen were scouring the shoreline along the bay when Anton fired his rifle as a signal. Captain Barber continued searching the shoreline for two days and negotiated the release of more victims from the Tlingits. When he determined that the search for more survivors was futile, he ordered the Unicorn to be brought about and turned west toward the setting sun and set full sail for the six hundred mile voyage to Alexandr Baranov's headquarters on Kodiak Island.

Chapter 19, BARANOV

Captain Barber was left with the grim mission to notify Baranov of the massacre and the destruction of his beachhead on Sitka. His second task was to deliver the survivors and the pelts, but not before securing a ransom for their rescue and return. Once he had obtained that ransom and conducted other trading business with Baranov, he would then be off to Petropavlosk.

On the upper deck of the Unicorn were two Russians. They were the only Russians besides Anton to survive the attack on the fort. They sat barefoot in ragged clothes apart from the others and held their knees against their chests and stared off into space. The twenty Aleuts gathered near the bow. Anton chose to sit with them. He tried speaking to them in Tlingit, but none of them understood the language. Many, however, spoke broken Russian. At first, they kept stoic looks on their faces when he tried to talk. He was Russian after all, like the ones who had taken their families hostage to secure their labor. But several were curious about the little totem in his belt, the Tlingit bow and arrow, and the bear claw necklace around his neck. They were brave enough to break the ice. Soon they crowded around him asking questions of the Russian who spoke the Tlingit language, carried three Russian scalps on his belt, wore clothing red with dry blood, carried an American rifle, and wondered if he was a Russian or something else.

The Unicorn plowed through the waves heading west toward Baranov's headquarters in St. Paul Harbor on Kodiak Island. Anton stood at the prow of the boat with a fresh wind blowing his lengthening hair and snapping it wildly behind his head. He watched as porpoises rode the energy wave of the ship as it plowed through the water. Large whales spouted and breached as they cruised through the water harvesting krill on the lee side of the ship. On the starboard side, he watched pods of killer whales with their tall black fins undulating through the seas as the predators patrolled the islands for seals. When the Unicorn passed the island the Tlingit called Tikh, a few sea otters and fur seals dotted the shoreline and bobbed in the shallows though their numbers had been decimated by the Russians. One of the Aleuts stood with Anton at the prow watching the sights. He told him that not many years ago the beaches on that island were full of the creatures — but no more.

"Now," he lamented, "the Russians have their eyes set on Sitka."

Eight days later the Unicorn pulled into St. Paul Harbor and moored at the main dock just after eight in the morning. The main buildings on the island other than the Orthodox church were a series of warehouses where Baranov stored the valuable furs gleaned by Russian hunters assisted by their Aleut slaves.

The largest of these warehouses was set on a small rise above the harbor. It was constructed simply with squared logs, a cedar plank roof, and was set two-hundred feet inland overseeing the bay which kept it safe from earthquake driven tidal waves. A wooden stairway led up the hill from the dock directly to the door suggesting that this was an important building. Nearby was the Russian Orthodox Church with its white walls and blue onion-shaped domes. Baranov himself lived modestly in a leaky wooden Yurt but did most of his work from an office in the main warehouse. On this morning Baranov was sitting at his desk by a window enjoying his morning tea and was surprised to see the unexpected arrival of a ship.

Captain Barber instructed his men to tie off the Unicorn to the pilings on the dock. The dock lacked the iron cleats found on most moorings. Given the weak pilings, he slid the ship in aft first in case he had to head out to sea to quickly to avoid the arrival of a sudden storm that would threaten the flimsy mooring at the dock. St. Paul harbor was a poor place. This far from civilization and readily available manufactured goods, the Russian America Company had to improvise on almost everything from iron for cleats, cloth for sails, and rope for rigging. Supplies coming overland from industrialized centers in Russia or Siberia took months to arrive in Okhotsk and were very expensive. And the only Russian ships available to ferry supplies to outposts like Petropavlosk, Kodiak, or Sitka were crudely built at Okhotsk or Yukatat, a Russian trading post on the Alaskan coast north of Sitka.

The only timber available was native larch which was not available at Okhotsk. While the shipwrights were reputedly skilled enough at ship-building, there were rumors of their excessive drinking of vodka throughout most of each workday rendering their work unreliable.

Most supplies did not come overland but came instead from foreign ships especially those from Boston and England. These Pacific trading vessels first had to sail around the perilous Cape Horn at the southern tip of South America. Then, once in the vast Pacific, they roved between trading destinations like China, Japan, Korea, India, Spanish American Missions, and the Russian America Company at Kodiak which traded furs for hard currency, food supplies, and luxuries like tea and sugar.

Now at the dock, Anton stood at the aft of the deck and leaned over the taffrail of the Unicorn to get a better view of the headquarters of the Russian American Company. He compared it in his mind to the Tlingit village of Puyuk and found it wanting. This place seemed dispirited, wet, muddy, overcast, and barren. *Who would live here*, he thought?

An Armed crew stepped forward and flanked the gangplank barring the rescued Russians and Aleuts from leaving the ship while Captain Barber disembarked with a bottle of Scotch as a gift to ply Baranov in his negotiations. He strode confidently down the dock and up the steps to the warehouse. The crude building ahead seemed the only likely one among the other nondescript buildings to find the leader of the Russian American Company.

What a miserable place these Russians have, thought Barber as he approached the building. *Hardly comparable to a commoner's privy.*

The captives on the ship watched from a distance as the door opened and Barber disappeared inside to deliver the news to Baranov about the destruction of Fort St. Michaels, his hard-won foothold on Tlingit soil. Then he would negotiate a ransom for the release of the rescued Russians and the furs he had managed to salvage from the outbuildings at Fort St. Michaels after the massacre. Baranov had worked diligently to establish his presence on Sitka and the news of its destruction was crushing to him. But he did not let his feelings known to Barber with whom he had business. The immediate matter at hand was obtaining the return of his men and the furs. He would deal with what to do about the massacre and the loss of the fort in time after careful calculation. He knew that would take years.

After pouring drinks intended to loosen up the negotiations, Barber proposed he be paid fifty-thousand Rubles for the three Russians, the furs, and the Aleuts.

Unruffled by Barber's opening gambit, Baranov the patient negotiator offered to fill Barber's glass in return and freely acknowledged the value of the furs and admitted he needed the return of the men. He gave nothing away since it was already widely known that he was always short of manpower. Few Russians were willing to sign up for the long journey to Alyeska and the dismal work that fur hunting required. Yes, he needed both the Russians and the Aleut slaves on board Barber's ship. So, he gave up little by admitting it.

But Barber thought these obvious admissions of need strengthened his hand and he betrayed a slight smile as he offered to fill Baranov's glass in return. But Barber's hopes of out drinking a Russian as part of a negotiating tactic were a fatal error. *We'll see how this British poppycock holds his liquor,* thought Baranov, the seasoned Siberian merchant and fur trader formerly from Irkutsk. He toasted the Captain and upped the ante on the whiskey while adopting a tactical slur to his speech. He laughed jovially at all Barber's sloppy attempts at humor lulling the man into thinking he was in control of the negotiation.

After waiting for the alcohol to sink into Barber's head, Baranov began a series of subtle stratagems. First, he asked Barber in a matter of fact conversational tone if it was true that his only out of pocket costs for his cargo of men and furs was six days of food for them as they sailed from Sitka to Kodiak. Since Barber could not think of any other costs with which he could pad his bill, he acceded to the fact. Baranov paused for a moment then pulled a piece of paper from the drawer of his desk, and made a short note but laid his hand over it when he finished. The costs were a minor part of Barber's ransom bid and it did not hurt him to concede it. But then Baranov built upon that admission by repeating a boastful revelation Barber had made earlier about his Royal assignment which was to sail to Kodiak and Petropavlosk in hopes of obtaining furs for trade with China. While on that mission he had just happened to see the burning fort and stopped briefly for survivors and salvaged furs. He had not gone much out of his way and had only been delayed for a few days. After Barber conceded the second point, Baranov jotted another note on the paper which was beginning to unnerve Barber.

But the deciding factor in the negotiations, along with the several additional shots of vodka poured by Baranov after the whiskey ran out, was Baranov's recital of Barber's historic folly six years earlier in the mid-Pacific. Baranov casually recounted to Barber the humiliating tale of his infamy for piloting the first shipwreck ever to be recorded on the Sandwich Islands. Baranov reprised the story recalling that Barber had run a British warship called the Arthur aground losing both the ship and six of his men who drowned. Then, as if to satisfy idle curiosity, he asked him if it was true with a lilt in his voice to the end of "true?"

Humiliated that news of his misadventure had traveled this far north, Barber was a vanquished man and defeated men negotiate poorly. Hours later, he emerged on whiskey and vodka impaired legs wobbling down the steep stairs leading back to the dock. He clutched the rails for balance with one hand and held an agreement from Baranov in his other. It said that he would only be paid ten thousand rubles for the delivery of the rescued captives and the furs: a mere twenty percent of Barber's first bid. Before leaving the warehouse, Barber could not resist asking to see the two notes Baranov had written down during their negotiation. Baranov did not deny him. He slid the paper across the desk, and Barber put his glasses on to read. There were just two words: "Check," and "Mate."

Anton had never met Baranov in-person and was over six thousand miles away in St. Petersburg when he enthusiastically accepted an appointment to work for him. It was a decision informed mainly by callow ideas about savages and a naïve yearning for adventure. He had obtained his post through letters between Headmaster of the First Cadets, Mikhail Kutuzov, and Baranov. The assignment, as presented to him, was to use his linguistic skills to learn the language of the Tlingit. He was to observe and report on their customs and practices, earn their trust, and assist Baranov to secure a peaceful relationship between the Tlingits and the Russian America Company's trading post called Fort St. Michaels on Sitka. The description of his assignment was tailored to suggest Baranov wanted a mutually beneficial arrangement for leading to peaceful trade between equals. But that was a lie.

As he prepared to challenge Baranov, he imagined a large powerful man, perhaps in the mold of Ivanov the bully at the First Cadets, or the largest of the three Russians who murdered Puyuk and Aluki. As he was having those thoughts, a fast-spreading rumor quickly ran through the ship's deck suggested that Barber had just been out-negotiated. This only added another level to Baranov's powerful mystique. Barber, after all, ranked high in British nobility and was a Naval Officer and Captain of a British ship, no less. And this rustic Russian fur merchant whose birthright was barely above the peasant class of society and who resided in a land north of everything civilized and whose place of business was a drab little hovel called Kodiak had bested him. Word spread that all the rescued Russians, Aleuts, and furs had been delivered and freed for a pittance negotiated by Baranov. Anton drew a deep breath, then set his sights on the door at the top of the stairs, and strode down the gangplank to the dock. With no safe place to store them on the ship, he walked carrying his rifle and two pistols in his belt, bow and arrows over his shoulder, and still wearing his pack as he walked up the stairs.

Baranov was back to sitting at his desk after dispensing with the British Captain when he heard a firm knock at the door. Thinking it must be Barber returning to renegotiate their deal, he donned an angry face and threw open the door only to see a young man in bloodstained clothing wearing a bear claw necklace, three scalps, and a toy totem. Quickly replacing his frown with a welcoming smile, and unruffled by the strange dress of the fully armed man before him, he tried to assess who his visitor might be.

He must be a survivor from the fort.

"Yes son, what can I do for you?"

Anton had been rehearsing what he was going to say to a man he expected would be large and formidable and was now speechless. Standing before him was a stooped fifty-five-year-old balding man of modest height with large sad eyes, pallid skin, and spindly legs wearing a heavy orthodox cross that hung from his neck that pulled his head forward so that he had to strain his eyeballs to look up to Anton.

"Come in stranger. Come in. Put your rifle and other arms over here." Spying the blood and the red-haired scalp on Anton's belt by his pistols, he squinted at it querulously, and asked: "injured at the fighting at the fort, were you?" When he noticed his long hair and his bear claw necklace he thought—*this is strange. He looks more like a Tlingit than a Russian.*

Still, without words, Anton allowed him to guide him to a chair in front of his desk while Baranov moved slowly to his chair on the other side where a pistol lay in the main drawer. Looking up with lamplight falling on his sad but kindly face, he asked empathetically: tea?" young man.

"Yes – Yes tea would be very good." The idea of hot tea made him suddenly realize that he had not been warm for several days, and he noticed he was shivering in the chair.

"Anna," commanded Baranov. "Two teas and some sugar please, and bring along the red blanket too."

Shortly later, Anton looked up to see a beautiful Aleut woman appear with a pot of tea, a bowl of sugar, small spoons, and a blanket folded over her left arm. After serving tea to both men, she looked at Anton then down to the red scalp and the pistols. Then she glanced up to Baranov before putting the blanket on Anton's shoulders and warmly tucking it into place.

Baranov thanked her for the tea with a "Thank You Princess,"

"Princess?" asked Anton.

"Oh, apologies all around. We have not yet introduced ourselves, have we? I am Alexandr Baranov, of course, as I believe you already know. This is my companion. She is known as Anna Grigoryevna. She is also called the Princess of Kenai as the daughter of a local chief.

"But she has a Russian name."

"Yes. As in the manner of Russia, conquered peoples are often given Russian names as a token of peace. Here she is called Anna. And may I have the pleasure of learning your name?"

"Anton-Anton Niktovich."

Baranov heard the name, but it did not register at first that this was his Anton Niktovich. Then suddenly realizing that it was his agent on Sitka, his eyes widened, and he exclaimed:

"You – you are Lt. Anton Niktovich," asking the question rhetorically?

"Yes sir."

Surprised to meet Anton so unexpectedly for the first time in-person and impressed by his luck at surviving the massacre he exclaimed almost in the formal manner of a court announcement:

"So, this is the noble son of Leonid Niktovich recommended by none other than Mikhail Kutuzov for an appointment to me and my mission on Sitka. I am so pleased to finally meet you in person and that you have survived the attack. You know, I have been receiving your reports every six months now for almost three years. I would have gone to meet you in person on one of my visits to the fort, but your cabin was too far and the path too steep for a man of my age. My apologies."

Anton had a worrying thought: *He's not acting like he has received my last letter resigning from my post. Does he know?*

It is good to greet you now. I see you are wearing the bear claw necklace and the small totem you described in your second report. You should know young man that through your reports we have learned much of value about the savage but crafty Tlingits."

Then, with a wince, he acknowledged the obvious. "The destruction of the fort and the loss of life is tragic and painful for me." Mustering a brave resolve, he said: "But I can assure you that I will be back. It may take years, but I will be back, and you will have been a great help in that effort. Rest assured young man, I will need you in these coming years."

No, the report has not arrived yet. He does not know I intend to resign.

Then, Baranov spoke excitedly in Aleut and announced to Anna who was with their giggling children on the other side of a pile of provisions. "Anna, this is Anton Niktovich!"

Unaware that Baranov had an Aleut mistress as well as three half-Aleut children by her, and also impressed by Baranov's facility in the Aleut language he remarked— "You know the tongue of the Aleut?"

"Yes, Anton. You look surprised."

"It's not what I expected from the head of the Russian America Company."

"What did you expect?" Ignoring the question, Anton asked: "Did you get my March Report?"

"No, I have not. But as you know, the mail is very unpredictable. Sometimes it comes by ships under foreign flags which stop at Okhotsk or Petropavlosk for mail coming from Russia, or they stop at Fort St. Michaels. The last report was October of last year when you reported on your invitation to the Potlatch. I was very impressed. Oh, and you mentioned a woman named Poouke and the girl slave, Uki."

"Puyuk and Aluki."

"Yes, that's it. How are they?"

"Dead"

"Dead? Killed by Tlingits?"

"By Russians."

"How do you know they were Russian?"

Anton was resolved not to hold anything back. "I spoke with them, and I found them drunk next to their raped and beaten bodies. They were still drinking, singing Russian songs, and laughing as if they had done nothing wrong.

Baranov tried to interject a word of condolence, but Anton kept talking.

"That was when I killed them and scalped them. One of them I scalped before he drew his last breath. He died a bad death."

"You say that as if you were describing the death of three dogs."

"No, not dogs. Dogs I would not have scalped. They murdered my friends."

"I see," said Baranov as he inched his hand a bit closer to the drawer. Then he asked slowly and deliberately a question whose answer seemed loaded with consequence: "And do you believe that I am your friend?"

Anton saw Baranov's hand inching toward the drawer but when Baranov saw him glaring into his eyes, he pulled his hand back.

"No, Mr. Baranov. You are not my friend. You are my employer."

"All right," said Baranov remaining wary of the man sitting across from him who had just admitted to killing three of his men and was still armed. And Baranov was not entirely sure of Anton's sanity or even his real purpose in meeting with him.

"I am sorry for the loss of your friends. You must understand that most of the men we get from Russia are criminals, prisoners, or other desperate men from Siberia. Often, they're brutes. Even then, we are still in need of Russians. We don't have enough of them to do the work. Thus, we are forced to enlist the Aleuts who do all of the hunting at sea."

"Enlist?"

"Yes, well they have to be induced. Call it forced conscription. Often, we ask for hostages to ensure they are committed to their work. Sometimes we must take hostages by force, but other times they readily submit when I tell them they will be paid.

"So, they're slaves."

"Ah, we get to the heart of the matter. Do I detect an idealist in my midst?"

Baranov was now beginning to sense why Anton had come to see him, and he heaved a sigh before answering and took a paternal tone laced with condescension.

"Life is complicated is it not? Is this the reason for your visit— Indian mistreatment, hostages, slaves, renegade Russians? At a certain age, you will find that nothing is all black or all white young man. Let me show you something, Anton."

Baranov got up and walked to the door and yelled "Alootook" to a man working on the adjacent building. Soon Alootook was at the entrance and Baranov invited him in.

"Alootook, this man is Lt. Niktovich. I want you to tell him the name given to me by my Aleut friends."

"You are called Nanuk."

“And what does that mean in Aleut?

“Great Hunter”

“And does Nanuk pay Aleuts when they hunt for him?

“Yes, he pays in iron.”

“And what if the Aleut refuses to hunt.”

Alootook looked at Baranov then to Anton. Then he stated matter of factly: “Nanuk take wife and children. Man have no choice but to do work for Nanuk.”

“Does Nanuk still pay the man with iron.”

“Yes.”

“So, my dear Lieutenant, ponder this. I am a Russian man upon whom was bestowed the honorific title of Nanuk by the very people he allegedly abuses. Sadly, it is my only title. Russia, as of yet, has granted me none despite the riches I bring them. Also to my credit and my benign view of the natives, I learned to speak their language. And I hold dear my Aleut princess who is the mother of my three children.

So, when this Great Hunter demands that some reluctant Aleuts work for him by taking his family hostage to enforce that demand I ask you: is that Aleut a slave, a peasant, or a free man? I assert it is all of them at once and it is of necessity to achieve the goals of the Russian American Company of which I am in charge.

"Mr. Baranov, It's not important what I think about slaves, serfs, peasants, or free men. What is important is what the Tlingit think. And I can tell you they call it slavery and they will not submit like the Aleuts who they believe are all slaves. Tlingits are warriors Mr. Baranov. They will yield to neither the taking of their freedom nor the robbery of their land, your moral view of your actions will be of no account to them."

Baranov knew that Anton was right and that the Lieutenant's opinion on it mattered little. What bothered Baranov was being lectured on his treatment of the Aleuts by a man born into privilege. That would not lie with Baranov, whose grievance with Russian nobility and its crushing effect upon him ran deep.

"Mr. Niktovich, you were born into privilege. Your perspective on life is from the perspective of privilege. I, on the other hand, was not born to nobility. Do you have any inkling what it is like to be Alexandr Baranov and have to scrape and bow to superiors who by virtue of the womb that cradled them have the power to lord over me with impunity even as I labor to make them rich? I suspect not.

"Your grievances over your social rank that rankle you so deeply and distort your sense of morality are none of my concern Mr. Baranov."

With that, Anton stood up and walked over to his rifle and slung it over his shoulder, signaling his departure. As he half-opened the door, he paused and turned to Baranov.

"When my last dispatch finally arrives you will see that I have resigned. Good luck to you Mr. Baranov."

And with that, Anton walked out the door toward the ship to discuss passage to Petropavlosk with Barber. He wanted to be rid of Kodiak and everything associated with Baranov. As he walked down the wooden stairway, he heard Baranov bellow behind him:

"Your superiors will hear of this Niktovich. You are deserting your post!"

Anton stiffened and stopped in mid-stair with his back to Baranov. Baranov did not know what Anton's pause might mean and backed into the warehouse, leaving the door open just a crack to protect himself as Anton went over the word *deserter* in his mind. Then he continued down toward the Unicorn. *He's right. I am a deserter.*

As the pier filled with survivors coming ashore, Anton walked in the opposite direction, elbowing through the crowd. Then he strode up the gangplank to board the ship to ask Barber for passage. Barber, still slurring his words, replied that conveniently for Anton, his next stop was Petropavlosk. From there, the Unicorn would sail on to Okhotsk where Anton could pick up the Okhotsk trail toward Irkutsk, and whatever future he might find there.

Letter from Baranov

To: Your Excellency, Mikhail Kutuzov
From: Alexandr Baranov, Chief Managing Officer of the Russian American Company

Date: July 5, 1802

Dear Sir:

May this letter find you in good spirits and good health. I write to you soon after a tragic incident that will affect the Russian America Company operations in the Americas. Our only foothold on the fur-rich island of Sitka was destroyed by a coordinated attack on Fort St. Michaels by several clans of the Tlingit tribe. Almost all the occupants of the fort were massacred.

As you know, you recommended Intelligence Officer Anton Niktovich to assist me in my efforts to establish a diplomatic channel with the Tlingits to convince them that our Russian presence on their Island was mutually beneficial. We being without sufficient armed force presently to take it from them now, diplomacy was our only option. Niktovich survived the attack. Prior to the massacre, he had done a superlative job of learning their language, documenting their culture, and earning their trust to the extent that he even attended secretive ceremonies as a friend of the Kiks.ádi clan. Unfortunately, I believe he has turned feral on us seemingly favoring the Tlingits over the interests of his homeland and his birthright. A few days ago, he resigned from his post, but not before killing three of my men in retribution for their abuse of some Tlingit women. I say feral, in part, because he scalped each one and had their scalps tied to his belt when he resigned in my presence here on Kodiak.

I tell you this primarily because I believe he is still an officer in the Russian Army. Since this may become a disciplinary matter, despite his noble status that likely will shield him from serious reprimand, I still believed I should notify you in advance so that you may be sufficiently informed on the matter should his family appeal to you as his former headmaster.

My second purpose in writing you this letter was to let you know that I will be taking military measures against the Tlingits as soon as it is practical. I estimate that will be at least a year and probably two in order to get the armaments and the ships needed to dislodge these stubborn and warlike people from the Island or at least put them on the defensive so that we can bargain from a position of strength. I will need all the support I can garner from our military. Your endorsement of my cause will go far among the General Officers of the Army and Navy.

Your humble servant,
Alexandr Baranov

Chapter 20, FAREWELL TO PETROPAVLOSK

Anton sailed back to Petropavlosk in early-July after Barber finished his trading with Baranov on Kodiak. It had been three years since he first arrived there and met the beautiful Nadia standing outside the dance studio in the summer sun. As he strode up the hill past the studio to his cottage, people stared at his bloody clothing and unkempt hair. He had not been able to bathe or change since killing the three Russians. He had the foresight to stuff the scalps into his pack to avoid scaring the townsfolk, and wondered if it was time to be rid of them. But he was not ready yet. For a reason he could not fathom, he wanted Ilya to see them. Maybe it was for the same reason Ilya had to tell him that he once killed Indians because he didn't know any better. Anton could almost hear him saying:

"Ilya no more kill Indians. No more forever."

No, that's not right. Killing the Russians was justice, not murder, but still, it was a killing. Maybe it's just the killing that I have to tell Ilya. Maybe there is a brotherhood between killers of men. No matter. I will tell him. Then I will bury their scalps and be rid of their stench.

Entering the cottage at mid-day, he closed the door behind him and felt the peace of a familiar place. As he walked toward his bed, he shed pieces of clothing, weapons, and boots one by one in a trail on the floor before flopping onto the mattress where he slept until the evening on the following day. Then he hiked through the forest on a starless night up to the nameless lake he and Nadia had baptized themselves in three years before. He entered the cold water and scrubbed his body until the years of sweat, blood, and a bit of the taint from Baranov were gone. Then he donned a grey Kosovorotka tunic with trousers to match, black knee-boots, and was clean. Then he returned to the cottage and slept again until dawn the next morning when he awoke to see the Unicorn still in the harbor. Dark circles surrounded his sunken eyes.

He gathered the sketches he had drawn over his three years of traveling across Siberia depicting the sights and people of Petropavlosk, Sitka, and the ships at sea and placed them inside of a leather brief and wrapped it in oilcloth. Then he pried up a false plank in the floor and retrieved his meager supply of Rubles to pay for his journey to Irkutsk that would begin soon with a voyage to Okhotsk on the Unicorn. There he would rent a riding horse and a pack animal to travel The Yakutsk-Okhotsk Trail, and then secure passage by boat along rivers and carriages on roads. He placed his rifle and his bow and arrows in the same nondescript wooden case he had brought with him from St. Petersburg. His few other items like spare clothing, the bear claw necklace, and Aluki's totem went into a seaman's bag that he could lash to his pack-horse. The only other things he needed to buy were food, cooking utensils, a canteen, a fire starter, a tent and blankets, and citronella and mugwort grass for mosquitos. While Irkutsk was not home, his hunger to see Nadia and Ilya ground in his stomach, and he felt that if he could just see them once more that he could breathe again, and then decide what to do with his life. As he walked down the path toward the Unicorn a woman with a furrowed brow hurried up the hill with her head down and she smashed into Anton's shoulder knocking both of them off-course.

"Sorry," volunteered Anton.

"You should be," said the young woman. You should watch where you are going."

"Yes. Good advice."

As he continued down the hill it dawned on him who she was. *It's that girl from Nadia's dance class. The nasty one. I thought she went to St. Petersburg years ago.*

July 18, 1802
Dear Father,
I have much to tell you but little time to tell it. You will be disappointed to know that I summarily left my post at Sitka which will no doubt be the end of my military career. The fort built by the Russian America Company that lay three miles below my cabin was

destroyed with most of the occupants killed by the Tlingits. I escaped. Captain Barber of the British ship the Unicorn happened by the fort and rescued me along with some others and we sailed on to Kodiak where I promptly resigned as Mr. Baranov's agent on Sitka. My reasons were personal but had to do with the fact that I succeeded in earning the confidence of the Tlingits as I was asked to do. But I came to understand that Mr. Baranov wanted me to go further and exploit that trust to mask the true purpose and intent of the Russian America Company which is to occupy Sitka and enslave the Tlingits. This I could not do.

There is also the matter of three Russian marauders. These men killed two of my Tlingit friends without cause in a most gruesome fashion after abusing them. I challenged them for the murder and rape of my friends, and all three of them are now dead at my hands. I fear that Baranov, who was unhappy with my resignation, may allege that I am likewise a murderer in my own right. He also threatened to claim I am a deserter. I assure you that I had just cause in my actions, my motive for revenge and justice notwithstanding.

My actions will no doubt have repercussions as I am still an Intelligence Officer for the Army. Kindly use your influence to soften any damage that might come my way as a result. In any case, I do not plan to return to St. Petersburg, but instead, I desire to build a life on the frontier where my noble rank will offer me little advantage. What life that will be I do not yet know, but understand that I have come to embrace the idea of making my own way. I know that this is not what a son of noble birth does with his life nor is it what you hoped for me as a military officer. But be confident that I will succeed since to your credit you raised me to be a resourceful man. After Christmas of this year, you may reach me for a time in Irkutsk at a hostel called Ilya's House by the River.

Your loving son,
Anton

Chapter 21, THE RETURN

The voyage from Petropavlosk to Okhotsk took six days. Hoisting his weapons box and duffel over each shoulder he went down the gangplank of the Unicorn and walked the dirt road to the livery to purchase a horse to ride and a pack-horse for his gear. It felt ironic to Anton to be doing the trail in reverse from when he came from the other direction as a novice with Ilya as his guide. All of it came back to him, except now he was a different person. He was three years older and more wizened in the ways of the world and by his time with the Tlingits. And thanks to Ilya and Puyuk, he was now skilled at living in nature. He laughed when he recalled Ilya's gruff lesson about kindling and Puyuk's patience when she showed him all the ways to predict weather and find his bearings by sun, moon, and stars. Now he was on the verge of using all those skills along the 700-mile Yakutsk-Okhotsk trail. He was anxious to start the journey and to test of all he had learned about living in the wild from his mentors.

As he negotiated with the man at the stables for the horses, he noticed a man lingering by a fencepost with a travel trunk lying beside him near the start of the Yakutsk-Okhotsk Trail.

"Who's the man with the trunk?" asked Anton of the livery-man.

"Don't know. He's been there three days now. Think he's waiting for his guide."

"Who is his guide?"

"Nobody I ever heard of."

The livery-man saddled the riding horse while Anton fixed the rigging for the pack horse and loaded his gear. After paying, he walked the horses over to the man standing at the fencepost. As he got closer, he determined that he was a few years older, but no more than thirty. His hands were small, and he did not have the look of a man that got outside much and was out of place in isolated Okhotsk.

"Hello," said Anton earning a nod and a tip of the hat. "You speak Russian?"

"Da. I am from Moscow."

"You're a long way from home my friend. My name is nobody."

"Sir?"

"Sorry, I was trying to be funny. My name is Anton – Anton Niktovich."

"I am Viktor Turetsky."

"You seem lost Mr. Turetsky. Can I help you?" *He seems a helpless lad.*

"My guide is over a week late."

"Sorry. It is seven hundred miles across the mountains to Yakutsk. And I do not recommend trying it without a guide. Hopefully, your guide will arrive soon," he said as he started to leave. *He'll never make it alone.*

"No, wait," he pleaded as he stepped closer toward Anton. You see my trip began by sea. I left St. Petersburg two years ago and sailed around Cape Hope arriving in China on a diplomatic trade mission. My work done, I decided to sail north to Petropavlosk, and from there to this desolate place where I stand. And here I am."

"Why not return to Moscow by ship the way you came or via the Mongolian route to the Siberian Track through Irkutsk and then on to Moscow? This is the long way."

"Yes, that is certain. But truth be told, I wanted a little adventure. I wanted to see what lies east of Moscow all the way to the Pacific. Few have ever written about it. It's an interest of mine."

"Adventure! Ha," laughing mainly at the word and himself. "Adventure you will have that for certain."

Still laughing, Anton put his foot in the stirrup and threw his other leg over the saddle and was sitting tall above the smaller man.

"Sorry, it looks like you picked the wrong guide."

Anton tugged on his reins to turn the horse up the trail. After going twenty feet he heard the man behind him shout.

"What about you? Would you guide me?"

Anton halted his horses and sat in his saddle for a moment and thought. In another life, he would not have uttered what he was about to ask. But this was his life now, and he had to make his way. So he stood up in his stirrups turned around and asked.

"How much will you pay?"

"How much do you ask?"

It was Anton's first success at earning a ruble other than the pittance that the army paid him causing him to don a wide grin.

"Did I say something funny?" asked Viktor.

"No. It was not about you." He searched his memory for what Ilya had charged him for the same journey and let Viktor know the price. Viktor looked puzzled.

"Is that not a fair price," queried Anton?

"More than fair. It's half what my guide was going to charge me," he blurted without thinking.

"Well then, I'll just take that fee instead. Agreed?"

Knowing that it was late in the travel season and that nobody was likely to help him this time of year, he grudgingly acceded to the price.

"Agreed," said Viktor.

Anton dismounted and walked Viktor and the horses back to the livery to get another horse for the journey. "Let's go over our gear. I have a tent for two. You will need blankets, a raincoat, food, a knife-fork-and plate, and a gun. We should be able to get all of that here."

"A gun?"

"You have no weapon?"

"No."

Anton pulled one of his pistols and gave it to Viktor, but Viktor looked at it as if he had never seen a pistol before.

"You don't know how to shoot do you?"

"No."

"You'll learn."

Anton reasoned that if they should meet up with any trouble on the desolate trail that having each of them armed was better than just one of them. Half the usefulness of a gun was showing the other side that you had one. That said, he still planned to give Viktor a few lessons with it as soon as they had put a few miles behind them.

The trail led from the Pacific shoreline up the drainage of the Ulya River. When they reached steep sections, the trail morphed into switchbacks that zigged and zagged to allow a moderate angle of rise to the tread. After three or four of such changes in direction, the view and the trail became tedious. Anton led the way with Viktor following behind the pack-horse. But whenever Viktor got close to Anton's pack-horse he caught wind of something foul coming from it. At first, he thought it just must be how horses smelled. But it smelled like death. When they finally reached the crest and could take in the view of the Pacific behind them and the valley stretching out below, Viktor could not hold back any longer.

"Sorry Anton, but something in your pack stinks. I think a rat may have died in there."

"Yes, maybe more than one. I am the one owing the apology. I'll take care of it when we camp."

Viktor fell back and kept his distance from Anton and the smell coming from his pack-horse and began to enjoy the view. He would have enjoyed it more if the mosquitos weren't so thick.

"Anton," he yelled from the distance. "You have anything for mosquitos?"

"Yes, wait for the camp," he answered, enjoying a subtle but cruel initiation rite for Viktor about the outdoors in Siberia.

Anton's habit which he learned from Ilya was to wait until an hour before sunset before deciding to pick a spot to camp. After then, he would settle on the very first adequate spot they came to even if it were not perfect. That was because to look for a better camp further down the trail might find them having to search in the dark and regret passing up the merely decent campsite they had greedily left behind. Fortunately, they quickly found a good site near a fast-moving stream fed by a glacier. Anton did the work of setting up the tent. Before preparing dinner, Anton wove some citronella and mugwort grass into a necklace for Viktor who donned it immediately. To his great relief, the buzzing invaders finally left him alone.

Dinner was hard-tack and some jerky. They would hunt for fresh game the next day. As Viktor chewed on the leathery meal, Anton went to his duffel and reached in to find the three scalps which he had wrapped in oilcloth thinking it would contain the smell. As he unwrapped them they gave off an odor of death so strong he almost wretched. Holding them as far away from his body as possible, he trudged up a hill and buried them under a pile of rocks then returned to the stream to scrub the smell off of his hands. He was surprised he would be so relieved to be rid of them this soon since they had meant so much to him after the killing of Aluki and Puyuk. Back then, he recalled, they were evidence of justice. Now they just stunk. He laughed when he remembered that he had wanted to show them to Ilya. But now he could not remember why. Now they seemed just one last piece of the last three years that he wanted far behind him.

"I took care of the stink."

"What was it?"

"Three rats. But it's a long story. Someday I might tell you. Maybe after I cook up a special stew of venison, wild onions, and red mushrooms."

"Red mushrooms?"

"Yes, very red and very rare."

"After that hard-tack and jerky, I'll be looking forward to that stew," complained Viktor. I think I lost a tooth."

Viktor slept fitfully, and jumped at every sound and crack of a twig.

"Did you hear that?"

"Go to sleep Viktor. It's probably just a field mouse."

Just then, a large rock in the creek tipped over from the force of the current and made a loud hollow bonking sound and Viktor was sure there was a bear afoot.

"What was that?"

"A rock. Go to sleep Viktor."

The next morning found a tired Anton and a sleepless Viktor. Anton felt that the best thing to do when you felt like that was to press on and not give in to it. Soon Anton had packed his gear and the tent, but Viktor was still wrestling with his blankets. Anton let him struggle until he packed them away and they were ready to go.

“Your pistol Viktor.”

Viktor looked down at his belt and realized he had not packed his pistol. Anton held it by the barrel and handed it butt first to him.

“You’ll need this.”

With that, they began their second day on the trail. As they got into the rhythm of the horses, Anton looked over his shoulder and asked Viktor about his life. Viktor explained that he was an attaché to a diplomat and had accompanied him on a mission to Canton. Before that he was a seminary student at the Slavic Greek Latin Academy housed in a former orthodox monastery in Moscow.

“So, you studied to be a priest and then you became a bureaucrat? So, should I call you “Father Turetsky” or Ambassador Turetsky?”

“Neither. Frankly both were boring. I would like to say that each was exciting, but they were not. The main reason I entered the diplomatic service was to see new places. You see, I bore easily. My real passion now is writing and traveling. I plan to write a book on my travels.”

Viktor seemed proud of his kaleidoscopic background, but to Anton, it betrayed a distinct lack of conviction and direction. But his mention of writing a travelogue intrigued him so he asked about the book Viktor was planning.

“You mean to write a book like Aleksander Radishchev?”

Surprised that Anton knew of Radishchev he asked: "you know his work?"

"Yes. I read a smuggled copy of his manuscript for *Journey from St. Petersburg to Moscow.* It made the rounds at the First Cadets in St. Petersburg."

"No, not a book like that. Too much political questioning about nobles versus serfs and social justice. He tried to disguise it as a travel book with the title, but its political content was clear. Empress Catherine exiled him you know. No, my book will be an illustrated volume about Siberia and its people. I have no plans to write myself into an exile or commit suicide as Radichev did. I rather like Moscow and have no plans to take my own life. But I do hope to travel to the place where he lived for seven years."

"Where is that?"

"North of Irkutsk near Lake Baikal in a town called Llimsk"

"Oh, well then. You are lucky. We will go near it on our way to Irkutsk. Tell me about the illustrations you plan for your book?" asked the artist in Anton: "Paintings or drawings?"

"First the writing. The illustrations will come in time."

While Viktor droned on about the book, Anton spied a Roe Deer on a distant hillside. He dismounted and removed the box containing his rifle and pulled it out almost like a swordsman pulling his blade from its scabbard. Checking his powder and his load, he laid the barrel on the rump of the horse and aimed. After taking three breaths, he exhaled and left his lungs empty of air and squeezed the trigger. The deer jumped, ran a hundred feet, then fell down while the horse bucked at the sudden report and the recoil of the rifle against his rump.

"I missed," Anton exclaimed.

Astonished that he had hit his target from so far away Viktor questioned his comment. "No, you hit it. I saw it go down."

"No, I missed his heart. Probably hit his lungs. Either way, it won't run far, and it will be our dinner for several days."

After dressing out the deer, Anton quartered it. The first quarter would be fresh meat for the next week as they traveled through the mountains. Anton rode up the side of a steep section to find patches of snow to pack the meat and keep it fresh in the mild alpine temperatures. The other three quarters would have to be dried into jerky by cutting it into thin strips, salting, and laying it out on a lattice on top of the pack-horse. That meat would last all the way across the flatlands after they descended the mountains toward Yakutsk.

Toward sunset, Anton started looking for a campsite. As they came over a rise he saw a familiar lone tree and a perfect campsite beside it. It was the same spot he and Ilya had camped at three years before. Ilya had called it "his" campsite. Viktor had by now mastered the art of erecting their tent which freed Anton to prepare dinner. But before gathering wild onions and sourdock at the creek for a venison stew, he wanted to capture an image of the site. It would be a gift to Ilya titled "Ilya's Spot." Settling down with his pen, ink, and paper on a good sitting rock, he looked east toward the peak where Ilya had seen the change in the sky portending the storm. It was now just before twilight at the end of a clear day as he captured the winding trail, the lone tree, tent, the grazing horses, the campfire, long shadows, and the alpenglow on the distant peak.

"You draw?" asked a curious Viktor.

"Yes. I draw."

Viktor peered over Anton's shoulder as the sketch came to life with a line here, a line there, and some hash-marks for shadows.

"You are quite good at this Anton."

"Thank you," Anton murmured absently while hoping Viktor would leave him alone to concentrate on his craft.

"Do you have any more of these?"

"In the leather valise over there."

Viktor fetched the leather bag and pulled out sketch after sketch. One showed Nadia standing in front of the studio in the bright summer sun in Petropavlosk. Another showed her nude by a lake under starlight. Then there was Ilya looking formidable sitting tall on his horse on a mountain trail. Two Indian women sat by a small lake with their feet in the water. There were sketches of towns cast in winter snow, whales coursing the sea, fierce Indian warriors, totems, and whole villages by the sea with decorated war canoes pulled up onto the sandy beaches. There was a man who looked just like Anton standing next to a cabin with an Indian totem beside it. Several of the sketches had bloodstains on them.

"It's a treasure."

"What?"

"Your work. It is a treasure. You have captured Siberia and beyond. You realize that no one has done this?"

Anton looked up from his art curious to see Viktor's face to discern if he was serious about what he had just said. He saw Viktor standing with the campfire light on his face holding one of the drawings with his eyes wide and his mouth slightly open. His face expressed intense fascination in what he saw as if he had found a map leading to gold.

After finishing the drawing, he stowed it into his valise with the others and went down to the creek to find onions and sourdock for the stew. Alone back at the camp, Viktor was curious about the new sketch that he had just finished and picked it out of the bag. He was surprised to see that it included a perfect likeness of him sitting by the fire. Pleased and impressed with it, he placed it back into the valise. Meanwhile, Anton was searching for the vegetables and quickly found the sourdock. Then he found some wild onions growing out of the bank with some red and white mushrooms beside them and almost laughed out loud at Ilya's prank years before. *No mushrooms tonight*, he thought, *not tonight.*

On their last day in the mountainous section, Anton spied movement a mile ahead. Travel season along the Yakutsk-Okhotsk trail was always light in summer due to rain, mud, bloodsucking biting midges, chomping horseflies, and mosquitos. The flats below the mountains that led to Yakutsk were often swampy making it very hard on the horses and even on the men when it got bad enough that they needed to dismount to relieve their steeds. So, seeing several horses with riders coming up the trail this time of year put Anton on alert. He stepped off his mount and removed his rifle from the pack-horse to have it at the ready.

Days before, he had taken time to train Viktor on how to load and shoot a pistol. It did not go well, and Anton thought that Nadia had better skill at it than him. Nevertheless, Viktor wore it conspicuously on his belt as Anton had showed him. Stepping back up on his horse, Anton carried the rifle crosswise in his lap to ensure it was visible as well. As they rode downhill to within a hundred yards of the riders, they came to a large outcropping of rock and the riders disappeared behind it. Anton halted his horse with Viktor behind him and then waited for them to appear again on the other side of the rocks. While they were still hidden by the outcropping, Anton whispered an order to Viktor.

"If they approach us in a single line one after the other along the trail, all should be well. But if they spread out and approach us abreast, we'll need to flank them.

"Flank them?"

"Yes, turn your horse to the right ride twenty feet then turn your horse to face them and ready your pistol. I will do the same to the left. That's a flanking move."

Viktor trembled at the words that suggested they might be in mortal danger and clung to the pistol shaking in fear while trying to look brave in the face of danger. Then they waited until they could hear the slow clip-clopping of the horses coming up the hill dislodging rocks as they came nearer and nearer. Five armed riders with pack horses in tow shortly appeared.

"Hello," boomed Anton with intent to startle them and take them off-guard.

The front horse pricked its ears toward Anton and took a step back as the rider yelled "Whoa" to his horse and then shouted back a "hello ahead" to Anton.

"Who's there."

"Nobody special," answered Anton. "Just some fellow sojourners. How's the trail ahead?"

"Miserable," said the rider—"just miserable. Even lost a horse. Broke its leg in the mud. You'll see him down the trail. Sad, had to shoot him."

"Sorry for your horse. We'll pull aside for you since you're coming up."

With the niceties out of the way, the five riders all armed with pistols slowly spread out ominously forming a skirmish line and began to come forward as a group toward Viktor and Anton. It was just as Anton had feared.

"Now," said Anton, and Viktor obediently turned his horse to the right and trotted twenty feet and then turned to face the riders while Anton did the same to his left.

Anton now saw that he was facing five desperately poor Russian fur hunters likely on their way to Alyeska to butcher fur seals, otters, and Tlingits for Baranov. What they might want with Anton and Viktor he did not know. But their maneuver to spread out their firepower was not a good sign, and Anton was in no mood to assume these Russians were their friends.

Viktor held his pistol visible while pointing it straight up at the ready. Anton did the same and made sure the Russians saw his long rifle as well. Anton and Viktor were outnumbered by five to two. The arms on his side were four, while the Russians appeared to be carrying only five pistols among them. The odds were not ideal on Anton's side, but the Russians recognized that they could not be sure of prevailing against the two armed men in front of them, so they took a conciliatory tone.

"No need to be concerned with us comrade. We are just on our way to Petropavlosk. With your permission, we will just proceed in peace. All right, friend?"

"Have a safe journey," Anton responded curtly.

After they passed, Viktor leaned over his saddle and vomited his lunch. When Anton could hear their distant hoof-beats on the loose rocks no more, he pushed down the trail with Viktor in tow.

"How did you know what to do?" asked Viktor.

"I was once a soldier."

A day later, they found a horse covered with flies shot dead in a bog. A dead man was trapped beneath it half-submerged in the muck. He had been shot through the head. His mouth was agape, and his eyes were open wide as if to watch travelers passing by. Viktor vomited his breakfast at the sight, and quietly praised his God that Anton was his guide over the Yakutsk-Okhotsk Trail.

It took two more weeks of hard slogging to get across the muddy flatlands and several more river crossings to get to Yakutsk and the Lena River that would take them south to Irkutsk. They were lucky. Despite the mud and bogs they didn't lose a horse and made good time. But Anton drew no sketches of this terrain and was glad to be rid of it when they finally reached Yakutsk on the banks of the Lena River on September 2nd, 1802.

Chapter 22, THE HOUSE OF ILYA

Nadia sat by the wavy glass window of Ilya's hostel and watched his Koryak girls, Cheyvyne and her little sister, Kamak play on the banks of the Irkut River as it flowed slowly toward the town Irkutsk and Lake Baikal to the east. The morning was cool, and the days and nights now had the aura of fall with its lengthening shadows and angled light. While keeping an eye on the girls, she re-read Anton's letter from Petropavlosk sent five months earlier in the spring of 1802 before he was to depart for Sitka for the summer. It was to be his last time on that Island he said. A sense of finality hovered over his words. She worried about his tone and felt he was troubled by something, but could not fathom what it was. She was disappointed that he had made no commitment to see her in Irkutsk and had even suggested that America might be his next destination. Oh well, she thought. *We were just a fantasy anyway – yes, but it seemed so real,* she countered to herself. *But if he does come, he will probably arrive months after his summer duty on Sitka – when is that - let's see - if he leaves Sitka in early fall, he might be here by Christmas. Oh, Anton. I do hope to see you again.*

Ilya had been working hard to make the hostel appeal to the wealthier merchant and military travelers. Most of them came along the Siberian Track that stretched from Moscow to Irkutsk and beyond including a route to the only official trading station between Russia and China at Khyatka south of the Siberian towns of Ulan-Ude and Irkutsk. A few traveled overland from eastern lands like Korea, China, Japan, and Mongolia. Some of these travelers had ties to the tea trade or simply had a penchant for exotic journeys—like the British. Ilya had combined his guide business for such wealthy travelers with a pleasant place for them to stay. He called it "The House of Ilya."

Private hostels were rare along the Siberian Track. Most travelers had to use the post stations along the way which had minimal services. By the rustic standards of a Siberian post station, Ilya's hostel was regal. Like most buildings in Irkutsk, it was constructed of squared logs cut from Sitka spruce. Large windows paned with glass were featured on all sides of the structure and were framed by shutters as was the style.

Ilya preferred his wood in its natural unpainted state except for the shutters which he painted sky blue. The contrast between the weathered orange of the logs and the blue shutters made the building vibrant in the setting sun on its riverside perch. Alongside the main building, he built a small stable to shelter horses since he was a few miles distant from Irkutsk and the Siberian Track that led there.

But the main things that set off his hostel from the mail stations dotted along the Track were humble yet effective. They included his Russian Stove, clean beds, and two outhouses. Just having more than one outhouse was a luxury. But his outhouses had even more added comforts. He built a covered passage made of the usual square logs that connected to the main building forming a long enclosed hall leading to each of the vented latrines. A dedicated door in the hostel labeled "Fligel" led to the passageways. That meant guests could avoid walking through blinding snow and bitter cold to do their business, a unique luxury in sub-zero Siberia that was much appreciated by his roomers.

The second unique thing was that each guest got their own rope latticed cot to sleep on. Even better, his sheets were clean and devoid of bedbugs. At many hostels, the bare floor was the bed. As for bedbugs, Ilya had two methods of ensuring his sheets and mattresses were free of pests. In winter he hung the bedding outside and the insects would fall dead onto the snow unable to tolerate the freezing weather. In summer the bedding was washed and dried in the sun fresh for each new guest. The cleanliness of his sheets and bug-free bedding were widely revered along the Track and brought in more and more business from those who could afford his rates.

But the main attraction was his lavish wood-fired Russian Stove which was the centerpiece of his one-room hostel. It was built by local *pechniki* craftsmen who he paid handsomely with blocks of Chinese tea that he had traded for gold on the black market. The wood-fired stove exhausted its superheated smoke and gasses through serpentine labyrinths. These tunnels were made of brick and ceramic. As the smoke past through the inner pathways of the structure, it left its heat along its brick lined walls allowing the warmth to radiate out into the room. Finally, after leaving much of its heat energy behind in the bricks, the spent exhaust exited the flue above the hostel. It was an efficient way to warm the whole room with radiant heat during the long Siberian winter nights. Ilya also had the *pechniki* leave a section of exposed brickwork along a shared wall with the livery to take the edge off cold nights for the horses next to the hostel.

The stove also provided means for baking fresh Siberian breads in the oven aperture and cooking the collective meals that he heated in pots hanging above the open fire. It was also efficient for drying foods for long-term storage. Using ingredients from his permafrost cellar, he gained a reputation for good food along the Track. His venison stew made with wild onions, garlic, potatoes, or pelmeni dumplings and mushrooms cooked in venison stock was regionally famous. A line of clean pots and pans on hooks hung above the multiple cooking areas, and the hostel always smelled of a pleasant myriad of wild herbs, pine logs, and Mongolian spice.

At the wavy window, Nadia's thoughts were rounding in her head in an endless circle like an incantation. C*ome home Anton - Please...* But her melancholy thoughts were mercifully interrupted by the piercing sound of, Cheyvyne and, Kamak bursting through the door shrieking like the little eleven and seven-year-old girls they were.

"Hello big sister," said the older Cheyvyne.

"Hello, little sister, replied Nadia. "And hello to you too baby sister," she said to Kamak.

"I'm not a baby."

"That is true. I made a mistake. You are huge."

"I'm not huge either."

"All right. What are you then?"

"I'm just right."

"Yes, you are baby sister."

"N-a-d-i-a," she whined again and then went off and sulked in a corner by the Russian Stove.

For weeks, Nadia had been watching the girls for Ilya. Since his hostel business was always slow in the summer, on most afternoons, Ilya was free to play chess with his friend, a wrinkled bent-over Ukrainian Jew that had been exiled from Kiev to Siberia as punishment for selling politically provocative books. Now settled in Irkutsk, Abraham had managed to start a new bookstore in the commercial section of town and carried a wide array of world literature in several languages. The authoritarian urge to censor was far weaker this distance from St. Petersburg. So far, he had eluded the watchful eyes of the local authorities with his avant-garde offering of books for sale. But even if he had raised their ire, officials in Irkutsk were usually amenable to looking the other way for a pinch of Chinese tea or a jar of Chinese vodka.

Not only was Abraham Ilya's chess partner, he was also Nadia's landlord. Six months earlier, soon after she first arrived at Ilya's hostel after her fall from grace in St. Petersburg, Ilya took her to meet Abraham. His purpose was to discuss renting a vacant building that Abraham owned adjacent to his bookstore for Nadia's dance studio.

"This is friend. Name Nadia," Ilya announced to Abraham.

"Hello, my dear young lady. I am pleased to meet you. My name is Abraham Altschul." Then with a twinkle in his eye and a wry smile, he said: "But my real name is Abraham Cohen."

"Sir?"

"Sit, I have a little story," he said in a German - Yiddish accent.

"When I was a baby, Russia not allow Jewish names. They say to my parents, you can no longer be Cohen. They say to pick good Russian or German name. So, parents choose Altschul. In Deutschland it means "Old School." Russians know Deutsch, but not know Yiddish. In Yiddish Altschul means Synagogue. Ha! So, Russia not like my Jewish name of Cohen, but all-right to call me Synagogue. My whole life is joke on Russian. My name and my books—big joke on Russians."

For reasons only Abraham knew, it was important for him to explain the story behind his name to anyone he met.

"So, you want I should rent you my building next door to Altschul's bookstore? Come in for some tea by the fire. It's cold. We talk."

Even though Nadia had fallen from grace amongst genteel society due to her convoluted pedigree, a few of the benefits of being born into nobility still adhered. Those benefits included financial support through the generosity of her Aunt Maria. "Auntie" had promised to finance her ambition to become a business owner. Unlike St. Petersburg, in Irkutsk, an Indian, a Jew, a Russian, and even a Cossack could become what they wanted. And if anyone were wont to talk of class here, it would have been the merchant class. To nobles in the urbane west, merchants were not much above the rank of a serf. But in Irkutsk, many of these merchants had made fortunes trading furs for Chinese goods at Khyatka, a Russian town on the Mongolian border approved by treaty to trade goods between Russia and China. Other merchants had made fortunes by clandestine means in the black market. They traded with like-minded free marketers on either side of the Amur and Shilka Rivers, which divided Russia from both Mongolia and China and escaped the customs and taxes collected by local authorities on behalf of St. Petersburg. It was the merchant class that owned the large homes built of spruce with expansive windows and brightly painted shutters.

After their talk, Nadia and Abraham agreed to look at the property for rent. Abraham carried a large set of keys that tinkled and clanked as he locked his bookstore and then limped next-door with Nadia to see if the building would work for Nadia's dance studio. The keys rang out again as he opened the wooden door to a wide-open space interrupted only by two vertical spruce pillars which supported the second floor.

As she walked over the roughhewn timbers that creaked under her feet, Nadia made mental notes as to what would be needed. Barre and Mirrors along the walls, a piano, flooring carefully planed and sanded to make it smooth and firm for the dancer's feet. Also needed was padding around the support pillars to protect the leaping and twirling students should they crash into one.

While Nadia was already an accomplished pianist, she would need to teach Cheyvyne how to play so that Nadia could be free to show students the steps and guide them through the postures and routines. Large windows were facing the roadway in the front and more in the rear which faced the alley. The windows would bring in plenty of light and entice potential customers strolling by on the boardwalk to look in.

Being next to a bookstore would help traffic the type of customers she needed. Her biggest worry was whether anyone this far east would even care about learning dance. It was, after all, the frontier as her former headmaster had reminded her. But she had faith. *It worked in Petropavlosk, why not in Irkutsk*, she thought. But her conclusion ignored the fact that Petropavlosk was home to families of military officers from the noble class, unlike Irkutsk where most of the upper class were mere merchants.

Abraham rattled his keys again and selected one for Nadia to use on the upstairs room. He held the selected key out to Nadia between his thumb and forefinger and pointed to it as he passed it to her. Then he gestured out the front window toward a stairwell that ran up the side of the building. Nadia left him downstairs as she walked up.

"Aren't you coming? she asked.

"No. I never go there now. You go."

As she reached the landing above, she pushed the key into the lock and opened the door only to be blinded by the afternoon light pouring in from windows on all sides on a cold sunny day. The bookstore next door was a single-story building. Its lower roof exposed a partial view of the confluence of the Irkut and the Angara Rivers. Both rivers flowed through and around the town.

The second floor had once been the home of Abraham's daughter and her husband. They drowned when their sledge broke through the spring ice and took them to the bottom of the Angara. Abraham had not entered the room since that day four years before.

Through the dust and cobwebs, she could see that the room was tastefully decorated. It had a large spring bed and a down mattress, carpets laid over the roughhewn flooring, a cast-iron wood stove, a table next to a window on one side, and a bookcase on the other. In a corner by another window was a large leather chair with an ottoman that she suspected the husband of Abraham's daughter had once claimed as his own. Nadia threw her gloves on the leather chair and allowed herself a little twirl and a smile as she walked about the room alone rubbing her hands together to warm them from the chill.

This will do. This will do nicely.

Then she allowed herself the image of a smiling Anton sitting by the window.

Stop it, she cautioned herself!

"How much do you ask?" inquired Nadia as she re-entered the downstairs room and surprised Ilya and Abraham who were sharing a few sips of vodka from a bottle with their Polish friend Alexy Kowalski who had just arrived. He was the village blacksmith, and was an exile from the First Polish Uprising during the Bar Confederation war with Russia.

"Oh, I'm so sorry. I didn't know you had a guest."

After introducing Nadia to the blacksmith, Abraham answered her question about the price.

"For friend of Ilya, you pay what you can. But promise me. You will not change the upstairs room until a year. Please: just one more year. Then we talk again. Yes?"

"Yes," she answered beaming a wide smile while jumping up to hug each of them, even the blacksmith whom she had just met as she verily hopped and clapped for joy. The old men blushed and were happy with her and poured each other another drink to toast the merriment.

Over the next several months Nadia supervised the improvements needed for her dance studio in the lower floor. The most difficult items to obtain this far away from commercial centers in the west were Mirrors.

China was a net importer of Russian Mirrors and had none to provide. And when Nadia tried to obtain them from Moscow, it was expensive and risked being diverted to Khyatka to trade for tea or other goods needed from China by Russia.

After a month of frustrating talks with local merchants who would not guarantee delivery, she wrote an express letter to Auntie who knew the regional governor Nikolai Petrovich Lebedev. He, in turn, persuaded a merchant to secure the needed mirrors for Nadia from Moscow and deliver the goods intact. By spring, the studio was complete except for the signage. One day while taking a walk by herself along the banks of the Irkut near Ilya's hostel she found her answer to the name of her studio. It would be The Kolosova at the Bolshoi Studio. She had it painted in gold lettering across the front window next to Altschul's bookstore, which was also painted in gold.

Seven months after arriving in Irkutsk the living space above the studio stayed vacant. Nadia found it lonely by herself and preferred to stay with Ilya, Cheyvyne, and Kamak at the hostel. She also sensed it was too soon for her to move in since Abraham seemed to still be in mourning for his daughter. So, she left it vacant for the moment, a considerate forbearance that did not go unnoticed by the old man.

So far, she had two dance students, and they could not afford to pay her. Their names were Cheyvyne and Kamak. Nadia believed that by holding dance lessons for the girls even when she did not have paying customers worked as an advertisement, which she hoped would eventually encourage some real clients. The sound of the piano was another draw for future customers, and she played it loud and often. Fortunately, she was not destitute, and thanks to Auntie, she had sufficient capital to be patient. In the meantime, Cheyvyne and Kamak were thriving under her tutelage and attention.

"So, show Ilya what you learn today," said Ilya from his favorite chair.

Squealing as they ran to the center of the room, both took their premiere en bas positions. Then, on Nadia's humming of their music, they clumsily performed a pas de bourree for papa Ilya to his loud applause and then collapsed into their own giggles. Ilya was even more pleased than Nadia.

"You know Ilya dance, Nyet?" he asked of Nadia.

Unsure of what Ilya was proposing to show Nadia and the girls, she asked querulously: "you dance ballet Ilya?"

"Nyet Ballet," he said almost angrily. "Ballet for pretty girl like Nadia and girls. Cossack dance is man dance. Ilya show. You look."

With that, Ilya stood tall with his hands on his hips in his starting position. He smiled at the three of them proud of what he was about to show them. From this standing position with his arms on hips, he dropped his huge frame quickly to a squat but now with his arms now crossed over his chest. Then immediately, he stood back up straight again, but with his arms raised out and above his sides, his legs spread as wide as his arms, and his feet now balanced on his heels.

From there, he dropped again to another flatfooted squat except this time he ended standing in a wide stance on his toes. His third variation was to do all the same movements except he ended with one foot on its heel and the other flat on the floor.

It was an athletic performance for the big man and he was out of breath. After just three repetitions, he sat down exhausted into his chair but earned a round of applause from the girls. After a short rest, Ilya rose to check on the Russian Stove but in mid-step, he remembered something and reached into his inside coat pocket. He pulled it out and held it out toward Nadia.

"Ilya forget. Letter come. Ilya not open."

Nadia took the envelope and read the address and return address. It was from Anton's father and it was addressed to Anton. She turned the letter over several times and sniffed it while looking blankly out a window until tears welled up in her eyes and her lips wrinkled and she sobbed.

He's coming.

Letter to Auntie

June 1802
Dear Auntie,

I hope this letter finds you happy and well. Thank you very much for your continued support of your grateful niece. I am pleased to report that we completed the studio some months ago, replete with the mirrors and barre that you most graciously helped to expedite. I call the place Kolosova at the Bolshoi Studio. Yes, it is pretentious, but I thought you might like it. I have two non-paying customers, namely the adopted children of Ilya. But I hope to attract paying patrons soon when people recognize that my services are available here on the frontier as they say.

I know you asked me about Anton in your last letter. Suffice to say I have no direct news either way of his plans. However, his father did send a letter addressed to him here in Irkutsk. It could mean he is on his way here, but I know nothing for sure. Perhaps I should take your advice and let go of him in my thoughts and dreams. Sad to say, I cannot, yet it pains me to stay in this dreary condition. Sometimes, in the uncertainty of my future, I knit. Perhaps I am just bored. But I think that if my business would grow, that I would be able to immerse myself in it and be rid of my melancholic obsession with Anton.

But that is enough about me. As I mentioned, gruff old Ilya has two adopted Indian girls, and they have become my little sisters. They are bright and happy though the reason for their adoption was the slaughter of their parents by Cossacks. I believe there is more to the story, but Ilya goes silent when I ask. The oldest seems to have little memory of the tragic circumstance that led to her parent's death, thank goodness. Ilya has been a wonderful grandfather to them. But I do have a fear that he is getting older even though he is quite robust for his age. Even now, he is out helping his friend trade with the Chinese and Mongolians. It is illegal, but he says it is safe enough. But what would happen to his girls should he be arrested or suddenly pass away? They are still very young. No doubt their big sister Nadia will have to step in. I would worry less about my ability to support them if my business was thriving. I can almost hear you, Auntie:

Patience, I know. Your confidence in me and my endeavor here is priceless, and I cannot thank you enough.

Your loving niece,
Nadia

Chapter 23, EARLY FALL ON THE LENA RIVER, 1802

After Anton and Viktor completed the trail from Okhotsk over the mountains and reached Yakutsk, Anton turned in the horses at the livery and secured passage on a small flat-bottomed shitik going south on the mile-wide Lena River. They would travel upstream in this boat, which was propelled by oars, sail, poles, a long rudder, and by cordelling where the crew pulled the little craft forward with ropes. While the shitik lacked a proper keel due to the uneven depth of the river, it did have a false keel that ran the length of the boat and served to protect the hull from rocks on the river bottom or thin ice later in the year. But it also allowed the shitik some ability to tack against the wind and thus make some forward progress even when the wind was not directly behind them. It was not as good as a deep keel for tacking, but it allowed them at least some flexibility when the wind was not perfectly aligned. Depending on the wind direction and currents, they hoped to reach the portage at Ust-Kut that led overland to Irkutsk before the river froze solid for the winter.

Compared to horse travel on the Yakutsk-Okhotsk Trail, floating up the wide Lena River was luxuriously slow and lazy at first. On the best days when the wind was behind them propelling them upstream, they made good time. But even under the best of wind conditions, their speed was not swift since they were always pushing against the flow even if it was mostly gentle and slow. And forward progress would nearly stop when the wind behind them was weak. Under these conditions, the crew compensated by poling. But when the wind blew directly against their faces, poling was ineffective, and tacking against a frontal wind was impossible because the false keel was no match for such force. When this happened, the little boat might go backwards, and the crew would need to scurry ashore to halt its rearward progress with ropes and then start pulling the boat forward using a technique called cordelling. Since the boatmen knew that the current always ran slower nearer to the riverbanks, they routinely hewed close to shore, hunting for the weakest flow on the river.

Succeeding at going upriver on the Lena was a matter of making the best forward progress possible by taking advantage of several methods and tactics. Slightly in their favor was their late-season start, which meant that the high volume of water from snowmelt at the river's source had ended months ago, and the remaining flow downriver was trickling downstream at a much slower rate. On the other hand, a late-season start also carried a big risk. The winter freeze was not far off.

Inside the covered cabin of the shitik, Viktor continued working on his journal which would form the basis of the book he planned to publish someday about traveling from Okhotsk on the Pacific across Siberia to Moscow. Anton continued to sketch what he saw, and there was much to see along the journey. However, he worried about the slow pace of their travel.

The first small settlement they came to was Pokrovsk, founded by Cossacks in the last century. Anton remembered Ilya telling him that he had come from that village as they made small talk along the Yakutsk-Okhotsk Trail three years ago. His fellow Cossacks had banished him for refusing orders to suppress the local Yakut population. It was the reason that he now lived in Irkutsk.

From shore, Pokrovsk looked like a bleak place with austere dwellings and the remains of a defensive fort. It was nothing like Nadia described of his hostel on the Irkut River in her letter. Then they passed another Cossack town called Olyokminsk where the Olyokma River intersected the Lena and led southeast toward the Amur River and China. Many Yakut Indian villages, most abandoned, dotted the shoreline on the way to Lensk, which was founded by Russian Fur traders. Then came Khamra and Peleduy, where the Tiaga forest of spruce began to grow thicker than the thinly spaced stunted pines on the muddy tundra near Yakutsk.

They did not reach the mid-point of their travel on the Lena until early October. And due to their slow progress, they were now in a race to reach Ust-Kut before the winter freeze stopped them. In any given year the Lena would be frozen over by mid-November. Sometimes it came earlier and sometimes later. Anton estimated that at the rate they were traveling that they would not reach the portage at Ust-Kut until sometime between November 5th and November 20th. There was a good chance that the river would freeze before that time forcing them to lay over for months until they could travel again by sledge up the frozen river to Ust-Kut.

As he worried about the coming freeze, he also reflected on his state of mind. In the weeks after the massacre at the fort, the deaths of Puyuk and Aluki, and his killing of the Russians, Anton would not have been in a mood to care about where he went next or how soon he arrived there.

But after the arduous horseback trip over the Yakutsk-Okhotsk Trail, the ritual burial of the rotting scalps, and the long tedious weeks on the river, Anton felt that he had worked through most of his grief and shed his malaise over the tragic events that had dragged him into a gloomy place. The dark circles under his eyes were gone, and he looked forward eagerly to seeing Nadia and Ilya and meeting his Koryak girls sooner than later. But now, he had taken to brooding at the prospect of having that reunion with them delayed.

To improve their chances of arriving at Ust-Kut before the river froze over, he and Viktor volunteered to help the crew when it was needed to speed up the pace. The small boat only had a five-man crew—one to steer with the rudder and the other four to man the sail, row, pole, or cordell the boat with ropes from shore. Larger flat-bottom boats were often pulled by horses. These larger boats transported the valuable furs called "soft gold" culled from tributaries along the Lena and from as far away as Alyeska. Smaller shitiks like the one they were in could usually manage with a much smaller crew and no animals to pull them. But with just four crewmen working at propelling the boat, their forward progress was meagre when the wind was not favorable. It was better than nothing. But with Viktor and Anton lending a hand their speed improved and the additional fraction of forward momentum that their manpower brought might make the difference between laying over for months waiting out the freeze or seeing Nadia in weeks.

Then, with just sixteen days left before the date of the freeze in mid-November, a freezing storm blew down from the north and the temperatures quickly dropped below zero. Fortunately, it came with a northerly wind which pushed the sail on the little craft forward to its fastest pace since leaving Yakutsk. The propelling wind was welcome, but if the sub-zero temperatures that came with it were to continue it would not be long before the river would soon begin to freeze despite bringing a wind in their favor.

Then, after two days of skidding forward pushed by the ice-cold northerly wind, things changed for the worse. The wind switched from the north behind their sails to the south dead ahead of their bow and the now useless sails had to be gathered up and furled.

Disappointingly, the southerly wind did not bring warmth. Frigid air and dense ice fog continued to waft over the boat, the river, and the land. Soon thin sheets of ice began to form over the slow-moving sections of the river near the banks and icicles formed on the ropes and rigging. The crew now had the added burden of hammering ice from the boat to prevent it from weighing it down deeper on the water making it unstable and slowing it even further due to the drag. Fortunately, the river ice was not yet thick enough to stop their travel, but it foreshadowed what was soon to come. Everyone on board now knew that the full freeze of the Lena was imminent. Donning their gloves and head coverings for their ears to protect from frostbite, Anton and Viktor jumped into the frigid water near shore, climbed up the banks, and helped the crew to drag the boat by pulling the ropes against hope that they would make it to Ust-Kut before the inevitable freeze.

Each time, after hours of hard pulling they waded back aboard with sweat-icicles hanging from their nostrils and earlobes, breath-frost on their beards, and with their trousers frozen and stiff like boards. But they were not deterred. After they warmed and thawed their bodies and clothing in the cabin for an hour, they went back out into the icy water and pulled again day after day until they tied off at midnight to rest for a few hours before starting again. Soon they had to break surface ice one inch thick just to make it to shore.

Then on November 8th, as Anton and Viktor wearily strained forward against the ropes, they looked up and saw the taller buildings of Ust-Kut rising above the ice fog on the right bank of the Lena. Within the hour, they reached the portage station that would take them overland to Irkutsk. Anton heaved a sigh of relief. His prospects for seeing Nadia soon were greatly improved.

Now all they had left to do was to wait for the track to freeze hard enough for a troika of horses to pull a sledge. When that happened, it would take just three more weeks to get to Irkutsk. But nature seemed to have a cruel sense of humor this year and was not yet fully committed to winter despite the late date. No sooner had the freeze begun, it stopped, and a fickle blanket of warm air settled in. They were forced to wait it out.

Anton and Viktor had little else to do in Ust-Kut except while away their time drinking Kvass beer and vodka at a tavern beside the natural steam baths on the west side of the small hamlet.

Marooned for the moment, Anton determined it would be as good a time as any to ponder his future. How would he live and what would he do to earn his way in Irkutsk or wherever he settled? The only thing he had firmly planned on was to see Nadia again. Hopefully, she would still be in Irkutsk, but he was not even sure of that. Just seeing her again would please him enough to justify his long journey but what would they do after their reunion?

What would Nadia think, he worried, of a man with no clear means of making his way. And what if she had given up her dream of starting a dance studio and returned to her parents in Petropavlosk since sending her last letter? She had written that letter almost a year ago, and much might have changed, he worried. And what, he feared most, if she had given up waiting for him?

Despite being unseated from his career in the army and probably unwelcome among members of his own class in society, Anton was still fastidious about what he would choose to do for a living. He envied Viktor who seemed already decided on a career since departing the diplomatic core. As Viktor busied himself with his writing, Anton went on with his unease about his future. But to distract himself from his worries which were solving nothing, he tried to be constructive in his thoughts. Thus, he began an inventory of what he liked, what he was good at, and what he could or could not tolerate in a new career as a disgraced Russian noble, and ex-army officer, and possibly a murderer looking for a meaningful role.

At the top of his list were honor and justice. Lofty words, but he believed in them. It was those ideas that drove him to take revenge and deliver justice to the Russians and give honor to Puyuk and Aluki. It was those ideas that caused him to revile Baranov for his abuse of the Aleuts, and the avarice that had infected his soul. He vowed he would never again allow himself to be part of anything unfair or oppressive to others.

Second, whatever he did for a living had to include wilderness. His three years on Sitka made it clear to him that the wilds were in his soul. He reflected on how he reveled in using his hard-won skills to survive in it. He also knew that wilderness was part of what made Nadia and him kindred spirits.

Third, he needed change and variety. He understood himself well enough that without new horizons, the childish side of him bored quickly. *Yes*, he thought, *you are a spoiled child. So be it.* It was a trait he was not proud of but one he could not ignore.

Fourth, and the part that was distinct from all the others, he loved his artistic temperament. It was this trait that found the wonder in the woods, the color of the sky, and the forms that surrounded him. His valise full of sketches was proof of that.

Fifth and last, though it wasn't a skill, or trait, or even an ideal he craved to have Nadia beside him for all that lay ahead. He wondered if she felt the same after their three long years apart. Except for her, all the parts of his being were disparate uncoordinated traits that swirled about with no discernable balance. Only with Nadia did he feel anchored with purpose. Closing his eyes, he saw her dancing by the lakeside and her face was as clear as the images he had drawn of her and taken with him to Sitka on his first voyage to the island.

The question was how did it all translate into an independent life for himself? And at a more practical level, would the Imperial Army forgive and forget that he left his post. Would he face charges for the killing of the Russians? Should he change his name to evade discovery in Irkutsk and hide from a military tribunal? Everything seemed unsettled and without direction. So, after worrying himself in circles, he ceased his fretting and settled on one thing—seeing Nadia. Perhaps just the sight of her might help to clear his mind.

As he was deep in thought over these important questions, Viktor brought him back into the present by exclaiming something with a bit of a slur in his voice from too much vodka.

"I've got it."

"You have what?" asked Anton.

"The beginning, middle, and end."

Anton responded tartly, somewhat annoyed at having his own thoughts interrupted.

"Everything that has a beginning has a middle and end. Sometimes the beginning is short, or the middle long, but there is always an end, and you can't avoid having a middle if you have a beginning and end.

These are self-evident, Victor. Not revelations." Heaving a sigh, he demurred politely to Viktor's opening gambit about beginnings, middles, and ends and offered a consolation: "but I suppose what you mean is that you have found a plot for your book about Siberia?"

"Yes. You see, I need to offer more than just the places I visited and their descriptions to make my story a story. If that were all I had, it would be tedious and boring. On the other hand, I don't want to go so far as to write my book of travels as a metaphor for something else a la *Journey from St. Petersburg to Moscow."*

"So, what have you decided, Viktor?"

"I decided that my travels need to be seen through the eyes of two very interesting characters. That way the reader will be invested in the people and the places they visit."

"I take it that you mean fictional persons, maybe like Odysseus and Polites and their travels?"

"Exactly:" bigger than life heroes on an epic journey."

"I think I understand, but give me a scene with your characters so that I am sure."

"All right. Here goes. *The boat was moving too slowly up the mighty river to make it to their destination in time to avoid the annual freeze-up. So Viktor…*"

"Wait a minute. You don't mean that your bigger than life persons are you and me?"

"That's quite what I mean. Oh, and by the way, your drawings would be priceless additions to my story."

Not surprised that his drawings were of interest to Viktor, he thought about the best way to seize on that interest to earn a few honest Rubles. "How much?"

"Pardon me?"

"How much are you willing to pay for my drawings?

"Oh. Well, Frankly, I can't pay you a kopek unless my book gets published. Anton, I can't pay you now. So here is a proposition. If the book sells, I will agree to pay you a third of my proceeds in return for the use of your drawings.

"How much will that be."

"Hard to say precisely, but if it sells who knows? Consider this fine list of predecessors:

Pausanius', *Description of Greece*; Marco Polo, *The Travels of Marco Polo*; Daniel Defoe, *A Tour Through the Whole Island of Britain*; Jonathan Swift, *Gulliver's Travels*; and yes, *The Odyssey*."

And make good note. Not one of these books covers Russia: especially Siberia. It's never been done before."

The skeptic in Anton was urging caution. Yet, Viktor seemed to have a good point. Siberia was unknown, but interest in it was growing fast if for no reason other than the fur trade and the arriving exiles sometimes coming with their families in-tow. Someone would have to be the first to publish a book for newcomers and the curious traveling to the provinces. It might as well be Viktor and him.

"Viktor, you have a good idea. But I won't take a third."

"I'm sorry to hear that Anton," his disappointment clearly intoned in his voice.

"It will have to be half."

"Half," he countered! "Why, I'm doing the writing?"

"Partly true, but you've left out the Americas. I've been there and you haven't. It's an important part of the story. You know we already have colonies there, and you cannot ignore it. It's a de facto part of the Russia you are aiming to depict. And that's where the fur trade is located not to mention the hordes of proselytizing priests on their mission to convert the natives. You can't tell the story of Siberia without including the Pacific and the lands we are now populating there, and only I can help you write that part. And only I can illustrate it all from the Americas to St. Petersburg. So, between my sketches and my experiences in Siberia and in America coupled with your travels from Okhotsk back to Moscow, we will have our book."

Viktor knew that the success of his groundbreaking travel book on Siberia depended on Anton's unprecedented images. He could write the best descriptions in the world, but they would be lifeless without the many fine works of art that would show the reader the places Viktor would be writing about. And Anton was also right about America. Without writing about that continent, the book would be incomplete. Thus, Viktor conceded to Anton's demand after realizing it was the only way.

"All right, we have a deal. A fifty-fifty split it is. And good luck to both of us on our book!"

With that, Anton poured two glasses of vodka while clanking the bottle loudly against each glass as he did. After they toasted their agreement, they began to work out the logistics. First on their agenda, was to select the illustrations. They could accomplish that part at Ilya's hostel once they got there. Second, Anton would need to write his contribution on the Americas and send it to Viktor. Then Viktor would need to cobble all the writing into an appealing whole. For the final draft, they could collaborate between Moscow and Irkutsk by mail. All the essential elements of their plan were complete except for one.

"Can I trust you Viktor?"

"Of course, but why do you ask?"

"Because you will have all my drawings in your hands when you go home to Moscow. No one will know who drew them but you and me. So, Viktor, I need you to answer me. Can I trust you?"

Viktor replied with a hand on Anton's shoulder and a big smile. "If you need me to say it out loud, here it is. You can trust me Anton."

"Good. I'm glad that's settled."

Anton never aspired to be a writer, an illustrator, nor anything else other than being an officer in the army. Russian nobles who wanted careers had three traditional paths. The first was the military, the second was the bureaucracy, and the third was the clergy. It never occurred to him that anyone would pay him to guide them across the mountains on the Yakutsk Okhotsk Track as a means of making a living.

He laughed at the thought of he and Ilya in business together to guide wealthy patrons across the wilds of Siberia. Closer to reality, Anton believed that the book had at least a chance at publication. After all, Viktor had already had success with his first book, a hymn to Catherine the Great titled *The Empress of Russia* whose sycophantic praise of the woman almost guaranteed its publication. The Georg Joachim Göschen publishing house in Leipzig had printed it.

Most important to Anton was that any success the travelogue garnered would help him transform from tarnished noble and ex-army man to something else. Perhaps even a writer and member of a small, but growing literati even if being part of such a group had its own dangers. The exile of Aleksander Radishchev to Siberia for his book of political satire was a good example of the peril that could arise when thoughts and opinions threatened the aristocratic class.

But exhausted from his worries about how he might fit into society anew, he closed his eyes. He daydreamed of simpler times with Nadia dancing barefoot beside a summer lake even though Christmas was only weeks away, and all the lakes in Siberia were freezing solid. It was time to take the last leg from Ust-

Kut to Irkutsk on the frozen track and see Nadia again for the first time in three years.

Chapter 24, THREE WEEKS TO CHRISTMAS, 1802

The next day Anton hired a troika sledge to take him to Irkutsk that lay 600 miles away at the southern end of Lake Baikal. The land route left the Lena heading overland over rough track until it reached the frozen Angara River, which would provide a smooth road-bed for the rest of the way to Irkutsk. Viktor, enamored with the exiled author Radishchev, chose to take a side trip to Llimsk 100 miles away to see the writer's Siberian home as a sort of pilgrimage to the famous man. After that, they agreed that he would then meet Anton at the House of Ilya about a week after Anton arrival there. Then they would work out the last details for the book before Viktor would depart for Moscow.

Covered by blankets and alone in the sledge, Anton watched the frozen trees go by to the sound of the driver's commands and the crack of his whip as the steeds strained to pull them up one hill and down the other side with a rush of speed fed by gravity. When they reached the smooth flat surface of the frozen Ankara, their pace increased and it marked just five more days in the sledge until they arrived in Irkutsk. On the fourth day, Anton felt butterflies floating around in his belly in anticipation of seeing Nadia, and then he threw up to the disdain of the driver who would have to clean it up. When he finally arrived at the House of Ilya, he felt as if it were a dream and nearly stumbled on weak legs as he unloaded his bags and his boxed weapons from the sledge and paid the driver with the last of his Rubles. Hearing the commotion outside,

Cheyvyne and Kamak ran to the door and flung it open. Anton then saw the two young Koryak girls run across the snow to greet him. They thought he was an arriving guest.

'Hello sir, can we help you?" asked the older one with the practiced smile of a hotelier.

"You must be Cheyvyne, he replied. And you must be Kamak?"

"Yes sir, but how did you know that?" they asked of the smelly bearded stranger who had not shaved or bathed since departing the hot springs at Ust-Kut three weeks before.

"That, little one, is a secret story about mushrooms."

"Mushrooms," they asked incredulously, seeing no connection between his answer and how he had come to know their names?

"Is Ilya here?"

"Ilya is out hunting Roe Deer. He will be back in a few days."

Perplexed, Cheyvyne asked: "excuse me sir, but what is your name?"

"Anton."

"Anton Niktovich?" they excitedly replied in unison while changing their demeanor from skeptical to intrigued. "You mean you are Nadia's Anton?"

"Well, that is a welcome compliment, and yes, I am Nadia's Anton."

With that, the girls each shrieked. They abandoned all pretense of being inn-keepers, grabbed both of his hands, and pulled Anton toward the entrance as if he were a long-lost member of the family.

"My bags," protested Anton.

"Don't worry, we'll get them. Come on in Anton."

Seeing that only the girls were home, he was disappointed not to see Nadia and asked where she was.

"Nadia is at the studio with her students."

"Students?"

"Yes, she is up to five now, and two more may be starting soon."

Anton took a breath. He was happy that Nadia's dream of having a dance studio was coming to pass. More than that, he was pleased that she was still in Irkutsk and had not returned to her parents' home in Petropavlosk. But mostly, he was heartened to be called Nadia's Anton. *Perhaps we still have a chance after these long years apart?*

"When does she come back from the studio?"

"Oh, in a few hours. She is closing early for Christmas Eve."

Anton felt a twinge of guilt for not bringing Christmas gifts but cured his omission quickly. He gave the totem to Kamak. It was the same one that he had first given to Aluki. To Cheyvyne, he gave the bear claw necklace that hung almost down to her waist. For Nadia, he would give the Tlingit bow and quiver of arrows he had made for her. He leaned them against the wall in the corner of the room opposite the entry. They would be the first thing she saw when she came through the door. *Artemis*, he thought fondly as he vividly recalled seeing her run through her forest haunts on feet so fleet, he imagined her chasing down deer. Despite the gifts, the girls were still focused on him, the long-suffering mythical sojourner who had finally arrived home.

Busily chattering, the girls peppered Anton with questions even as they rushed to put on several pots of water on the Russian Stove to heat his bath. The tub was outside near the back of the hostel hidden from view. And since Anton had no change of clothing, they gathered a clean pair of Ilya's trousers and a shirt and hung them on pegs by the tub next to a bench with soap and a sponge. Though Anton was a tall man, he would still have to roll up the pant-legs and shirtsleeves to make Ilya's clothing fit his smaller frame. And he would need a rope to keep the pants from falling to his knees. Soon the girls announced the bath was hot and ready. After undressing on the bench, he stood barefoot on fresh snow in the minus ten-degree air before stepping into the hot bath. Snowflakes swirled around his face and vanished into the steaming bathwater.

Chapter 25, ROE DEER AGAIN

Ilya had been gone for two weeks hunting for Roe Deer as he waited for the freeze to set in solid. That event would signal it was time to begin guiding travelers to Yakutsk and beyond again. Traveling over the frozen rivers was his preferred mode of travel with guests. Summer travel was too long, too many mosquitos, too tedious, and too dependent on fickle winds, currents, rain, lack of rain, and mud.

He had not guided another client in summer since shepherding Nadia to St. Petersburg three years before from Petropavlosk. To hunt Roe Deer this year, he decided not to take the dugout to the south side of the Sayan Mountains as he usually did. Had he chosen to do that—the Irkut River might well have frozen over during his hunt. The ice would have blocked his way back and forced him to abandon the dugout and return eighty miles on foot over a freshly frozen river with the danger that the river ice was not yet solid enough to support his weight.

To avoid those dangers, he decided to ride on his horse to the far eastern end of the Sayans nearest to Irkutsk and then follow north side of the east-west mountain range. It was an easy ride of just two or three days on his trusty steed Kassandrov.

As always, Ilya had no real need to be out in the wilderness for so long just to hunt deer. Instead, it was only a thin excuse that allowed him to reconnect with his old life as a marauding Cossack riding heedless of cold, danger from Indians, or stalking four-footed beasts that wanted to eat him. Age had not slowed down his urge to be immersed in the wilds though a prudent man like his friend Abraham the bookseller counseled him otherwise.

"So, you need a deer. I get you deer. They sell over there," pointed Abraham out the window to the butcher shop. "You're not some wild young Cossack anymore *mein lieber freund*. Soon you be an *älter* man like me. Not too long I tell you," he warned!

Ilya liked Abraham, but they could not have been more different. Abraham grew up in cities while Ilya grew up in a Cossack Fortress on the Lena River surrounded by hostile Indian villages that he and his comrades suppressed by force. Abraham had never used force in his life. All he had was his tongue and his sense of right and wrong. Yet they shared a bond. Ilya gave Abraham a slice of the untamed world, and Abraham gave Ilya a view into the world of the civilized. Between the extremes, they bonded through two things. First was chess, a pure game that required no knowledge of the world, no science, no book but only the rules of the game and a brain. Second, was a moral code. Their codes may have been different, but they hewed to them each in their own way that earned a mutual respect. Altschul had his Torah, and Ilya his Cossack code of honor.

Before he left on his hunting trip, Ilya visited Abraham and asked him a favor.

"Abraham, you smart friend. I need you listen."

"All-right. I'm listening," said the old man who sat in a chair opposite Ilya and crossed his arms across his chest already guarding against what Ilya had to say.

"Ilya have dream."

"Ya, so, we all dream. Tell me something I don't know my friend."

"I see Ilya die."

Hesitating to respond too quickly to the seriousness of his tone, Abraham was careful with his words. "You mean you imagine you get old and die. Or you mean you see your death in *eine Traum.*"

"Ilya die in dream. Dream real. Ilya die soon."

"Ilya —Ilya mein freund. You remember when you say the Lena freeze in October last year? It freeze in November. You not always right Ilya.

"Ilya right this time."

"Ach so, we all dream Ilya. Nothing special about *die träumend.* I dream once that I am einer jünger in bed with woman…"

Ilya stopped him from talking further and insisted. "Nyet Abraham. This dream true. Ilya see for his people. Ilya see good things see bad things. Now Ilya see Ilya die. To die is all-right. I die. But Ilya have girls. Tell Ilya, how Ilya protect girls?"

Acquiescing to the earnestness of his question, Abraham had two words: "A will."

Da, where Ilya get will?"

"Don't worry, I write. What else does Ilya see?"

"Ilya beat Abraham at chess one more time. I be back in one month."

Ilya and his horse Kassandrov had been together for a decade and each had great trust in the other. As winter was closing in they were weeks out into their meandering hunt along the northern slope of the Sayans when Kassandrov pricked her ears toward a small creek coming down the north side of the mountains. Halting for the moment, Ilya and the horse listened but heard nothing except the gurgle of water flowing over the rocks in the stream beside them. Steam blew from the horse's nostrils and she snorted an alert at whatever was ahead.

Pulling left on the reins, Ilya decided to follow Kassandrov's ears up the creek toward the mountain. Then, not far from where they turned off the main trail, they came to an abandoned village with houses made of birch bark. Beside them, were other houses made of animal hides. Ilya knew by the structures that these were the summer and winter dwellings of a nomadic tribe called the Tofalars. They had been subdued almost to extinction by his Cossack comrades over the last centuries. Not many lived in the wild this close to Irkutsk. But Ilya was certain this was once a Tofalar village.

Surmising that it had been abandoned long ago, he turned Kassandrov back toward the main trail leading up the north side of the Sayans. As Kassandrov clipped and clopped, she pricked her ears again to their left. Trusting Kassandrov's alert, Ilya pulled a pistol from his belt and let Kassandrov take the reins and follow the sound. Pushing through the brush and the stunted spruce they came to a scraggly meadow of snow-covered tundra. Somehow, the scene was familiar to Ilya. All was quiet.

Standing on his stirrups for a better view and looking left and right to survey the surrounds, he suddenly felt a pain in his belly then looked down to see a weathered silver-tipped Cossack spear that had run through his liver and out his back. Momentarily in disbelief that this had actually happened, he sat back down in his saddle and contemplated what he was seeing. *Is this dream?* In seconds the pain told him it was not a dream. He had been speared and with a Cossack spear no less, and he bellowed aloud at the irony.

Ha! Ilya die of Cossack spear just like Cossack kill Koryak. God play joke on Ilya. Good joke god!

Resigning to fate, he took no care that another spear or arrow might be coming and took out his long-bladed knife from his belt and whacked at the weathered woody shaft protruding out of his belly as he still sat in his saddle. Soon he had cut down that part of the spear to twelve inches, and the remnant fell quietly into the shallow snow. But the silver point still protruded another foot out from his back. Ilya could not reach it, but it had to come out if Ilya was to have a chance at living. Then suddenly, Kassandrov pricked her ears to some scrub on their right. Between the branches and leaves, Ilya looked and waited for a second wave of attack but only saw a single human face painted with fear.

"Come out," he commanded. "Come see what you do to Ilya," he boomed.

Slowly, an emaciated man with lines on his forehead and fear in his eyes stepped out in a crouch from the cover of the bushes. He did not have the look of a warrior. Rather, he had the appearance of a defeated man terrified of the tall Cossack before him on horseback. To him, Ilya was one more Cossack following centuries of Cossacks riding in to kill Tofalars. Ilya knew the man probably believed he was about to be another victim of a Cossack. Pointing his finger at the man, Ilya gave another command.

"You Come. Push out of Ilya."

The Tofalar knew nothing of what was said and shook his head from side to side as he stood in front of the man he had mortally wounded. Ilya pointed to the spear in his belly and asked him to push it out the other side. Beginning to understand Ilya, the man walked tentatively over to the horse and reached up with his arms to help Ilya out of his saddle. Now facing each other, Ilya towered over the Tofalar and gave the instruction again by pointing to the spear and gesturing.

"Push out."

The Tofalar looked at the end of the spear that Ilya had chopped off and put his hand on it while looking up at Ilya.

"Da, Push," he said, nodding in approval.

With that, the man pushed the splintered end as far as he could while Ilya grimaced but only looked ahead with clenched teeth and said nothing after stumbling back from the force. Then the Tofalar went behind Ilya and said something Ilya could not understand. Ilya guessed at his meaning.

"Da, Pull."

Ilya watched the splintered end disappear inside his belly then heard excitement behind him as the Tofalar held the remnant of the bloody spear he had pulled from Ilya's back. Ilya re-mounted his horse and then pointed at his saddlebag and commanded the Tofalar to open it. Looking inside, the Tofalar found Ilya's fur coat. Ilya gestured for the man to pull it out and give it to him as he slumped in the saddle. Ilya donned the coat, which comforted him as he began to feel weak and vulnerable to the cold.

Then, grimacing in pain and feeling faint as blood leaked from his wounds, Ilya heard rustling in the bushes and raised his pistol pointed it with a weak arm toward the noise. Then, two young girls stepped out huddled together along with the wife of the Tofalar man. The woman was nodding at Ilya in a manner that Ilya took as an apology or maybe a plea not to harm them. Ilya heaved a sigh and said: "Ilya no kill Indians no more - No more forever."

Though he knew she could not have understood the words, he raised his hand to his heart, nodded, and turned his horse away while putting his pistol back into his belt. *God is funny*, he thought again. *There. You see god. Ilya no kill Indian. Ilya good Cossack. Go to heaven maybe?*

After riding a few hundred yards, Ilya dismounted, removed his coat, and pulled out a pistol and emptied the frizzen of its powder into his hand.

Taking out his knife, he divided the powder into two mounds. The first mound he pressed into his stomach wound. It mixed with his blood making a red mud. Then he did the same with the hole in his back. Reaching into his pack, he pulled the flint and steel fire starter and struck it near the powder in his belly and a flash fire erupted. Ilya groaned, but the external bleeding stopped. He did the same with the hole in his back. The cauterization of his wounds gave him a chance, but there was no telling how much he was still bleeding internally or whether the spear had ripped open an intestine that would lead inexorably to sepsis. He now had three days or less to cover sixty miles and get home or die on the trail alone - the kind of death no Cossack welcomed. He put his faith in Kassandrov and conserved his strength as his horse walked him gently back toward Irkutsk and the temperatures began to plummet.

Chapter 26, CHRISTMAS EVE, 1802

Anton felt fresh and clean after his bath, shaving his beard, and trimming his hair. After drying himself in the frigid air, he stood barefoot on the snow as he pulled up Ilya's oversize trousers. Suddenly, his senses were struck still by the muffled silence of the snow-covered landscape. Still shirtless and shoeless, he listened for any sound coming from the forest or the river that ran below the hostel. But the Irkut had frozen over and there was no sound of flowing water - not the slightest gurgle. The forest too was silent. There was no wind to whisper through its pine. The only sounds to be heard were snowflakes falling gently on fresh snow. It was the sort of quiet roar that goes unheard unless you hush your heart and listen for the low rumble of flakes falling on flakes. Puyuk had taught him that, and he was pleased to remember her in the near silence of the land as the aurora borealis cast a green-yellow glow on the clouds above the falling snow.

As he clung to that moment, the girls burst out the door catching Anton standing agape, shirtless, and barefoot on the snow next to the tub. Giggling and putting their hands over their mouths at the image Anton presented, they turned around and ran back through the door. All Anton could do was laugh at himself, finish dressing, and go inside leaving his quiet moment behind. As he entered, he noticed the girls had covered the main table with a white cloth and strewn hay over it in imitation of the manger. It was Christmas Eve.

"Do you know how to play *ajagaak*?" asked Cheyvyne.

"No, I've never heard of that game."

"Nadia says it's a game the Inuits play."

"How does she know it's an Inuit game?"

"Because of one of the children at her studio. Her mother is Inuit, and her father is Russian."

"I see. Show me the game then."

Cheyvyne opened a trunk and pulled out an object made of two pieces of bone tied together by animal sinew. One of the bone pieces was sharp like a small spear eight inches long. The other was a piece of leg bone with many holes drilled into it and was about a foot long. The object of the game, explained Cheyvyne, was to hold the leg bone and flip the spear up as far as the sinew would let it go and then have it fall back down and pierce through one of the small holes drilled into the leg bone.

"I'll show you," offered an eager Kamak.

"No, I'll show," countered Cheyvyne.

To settle the argument, Anton got up from his chair and teased it out of the hands of Cheyvyne.

"Let me try. I think I know how this works."

With that, he flipped the sharp piece up and then tried to catch it with the leg bone on the way down. Instead, the sharp piece cut into his wrist and caused the girls to laugh in derision at his poor skill at the game.

"Let me, let me," pleaded Kamak.

Anton bent over and asked: "Say please?"

"Please"

Smiling with joy, little Kamak showed off her skill at the game by catching the point in one of the holes in the leg bone to the disdain of her older sister.

"I don't want to play this game anymore," pouted Cheyvyne. "I want to play *aarraq*.

"I've never heard of that either," Anton replied.

"Nadia says it's an Aleut game."

"Yes, well, please show me that game too. This time it's your turn, Cheyvyne."

Pleased to be recognized, Cheyvyne pulled a piece of string out of the trunk and tied the two ends together. Then she stretched the loop between her thumb and first finger on each hand and then thrust it into Anton's face.

"I know this game. It's called Cat's Cradle," remarked Anton.

"No, it's an Aleut game called aarraq. But all right, it's your turn," Cheyvyne said as she held it in front of him waiting for his counter.

Anton selected a strategy for his first move and lifted the stretched string out of Cheyvyne's hands, and he took it back creating his own pattern.

"You do know the game," observed an incredulous Kamak. "Me next - me next."

Still stretching the string, Anton turned to Kamak who created a new pattern and then offered it back immediately to Anton. Then, just as he was taking it back from her, the front door opened – and there was Nadia with none of the fanfare Anton imagined would precede their reunion after three long years. Instead, Nadia merely stumbled through the entrance into a child's game of cat's cradle and said "hello Anton" as if he were an expected guest.

"Nadia, Nadia, Nadia," screamed the girls who ran to her at the door. "Anton is here!"

"And so, he is," she said as both a fact and a wonderment though her heavy breathing betrayed more emotion than she felt she could safely show.

Anton was still sitting with both of his hands out holding the taut string looking as if he had been caught in a guilty pose and had no idea what to say to Nadia. But both held an honest steady gaze into each other's eyes that warmed the room so quickly that the girls fell silent and looked back and forth at the two of them in a child's version of awe.

"I've been thinking a lot about fern flowers," said Nadia in a soft voice that rose barely above the crackle of the fire in the stove.

"I'm not sure that ferns have flowers, Miss."

"Hmm—I used to doubt them too. I suppose I've softened a bit. Now I think the world should make some room for a few fern flowers here and there even if only in the mind."

"Well then, it must be true. Ferns do flower, but maybe only in Siberia—in mid-winter.

What do you think?" he asked.

"Winter is the best season in Siberia. It would be the best time to roam the forest looking for one that bloomed."

"Yes. Well maybe we can do that together some brisk evening—a walk on the river at midnight perhaps," Anton invited?

Without answering, Nadia asked: "Have you ever jumped barefoot over a bonfire?"

"Just once. I jumped together with my best friend holding hands."

"And what happened?"

"We never lost our grip though we fell, we rolled, we skinned our knees, and we bled a little on the other side, but we never let go."

"So, you both survived."

"Yes, we both survived."

"Still holding hands?"

"I never let go. And you?"

Then, changing the subject entirely, Nadia asked bluntly: "can you skip rocks across a lake?"

"Yes. They say I am very good at skipping rocks. And what about you?"

"Only fair. But I can shoot a .32 caliber pistol."

"Impressive."

"Yes. I had a wonderful teacher."

"The girls tell me you have a dance studio?"

"Yes, I must show it to you someday."

"Tomorrow?"

"Yes. That's just what I was thinking. Are you staying for dinner?"

"That depends. What are you having?

"Kuya, of course. It's Christmas, so it must be Kuya. I make it with wheat berries, sunflower seeds, milk, and honey. I'll be having it with the most handsome man I have ever had the pleasure of meeting.

"What's his name?" he asked as he dropped the cat's cradle and began to stand.

"His name is Anton," she answered. And with that, she finally let go of the safety of their banter and ran to throw her arms around him kissing his face, nose, and cheeks and knocking him back into the chair where he landed with a thud and with Nadia on top of him squirming like a little girl. "Oh god, Anton, it is good to see you."

"You don't know how much I missed you, Nadia," as his smile broadened, and his eyes filled with tears.

Hitting his shoulder three times, she demanded: "don't – don't – don't ever - ever leave me again Anton. Never!"

Cheyvyne and Kamak watched the entire interaction understanding little of the words. But they felt the bond between their big sister and the mythical man called Anton who had traveled to faraway places but would someday come back for Nadia like a bruised and battered hero of old clawing his way home to his love. And now it was all true just as Nadia had told them, and just had Ilya had predicted on the day Nadia first arrived from St. Petersburg with one bag of luggage.

For the next two hours, they sat together curled up before the radiant fire in the Russian Stove and said nothing while Nadia silently preened Anton's hair and they breathed in each other's breath and wept gentle tears. Cheyvyne and Kamak had gone to their bunks, pulled the curtains on their beds, and had fallen asleep. Firelight flickered on the flannel coverings making them cozy. But despite enjoying the calm, Anton could no longer contain the urge to break the silence with words he had to say and questions he had to ask.

"I'm not the same person you met at Kupala three years ago. I…."

"Shhhh," hushed Nadia. We will talk of your changes, my changes, our changes—tomorrow—the next day—the next month, the next year, but the answer will be the same. You are my Anton, and I am your Nadia. Then, pulling away slightly with a worried look she added:

"If you don't think that, you must let me know now as tears began to well."

Anton smiled and brushed her black hair gently back from her face to look into her eyes as they darted back and forth waiting for an answer. Nadia had made it simple and he answered simply in return. "You are my Nadia. You will always be my Nadia."

And with that, they made love on the floor in front of a roaring fire, with outside temperatures dropping to forty degrees below zero under a clear sky and the aurora borealis painting the snow with greenish-yellow ribbons of undulating light.

Near a distant mountain, Ilya's body stiffened in the cold as he clung to life still mounted on Kassandrov who struggled on without eating or drinking or stopping for rest as she pushed through deepening snowdrifts carrying Ilya back to Irkutsk.

Chapter 27, CHRISTMAS DAY, 1802

Early in the morning, Nadia rose from her warm bed beside Anton and began to busy herself by adding logs, re-lighting the Russian Stove, and donning an apron. It was time to bake a Bird-cherry chocolate cake for their Christmas dinner dessert.

Rousing the girls, she sent them to town on a horse to gather ingredients for the main course. Ilya had stored plenty of venison in the cold cellar, but she needed dried mushrooms, dried onion, and some of the special Mongolian spice for the venison stew Ilya loved so much. Fresh onions and mushrooms by the river were unavailable. They were already covered with snow so dried would have to do.

After they rubbed the sleep from their eyes and put on their warm clothing, she asked the girls to stop by Abraham's house in town and remind him of her invitation to a Christmas dinner at the House of Ilya. She imagined he might be lonely on this day though she knew he was not Christian.

“Jesus was a Jew you know,” she cajoled, trying to persuade him to a Christian gathering the week before.

“Ja, Ja, Ja,” he answered like a curmudgeon. A magic Jew who die and come back. Tell me, will Ilya be there?

“We hope so. He should have been back already. Perhaps he will be back for Christmas,” she answered as she struck a positive tone with her voice. “So, you will come?”

“Da, I come for Christmas dinner. What time?”

“Nightfall.”

Anton was the last to rise from his bed. Lying next to Nadia all night was a pleasure he luxuriated in and he wanted it to become habit. As he sniffed the scent of her drifting up from his bed-shirt and their sheets, he felt a peace that he had never felt before.

“Morning Ms. Nadia.”

“Morning Mr. Anton,” she smiled.

“Can I help?

“Are you good with a broom?”

“No, but I could learn.”

“Good. The girls bring in wet snow and debris all the time, so it has to be done every day, and especially this day since its Christmas with a guest coming for dinner. You sweep, I'll cook."

"That sounds like a bargain. Who's coming?"

"Ilya's best friend, Abraham. They play chess almost every day in spring, summer, and fall."

"What about winter."

"Ilya still has his guide business, but now he only does that work when the rivers and tracks are frozen. Traveling is faster and easier then. His time on the trail and in the sledge is much less, so we get to see more of him, and he does not have to deal with mud or mosquitos. I also think he likes to get away every once in a while. It's his wild side or maybe it's just his Cossack blood. His only complaint is that he has to deal with spoiled clients.

"As Ilya is wont to say about his clients—they talk much but know little."

Anton remembered that Ilya had said that very thing about him years before. As he suppressed a laugh at his former self, he was reminded of his admiration for the old man and secretly hoped Ilya might even take him on one of his trips next winter, though he still wondered why he chose him to tell the sad story about his girls and how he came to adopt them.

"Yes, Ilya is a lucky man. He's paid well, loves what he does, has a wonderful house on the river, and two happy little girls—not to mention, their beautiful big sister," said an admiring Anton as Nadia looked up from her work with a contented smile.

As the day went on, the house filled with the smells of Christmas foods baking in the oven aperture and simmering in pots hanging over the main fire. Anton breathed it in like holy incense swinging over pews - deliciously warm and deeply familial. Yet despite the glowing feelings Christmas day brought with it, Anton still worried about his future.

Nadia's belief that in saying the words "You are my Anton" and "You are my Nadia" solved all the challenges that might be ahead for them was temptingly sweet but unpersuasive. It felt good to utter the words and the suggestion of togetherness they assumed, but they were not magic incantations against the machinations of a prosecutor and the possible charge of desertion or the murder of three Russians. He knew their love would not make these things go away. But he did his best to enjoy the moment even as he knew that he and Nadia would have to have a serious talk soon.

"Why the sour look Anton?"

"Oh, I was just thinking about something sad. Something I will tell you later. Today—today is Christmas and I will talk of nothing else on this day."

"Well then. You need to get busy. Here, stir this."

Late in the day while decorating the cake Nadia looked up with a start and remembered that a letter had arrived for Anton from his father.

"Oh, I forgot. You have a letter. It's from your father."

Anton had dipped a spoon in the stew pot and was about to give it a taste when Nadia blurted out the news of the letter. When he heard it was from his father, he dropped the spoon into the pot and splashed broth on the floor.

Suddenly distant and quiet, Anton's face took on a look of apprehension as if danger lurked inside the envelope. It was the first letter his father had ever written to him. As she held it out to Anton, she saw him take it in a trembling hand and walk to a corner of the room. Like a man removing the powder fuse from a loaded cannonball, he opened the envelope slowly and unfolded the letter alone by a window.

Nadia glanced over at him several times as she tended the stove, trying to discern what his father might have written and why it had caused Anton to tremble in fear. The first thing Anton saw as the letter emerged from the envelope was the bold letterhead signifying it was official business written on Russian Imperial Navy stationery.

THE OFFICE OF THE RUSSIAN IMPERIAL NAVY

Leonid Niktovich, Vice Admiral Russian Imperial Navy

October 15, 1802

My Dear Son,

The thought of never seeing you again is unbearable, and I hope that the news I bring with this letter and the letter I attach with it will free us to reunite in-time.

The attachment from the Coroner will be self-explanatory. As of the date of its dispatch, you no longer exist as an officer in the Imperial Army because you have been declared dead, a victim of the Tlingit attack on Fort St. Michaels. You may thank Kutuzov for managing this feat of magic. As for the Russians you mentioned, they have been officially declared victims as well.

As a dead man, you are now free to pursue your new life on the frontier without fear of prosecution by military authorities. I know that you will live up to the high hopes I have of you as a man. I trust you did what you had to do in defending the honor of your friends and bringing justice to them. Irrespective of its effect on your military career, that was a noble thing to do and I commend you for letting your moral compass guide you.

Sincerely,

Your father, Leonid

Attachment: Letter from Dept. of Mortuary Affairs

Anton wept quietly as he digested the import of the words and Nadia came over to him and placed her hands on his shoulders but said nothing as Anton unfolded the second letter in the envelope. The letter bore the Department of Mortuary Affairs.

The Department of Mortuary Affairs, Russian Imperial Army

To: Leonid Niktovich, Vice Admiral Russian Imperial Navy

July 4, 1802

Dear Sir:

It is my sad duty to inform you of your son's death in the service of the Russian Imperial Army. Lieutenant Anton Niktovich was sent as an intelligence officer to the island of Sitka and assigned to the Russian America Company.

In that role, he fulfilled his duty to the empire but was unfortunately lost in an attack by the hostiles known as the Tlingits. These savages attacked the Russian America Company trading post and fort killing nearly all the inhabitants and burning it to the ground.

We received one written report from the Russian America Company that he survived the attack by deserting his post. However, that report was not true. A second report confirmed his death. Your son had been doing his work from an isolated cabin located a few miles from the fort. Like the fort, his cabin was also burned to the ground. Charred and scattered human remains were located inside the burned cabin accounting for at least one but possibly two persons. A sturdy door partly survived the flames. Near the defensive firing slot in the door, we found seventeen Tlingit style arrow points. It was obvious that your son died defending his shelter though there was no trace of his weapons inside.

In addition to your son, three other Russian victims of the attack were found not far from the cabin indicating that the Tlingit attack was pervasive and savage throughout the area.

Your son's remains were interred with honors on the Island of Sitka near his cabin on the lake on July 28th, 1802.

We thank you for your son's service to the Empire.

Sincerely,

Lieutenant Andrey Oblonsky, Department of Mortuary Affairs

cc. Mikhail Illarionovich Golenishchev-Kutuzov,
Headmaster of the First Cadets

Still standing behind him with her hands on his tense shoulders, Nadia felt Anton's body relax then slump into the chair.

"What is it, Anton?"

"Here," was all he could say - holding out both letters toward her.

Nadia took the letters and read. Soon she was holding her hand over her mouth as her eyes flickered back and forth and she tried to comprehend what was being said.

"You died? That cannot be. What does it mean, Anton?"

"It means that you are my Nadia, and I am your Anton."

"What?

"Remember what you said last night? You said: We will talk of your changes, my changes, our changes —tomorrow —the next day—the next month, but the answer will be the same. You are my Anton, and I am your Nadia. And because of those letters, those words are truer now than you can know.

"But."

"No buts today love. Today is Christmas, and tomorrow —well tomorrow is now possible.

"Still perplexed at the enigmatic words in the letter and Anton's seeming relief when he read them, she started to protest when Anton suddenly kissed her and throttled the question she was about to ask.

"Trust me?" he asked.

Looking back at the letter in her hand and then back at Anton her face relaxed as she said "all-right, I trust you."

Just then there was a knock at the door. Anton strode over and opened it and looked down to see a withered old Abraham standing with a cane and a small package for Nadia and the girls as his hired sleigh slid away with bells jingling. It would return the next morning to bring Abraham back to his bookstore.

"Hello, young man. You must be Nadia's Anton I hear too much about."

"Yes, I am, and you must be Abraham, Ilya's good friend that I hear too much about."

Smiling at the quick retort, he asked: "is he back yet?" as he lifted his chin and eyebrows hoping to hear good news?

"No, not yet."

"Come in out of the cold," said Anton as Abraham shuffled through the door.

"Papi, Papi," called out the girls, the name they had bestowed on Abraham, a frequent visitor to the House. What do you have for us?"

"Something very special," he teased. Something very special for our dinner."

Abraham touched Nadia on the arm and whispered into her ear — "latkes."

"Latkes?"

"Small potato cake with honey," he explained while lapsing into Yiddish as he often did. Then he added. "Madtshens will love."

Not sure she understood what he meant by madtshens, she looked over at Anton quizzically. "Mädchen means *girls* in German. Yiddish is mostly German," Anton answered matter of factly.

"Ja, the boy is right. Smart boy this Anton is."

"Come, sit down by the fire. Let me take your coat," offered Anton.

No sooner had Abraham sat down than there was another knock at the door.

"It must be Ilya," said Nadia.

"About time," grumbled Abraham.

Anton went to the door and to his surprise found Viktor, his traveling companion, and erstwhile client for his trip from Okhotsk to Irkutsk.

"Ah, Viktor my friend," said Anton as they gave each other bear hugs and slaps on the back. "You made it."

All the others in the room were quietly wondering who this Viktor was. Anton, for his part, suddenly realized introductions were necessary.

"A thousand pardons. This is Viktor. We traveled together to Irkutsk until Viktor made a small side trip to Limsk to visit the house of Radishchev."

"Radishchev?" asked Abraham.

"Yes, the great author. You know of him," asked Viktor.

"Ya. Radishchev ist alten freund."

"Abraham means to say that Radishchev is an old friend," whispered Anton into Nadia's ear."

Dumbstruck, Viktor excitedly dragged old Abraham by the shoulders over to a quiet table in the corner and began peppering the old man with questions. Anton overheard a few snippets of what was said starting with Viktor saying something about a travel book. He suspected the malleable and impressionable monk, bureaucrat, and now travel-writer Viktor would be pushed and pulled into still another direction by the persistent and opinionated bookseller. But he left Viktor to his fate.

Meanwhile, Anton explained to the others how he and Viktor met and let Viktor and Abraham continue their lively conversation even though it would probably make dinner a little late. Shrugging his shoulders at Nadia, she looked annoyed as she went back to tending the food to make sure nothing burned.

Finally, the big meal came. The mushrooms and onions had reconstituted and tasted almost as if they had just been plucked from the side of the river on a summer day. The Venison had mellowed and softened in the slow cooking broth while the Russian Stove glowed unusually bright as such stoves always do on Christmas.

Plenty of Chinese vodka flowed between the men. Even Nadia sipped a little. The girls learned what Latkes were and poured liberal amounts of honey on them, and no one saw a need to object. After all, it was Christmas. Then came Nadia's favorite—the cake. It all felt like a real Christmas, even to Abraham who once more conceded to Nadia that Jesus was indeed a magic Jew. Then with too much vodka in his belly, Abraham added a toast to something that no one but Abraham understood.

"And lo, they shall be wanderers among the nations."

Though it sounded like it might have been a toast to a tribe of nomads, they all raised a glass without understanding a word of what he said, or why he felt the urge to say it. Nadia made a mental note to ask him later.

As the evening wore on and conversation slowed, Anton put on his warmest coat, mittens, and hat and strolled down by the river and then turned around to take in a broader view of the house at night. His breath froze quickly on the stubble of beard on his face and the silver-colored wolf fur that shrouded his coat. It was thirty below zero. Looking back through the luminous windows, he saw everything and everyone he loved except Ilya.

There was Nadia bustling about giving orders to the girls as pots and dishes were cleaned and put away. Through another window were Abraham and Viktor continuing their animated conversation about Radishchev, and it gave Anton a little laugh. He knew that the impressionable Viktor had probably already been persuaded by Abraham to follow Radishchev and inject some politics into his erstwhile travelogue.

But outside in the snow, Anton was equally confident that he could persuade Viktor that his change in plans for the book might get him in jail or worse. He would remind Viktor that Radischev's original punishment was death and that it was only through the intervention of an influential friend that had he been given the lesser punishment of exile to the provinces of Siberia. Better to go with the original plan—a story of two friends on a journey spanning the Americas across the Pacific to Siberia and on to Moscow and St. Petersburg.

After watching Abraham and Viktor for several minutes, he turned his attention to the children who were busy giving kisses to everyone as they got ready for bed. He stayed outside for an hour stamping his feet on the snow to keep the blood flowing to his toes. As Anton basked in the thought that he was a fortunate man, the door opened and little Kamak stepped out onto the porch silhouetted by the warm lights behind her but surrounded by icy darkness.

"Anton. Are you out there? Come back inside, Nadia wants you, and she says it's too cold."

With that, she quickly ran back into the house, and the heavy door slammed behind her. Quickly, all became quiet again as light snow began to fall, and Anton was not yet ready to let go of the peace of the wilderness around him. He found a rock to sit on and listened to the whispering of snow falling on snow again.

That was when he heard the lonely sound of horse hooves clomping over the frozen Irkut river toward the House of Ilya. As Anton stood up, he peered into the dark, and a slow-moving horse came into view. As it came closer, he saw that it was Ilya's horse Kassandrov, but Ilya, who was always tall in the saddle, could not be seen. Anton took a few hesitant steps toward the river and then began to run across the ice to the horse with his heart full of dread.

There, partly by feel and partly by sight, he found Ilya slumped over in the saddle clutching the mane of Kassandrov. Ilya's face was turned away on the other side of Kassandrov, so Anton stepped over and saw that his eyes were closed, and he was pale but shiny with sweat even in the harsh cold.

"Ilya," he said quietly as if to wake him gently. Getting no response, he yelled: "Ilya."

"Da. Da! Ilya hear. Ears work good. Just have hole in belly."

"A hole in your belly?"

"Good to see Anton. Ilya happy. But get Ilya to house. Ilya little bit cold."

Anton rushed to grab the reins of the horse half crying and led Kassandrov to the livery.

"Viktor," he screamed. "Victor come outside. I need help."

The door opened and a shaft of light hit Ilya's frozen face and his crumpled body slumped over Kassandrov's neck.

"Viktor. We need to get Ilya into the house. Tell Nadia to get his bed ready but try not to frighten the children."

Viktor disappeared into the house for a moment and quickly returned with a blanket. Nadia followed as Abraham stood at the doorway. Anton lifted Ilya gently off Kassandrov with the help of Viktor and they wrapped his stiff body with a blanket and then carried him into the house and laid him onto his bed. Anton sent Viktor back out to take care of Kassandrov and get her into the enclosed livery stable and covered in a blanket. Viktor gave her fresh hay. The gaunt horse looked like she hadn't eaten for days.

"What do you mean you have a hole?" asked Anton as Nadia winced and held both hands to cover her mouth.

"Da, Ilya have little hole through liver and out his back. He gestured to bring Anton close to his face so that only Anton could hear. "I see this many times. Sorry boy, Ilya die soon. But Ilya happy to die old man with friends."

"Abraham – Abraham. You here Altschul? What I tell you old man. Does Ilya see or does Ilya see. Have drink with Ilya. One more drink together eh?

Nadia cried softly in the background while comforting the girls and let the men tend to Ilya who steadfastly refused to allow them to see his wounds. It would not do any good he said. He had seen this injury before in battles and no one survived such wounds. He was content to be warm in the house, drinking sips of vodka with his friends, and smelling the remnants of venison stew that he loved so much.

Ilya began to go in and out of consciousness even as he uttered a sentence that trailed off and did not finish. When he awoke again, he looked around the room with a look of surprise until he remembered where he was, and with that, he donned a happy grin.

"Old man, bring my chessboard. We play one last game eh —just like I say. We see who win. "Prop Ilya up, Anton. Help Ilya play chess with old friend Abraham.

Then turning to Nadia and the girls, Ilya boomed. "No cry girls. Ilya lucky. Old Cossack die like good Cossack with friends, not on trail alone."

Then, quickly changing the subject, he announced with urgency: "Kassandrov good horse. You take care of horse eh Anton as he tugged at Anton's shirt?"

"Yes, Ilya. You know I will take good care of the old girl."

Then back to Nadia he said: "You marry Anton missy? Or you find another boy just as good? Ilya think maybe you marry Anton," he said smugly as if he had won an old argument. Still talking with Nadia but looking Anton in the eye he winked and said: "He good boy. He talk much and know little. Ha."

Nadia remembered the prophetic words he uttered in front of Auntie in St. Petersburg and buried her face in Anton's shoulder to muffle her tears.

"Abraham, where that chessboard," he demanded?

"Ich Kom mein freund. Du alten vild Mensch. Coming!

Abraham ambled across the room and set the chessboard gently down on Ilya's belly as he lay on the bed. Then he put the pieces in their proper places and sat beside his old friend.

"Your move," said Abraham.

Ilya chose white and moved his pawn from E2 to E4.

"Ah, the Ruy Lopez opener. Sehr gut mein freund," congratulated Abraham.

Abraham studied his defense to Ilya's opening move with his left hand buried in his gray goatee as his other hand hovered over the board. Then, just as his hand descended to reach for his pawn to move it from E5 to E7 and block, Ilya uttered a sad moan, shuddered, and his body went limp dumping all the chess pieces to the wood floor clattering in all directions.

As Abraham leaned over to see Ilya's face, he watched until the light had faded from Ilya's eyes. Then, he sat back up in his chair in tears saying over and over: "You good friend you big old Cossack. You good friend." Then, after a long pause, he patted Ilya's hand and said: "Ilya pretty good at seeing future. But not so good when it come to chess."

Nobody win today my good friend. Both lose.

Chapter 28, THE BURIAL OF ILYA

For the rest of Christmas night, Ilya lay on his bed surrounded by family who stood vigil over his body, drank vodka, and snacked on the remnants of honey laden latkes and Bird-Cherry Chocolate Cake. Each told their stories about how and why they came to love the gruff old Cossack.

The next morning Anton busied himself with building a spruce coffin large enough for the big man. Nadia went about making a white headband made of cloth to place on his forehead. She also made a white robe and a white belt to dress him in but left the robe unhemmed and unfinished as a sign that he now belonged to another world as was the Cossack custom.

She and Anton washed his body. It was a painful but loving task of cleansing the punctures that had killed him. Red lines radiated from both wounds evidencing the sepsis that took his life. When all that was done, Anton and Viktor lifted Ilya into the coffin and set him on the main table in the hostel where it would rest for the next three days of mourning. Along with the body, Anton placed one of Ilya's fifty caliber pistols and his long knife in the coffin beside him. Abraham for his part told Anton that one of Ilya's last wishes was to be buried in a wild place, not in the church cemetery and Anton nodded as if he already knew.

"The Sayans?" asked Anton.

"Yes. A view would be di beste."

At dawn on the third day, Ilya's body was loaded in its pine coffin on to a rented sledge with a troika of horses to pull it quickly over the frozen surface of the Irkut River toward the Sayans. Expecting an overnight stay, Anton packed a tent for him and the driver and took along his Kentucky rifle and Ilya's other fifty-caliber pistol. Anton tied Kassandrov to the rear and boarded the sledge next to the driver while Nadia, Abraham, the girls, and Viktor said their final goodbyes by patting the top of the coffin. Then they were off with sleigh bells pealing out across the snow. After a few hundred yards of travel, Anton stuffed the bells with a piece of cloth to silence the ringing to the displeasure of the driver, who displayed a frown.

"It's a funeral," snapped Anton looking him in the eye.

Anton expected to search until he found a spot on high ground with a good view of Ilya's beloved mountains. He did not have to go far since the eastern edge of the Sayans were only sixty miles from Irkutsk, and their snow-capped peaks were even visible from the southern shore of Lake Baikal. Anton estimated one day out and one day back without need for a change of horses. Kassandrov was used to such daily distances even with a heavy rider like Ilya. Then, with a few hours of daylight left, they found a large unnamed island in the middle of the river that rose thirty feet above the Irkut. It had steep sides on its north and south and was covered with spruce. A barren clearing on the west side allowed the troika to pull the sled up to the highest spot on the island. The view was expansive. In the distance to the east was Lake Baikal, and to the west was an unobstructed view of the snowy Sayans which were beginning to show Alpenglow late in the day. Anton knew Ilya would have approved. Though there were more trees, it had the same feel as the camp Ilya called "his spot" when they first traversed the Yakutsk-Okhotsk trail together.

Anton and the driver lifted Ilya down to the snow along with Anton's gear and a shovel. Kassandrov was hobbled and given oats and two blankets for the night even though she was a Yakutian with a long coat of hair and well-adapted to the frigid temperatures. The hobble was probably unnecessary as well since Kassandrov was unlikely to wander far from the scent of Ilya.

Anton picked up the spade, but it wasn't for digging a grave. The ground was too hard for that. Instead, it was to remove snow so that the coffin would be resting on solid ground. After placing it there, Anton planned to cover it completely with white river stones to make a burial cairn.

The driver decided that it was not necessary to stay the night since they had not travelled far up the Irkut before finding the island. There was still a little daylight left, and his horses would be fresh enough for the trip back so long as he went slowly. After Anton paid him, he was off down the Irkut. After a few hundred yards, he removed the cloth that Anton had used to muffle the bells and Anton could hear them ringing until he rounded the first serpentine bend on the river.

Anton worked into the night carrying stones. He uncovered them from the snow with his shovel near the river's edge and carried them one by one up the hill to Ilya's promontory. Each rock found, carried, and placed on the coffin felt like an act of love, a penance, or some sort of devotion. Anton couldn't tell which, but he was honored to do it and it felt like a holy act. Soon he was telling Ilya about the stones.

"This smooth round one is from Nadia," he told him. "And this one with the ragged edges is from me." Then, after trudging up from the river to place another, he said "this one is from Abraham."

If he carried two smaller stones, he told Ilya they were from the girls, Kamak and Cheyvyne. He even set one for Viktor who only knew him for a few hours before he passed, and another for the Polish exile Ilya and Abraham knew in Irkutsk. Then he would begin naming the additional stones all over again, one by one as he added them to the cairn.

At the end of the evening, Ilya was covered snug in a raised pile of white river rocks each named after one of those he loved. Anton was unsure of which direction Ilya should lay in. But in the absence of a priest to advise him, he used his own counsel and decided it was best to have Ilya's head pointed west toward the Sayans and his feet toward the House of Ilya. Either way, he thought Ilya would approve. Then, after erecting his shelter and starting a fire, he sat beside the Cairn and talked with Ilya while drinking Chinese vodka and as Kassandrov munched on oats. Anton balanced an empty glass for Ilya atop a flat rock on the grave.

"And so, my friend, why did you choose me to tell your sad story of the killing of the innocents? Was it because you knew we shared kindred souls as killers of men? Was it because we were soldiers, scouts, or hunters of Roe Deer? Was there something in my spirit that only the eyes of a Cossack seer could divine? Or did you think I was some wilderness priest who could absolve you for your killing? No matter my friend. If redemption is due to anyone in this world, it is you. You saved the girls. And, if I am your priest, I forgive you."

With that, he raised a toast above the grave as firelight glinted on his glass, warmed his face, and reflected in the glowing eyes of a creature barely hidden among the spruce.

"And so you may rest in peace, know this. When Nadia and I marry, we will take the girls in as our own. But you knew this already, didn't you?"

Having said all he wanted to say to Ilya, Anton poured vodka for himself and for Ilya into two glasses and recited three toasts. After each toast, he emptied Ilya's glass onto his grave. The first toast was to friendship. The second was to women. And the third was to the dead - to Puyuk, to Aluki, and now to Ilya. After the last toast, Anton crawled into his tent and passed out while Kassandrov licked the snowy vodka from the cairn and then lay down in the snow feeling drowsy. The next morning, he awoke at dawn and noticed wolf prints around the cairn.

The Last Will and Testament of Ilya Kalnyshevsky

I, Ilya Kalnyshevsky being of sound mind and good health but anticipating death as the natural consequence of life do hereby declare this to be my Last Will and Testament to my entire estate. Ilya lived a good life and as a seer of his people he know already he will soon die a good death. God knows what I have done that was good with my life, and he knows of my sorrows and regret. In the manner of my death, and in the saving of my girls may God grant me redemption for what I did not know when I was too young to know.

To God I give my soul and plead forgiveness for my deeds

To Abraham I give my Books and my Chessboard

To Anton I bequeath my guide business, my wolf-skin hat, and my horse Kassandrov because boy get too bored running hostel.

To Nadia I give love and apology. Anton will only be gone for part of each winter on trail to Okhotsk. Don't worry, he live long life and always come back.

Of Anton I ask he bury me in wild place close to Sayans. He will know where.

To all of you I ask you visit me at my grave once a year. Ilya is Cossack. Cossack get mad nobody visit. Bring Ilya a little cake, tea, roe deer, and vodka.

To Anton and Nadia together I give the House of Ilya and all that is in it on Kupala June 22, 1803. But this have condition. Must adopt Cheyvyne and Kamak as their children and love them forever. Abraham do words on paper.

Signed X Witness: Abraham Altschul Cohen Date: November 25, 1802

Chapter 29, THE CLIENT, WINTER, 1803

Anton led his first client, a second-year army officer down the frozen Lena from Irkutsk to Yakutsk and then over the Yakutsk-Okhotsk Trail in the winter of 1803. He had little to say to the lieutenant who not only bored him but looked down on Anton as his hired-hand. The young man wore his social class like a shining medal for all to see and bow to. As they rode horseback over the mountain trail from Yakutsk, Anton tried to ignore the officer's constant chatter and boasts of his military prowess.

"Have you ever been in the military, my man?"

"Da, Anton replied tersely."

"Do I detect a tone of disapproval? Well, I suppose being an infantryman is much different than being an officer, but I rather like the military. The uniform is smart. I serve the empire. I suppress savages, tame the wilderness, lead men into battle. I say, have you ever killed a man in battle?"

"That's not a question you are supposed to ask."
"Why not?"

"It's unseemly."

"So, what you really mean is that you have never killed a man?"

"No, I did not say that."

"So, how many then?"

"Three if you must know."

"Three? And what battle might that have been?"

"The battle for Redoubt St. Michael on Sitka."

"Oh, my man. You must know that all of our men were killed except three."

"That's right."

"So, you were one of the three survivors on our side?"

"No, I was just a scout. I didn't count."

"That's a silly riddle. What does that mean?"

Anton gave no answer, and then trotted ahead to put some distance between himself and the annoying officer. Then he thought better of it and wheeled his horse back to confront him. As he approached, the lieutenant's horse took a step backwards, and then stamped his feet nervously on the trail.

"It means I did my best to scout a path between the sides, but I failed. So, I scalped them."

"Scalped who?"

"The Russians."

"Our Russians?"

"No, their Russians."

"Scalped?" asked the Lieutenant who was now unsure if Anton's words were gibberish, evidence of insanity, or wisdom taken from a source on high. *Either way*, he pondered, *what did scalping have to do with being a scout or taking a side?* In the end, he thought it best not to ask anything more about it. The man sounded dangerous.

Then, as they were settling back into the rhythm of the trail, Anton mused on something that bookish Altschul had told him once. He said that what you find annoying in another man is likely what you hate or hated once in yourself. *The old man was right. Thank god I'm past being a prig like this one. What was it Ilya said? Oh yes, he talk much but know little. Ha!*

Suddenly Anton was yanked away from his musings on the past and pulled back into the present. As he rode peacefully up a gradual slope, the loud report of a musket firing behind him caused his horse to rear and nearly buck him out of his saddle. The officer had pulled his musket and fired carelessly at a Roe deer grazing a hundred yards up the hillside.

"I think I almost got him," announced the client proudly with a wide grin.

"Almost means you missed."

"What?"

"I said you missed."

"Well, I..."

"You shot from horseback using a musket that's accurate to a hundred yards at best. What did you expect? Worse, what if you had only wounded him? That's a cruel waste of life."

"Hold on my man. You are saying you would have hit the deer?"

"I didn't say anything about me shooting at the deer. But if I had shot at the deer, I would have hit his heart at that range."

Stuttering in anger, the lieutenant issued a dare. "Prove it then. There's another Roe further up the hill. I guess he's two hundred yards out. Hit him if you are so good with your rifle."

"I don't kill to prove anything," he retorted righteously."

Then he reconsidered whether it was worth proving or not. Despite a deep misgiving that it would be a waste of time, Anton felt a strong urge to put the prig in his place and answered the challenge laid down by the Lieutenant.

"See that lone branch on the blackened tree burned by lightning a hundred yards away?"

The officer strained his eyes to see it then said, "yes."

"I'll hit the branch."

"Impossible. That branch is only two inches thick."

"Yes, and it will fall to the ground."

"I don't believe you can do it."

With that, Anton dismounted and pulled out his Kentucky long. After checking the powder, he rested it on the rump of his horse. Then, he factored in the distance to the tree and aimed, took his breaths, paused, and then fired. The loud report of the rifle echoed down the valley causing a covey of birds to take flight. Less than a second later, there was a faint sound of a bullet hitting dead wood.

"You missed."

"I don't think so," Anton responded as he fit his rifle back into its scabbard without looking up.

The branch was hit but it was kept from falling by a few remaining splinters of wood. Cupping his eyes from the glare of the sun the Lieutenant saw the branch swinging slightly back and forth though there was no wind. Finally, the last splinter gave way and it fell to the ground with a soft hollow thud. Anton heard it and then scolded himself for needing to prove anything to the annoying Lieutenant. *Next time just say he's right!*

The officer sulked all the way to Okhotsk. Despite his best effort, he could not conjure a sufficient retort to Anton's performance that would save his face. When it came time to pay Anton, the young man placed rubles one by one into Anton's open hand as if giving alms to a beggar. After he was finished, Anton dropped them into a bag, cinched it shut, then swung his horse around quickly causing it to snort in protest and then trotted up the trail to return to Nadia. He hoped that his next client wouldn't be like this one.

On the way back, Anton had time to ponder many things. But mostly, he thought about a story Ilya had told him when he guided him to Okhotsk three years before. It never made sense to him. He recalled the tale as best he could since he heard it several years before.

Once upon a time a Cossack scout was alone on a trail that led over the mountains and he met a lone wolf coming toward him. To his amazement, the wolf could talk, and the wolf asked the Cossack "who goes there?"

To which the Cossack answered. "I am called Perevertni. I am from the people between."

"Well, Perevertni from the people between, what a coincidence, said the wolf. I too am called Perevertni, but once I was called Perevertni."

The Cossack laughed and said: "That is silly. You say you have two names, but both names are the same."

"Yes, and that is why I am you and you are me." We have the same name because we are both Perevertni.

The Cossack slapped his head and said: "Stop wolf, you are hurting my head."

It was late in the day and the sun was about to set when the wolf answered:

"You do not believe me, so, I will show you."

As the Cossack stood in front of the wolf, he squinted with the glow of sunset on his face. Then, suddenly he found himself facing the other direction. And where he stood a second before, he saw the wolf with the glow of sunset on his black nose and his silvery grey fur.

"Wolf, you have changed your shape and your position."

"No, Cossack, you have changed yours."

After the telling, Ilya seemed embarrassed and added— "Crazy story Da? Anton forget. Just a story," he said while sneaking a look at Anton to see his reaction.

Chapter 30, GOLD

The day of the wedding was balmy and heavy with clouds of mosquitos which the happy couple warded off with necklaces of citronella grass laced with mugwort, spring flowers and drops of oils pressed from sage and rosemary. Nadia and Anton had forestalled their wedding date until Kupala in honor of how they had first met. Nadia forsook the trappings of her putative aristocratic status and went forth barefoot like a peasant and wore the same white dress she had worn three years earlier at Kupala in Petropavlosk. Upon her head was a spring garland fit for a princess or perhaps a ballerina.

Anton wore his cleanest white shirt with a simple white cravat at his neck, red trousers, a red sash, and

Ilya's Zaporizhian Cossack boots and his silver wolf hat as a symbol of his presence.

The girls wore copies of Nadia's dress and each carried a ring on a pillow. Each ring was hand-forged by Anton from placer gold. The girls bickered over which one would carry Nadia's ring and which would carry Anton's even though, except for the size, each one looked the same. Abraham had come by hired carriage the day before and was wearing his formal suit for the first time since the burial of his daughter after she and her husband had drowned when their sledge broke through the spring ice on the Angara River near his bookstore.

Even Viktor attended the festivities. He had stayed over in Irkutsk still obsessed with the stories of Radishchev that Abraham seemed never to tire of repeating to his eager student. Viktor had taken the room above the studio Nadia had rented but never lived in. He and the old man talked every day sitting on stools, drinking tea, and playing chess in the old man's bookstore.

They were interrupted only by the occasional customer and the hollow sandy sound of dancing feet sliding over the wooden floor next-door at the Kolosova at the Bolshoi dance studio. Anton was beginning to wonder if his friend would ever leave. But then, Viktor suddenly announced it was urgent that he and Anton go over Anton's drawings in preparation for his imminent departure back to Moscow to complete their book.

Viktor mounted his horse and started down the path toward the Irkutsk to fetch the valise of drawings waving goodbye to everyone including Abraham who had already arrived. Halfway down the trail he passed an official looking man riding toward the House of Ilya. Probably a hostel guest, he thought, although travelers were rare this time of year due to the muddy summer roads and mosquitos.

As the man neared the house the girls came running out to greet him.

"Is this the House of Ilya?" he asked.

"Yes, but Ilya died last winter. But if you need a place to stay, we can help you."

"No, I won't be staying. Is Anton Niktovich here?"

"Yes, we'll get him for you. Can we take your horse to the stable?

"That's very kind. Thank you."

Minutes later, Anton appeared in his wedding garb with a pistol thrust into his red sash. The girls had told him of the stranger and that he had asked about him and Ilya.

"Did he ask for a room?"

"No. He just said he wanted to talk to you."

"Thank you. Now stay inside and close the door behind me."

The girls watched through a window as Anton walked toward the well-dressed man. Anton approached him with deliberate steps and cocked his head to the side to take the full measure of the stranger.

"I am Anton Niktovich. You want to talk to me?

"Yes," he said as he looked around and took in the view. "Nice place you have here by the river."

"And how can I help you Mr…"

"Oh, yes. Pardon me. My name is Vasili Menschevich."

"I have a good friend who is a mensch. Are you also a mensch Mr. Menschevich?"

"It would be impertinent to call myself a mensch."

"But you already are calling yourself the son of a mensch."

"It's a common name in Russia Mr. Niktovich. It implies nothing about me being a mensch. But enough about me, I have some business with you."

"Yes, I know."

"It's about gold."

"It's my wedding day. Can this be postponed?"

Suddenly Abraham came out the door walking as fast as he could with his cane and gesticulating wildly as he limped forward toward Anton and the well-dressed man.

“Menshevich, you old mensch. You have come to wedding?”

Sighing, he answered. “Hello Abraham. No, not precisely.”

“Then what? No business today,” scolded Abraham while waving a shaming finger in Menschevich’s face. “Meine guten freunde marry today. What government business could you possibly have that cannot wait?”

“Gold —Anton was seen paying for a chicken with gold nuggets.”

“So, what’s a little gold between friends?”

“It’s the Emperor’s gold.”

“Ja, ja, my sour old friend. Ilya tell me that over and over —zuviel. So, what you do now. Send Anton to Siberia. Further east maybe. Shoot him?”

“It’s the Emperor’s gold.”

Abraham sighed and then put his arm around the man who was a low ranking bureaucrat and occasional enforcer of the law. Then he dragged him away from Anton toward the river talking all the way and gesticulating with his free hand.

“So, what you think. Does the Emperor like Chinese Vodka maybe?

Looking both ways before speaking as if a townsperson might be near enough to overhear, he answered in a hushed tone. "He might."

"Well then. It's settled. The House of Ilya will give you a bottle of Chinese Vodka to take to the Emperor in exchange for peace and quiet. What do you think? Will the Emperor be happy with that?"

"Oh, I think so. But I think he would be happier with two bottles. Yes, indeed. Two would make him very happy."

"It seems you know the emperor well. So, for how long might the emperor be happy with two bottles of vodka?"

"Oh, for six months maybe?"

"You are a mensch my friend. Truly, you are a mensch like no other to be so concerned about the Emperor and his gold."

Still with his arm on Menschevich's shoulder he called back to Anton.

"Anton. This is my friend Vasili Menshevich. Can he stay for the wedding?"

"What about the gold?"

"What gold?"

Chapter 31, THE WEDDING, JUNE 22, 1803

In the eyes of the Orthodox Church, Anton and Nadia had been living in sin for more than six months — ever since Anton had arrived at Christmas the year before and stayed. Irrespective of the ire of the holy church, the customary blessings from the parents for the nuptial were also absent.

But the lack of blessings was understandable and forgivable due to their vast distances away from Irkutsk in Petropavlosk and St. Petersburg. Auntie, however, had responded with her own blessings by letter to Nadia from St. Petersburg. Despite the lack of blessings from the parents, there were two things that followed custom.

The first was that the wedding day was on a Friday and avoided Tuesday, Thursday, and Saturday which were forbidden by the Orthodox Church. This was accidental, however, since the wedding couple had committed to have their wedding on Ivan Kupala which happened to be a Friday this year.

The second was that they had courted during Ivan Kupala. Through this irrepressible pagan tradition that had been long frowned upon by the church, it was a day that a future bride and groom might see meet each other without supervision which would have been otherwise required.

But in the end, three years of jarring change had left both Nadia and Anton too jaded to care about following the laws of God for their wedding. Instead, they found comfort in the laws of nature and their mutually beloved wilderness. Even so, they reluctantly conceded to Abraham's desire to have the priest of the Spasskaya Orthodox Church preside over the wedding.

"God must bless," Abraham insisted. "Even if not my God."

Abraham approached the priest and asked if he would marry the lovers. The priest agreed on one condition. Father Poplowski insisted that the wedding be held at the Spasskaya Church in town. But he lost the argument.

"God will be by the river," Abraham asserted.

"Yes, and God is in the rafters of the Church."

Poplowski was a stubborn Pole exiled for a sermon he gave on the plight of serfs in his parish. Despite his insistence on having the wedding at the Spasskaya, he sensed that Anton was firm in his resolve to have the wedding by the river Irkut at the House of Ilya instead of the church. But he only relented after Abraham began visiting him twice a day with freshly baked Polish bagels.

After three weeks, Poplowski flung the church door open one sunny spring morning and saw Abraham limping up the pathway with his cane in one hand and a bag of bagels in the other

"Ah, Poplowski my friend. I bring you breakfast bagels."

"Enough," shouted the Priest at Abraham. "Have you no shame. I will never want another bagel in my life because of your persistence. Tell Anton I will bring God to the House of Ilya on the day of Ivan Kupala, and I hope you are all satisfied."

The priest arrived by carriage near the time of the ceremony and stepped down near a table filled with wedding feasts strewn over a white tablecloth and dappled by noonday sun. In the center of the table was a bird-cherry-chocolate-cake. From inside the House of Ilya, the aroma of venison stew simmering alongside potatoes, onions, and mushrooms spilled out the open windows and drifted over the wedding guests making everyone hungry.

The priest wore a black Skufia with a silver cross and black vestments that hung down to his feet. As the midday sun bore down, perspiration was soon dripping down his long black beard and his uncut hair that hung down from his Skufia hat.

Nadia took pity and gave him a chair and a glass of ice-cold river water in the shade of a tall spruce. Though still a young man, he was short and portly and had to lean on his crozier as he sat down out of the sun. Nadia asked the girls to take his prayer rug and roll it out under the shade of another tree and nodded at Anton to gather the guests near the carpet. Soon the wedding began with the priest standing on the rug facing the couple and the girls who stood behind them with rings and crowns on pillows. Then he began an abridged service due to the summer warmth and everyone's desire to begin the feast. That was especially true of Poplowski whose belly betrayed one of the seven deadly sins.

O Lord, our God, who didst accompany the servant of the patriarch Abraham into Mesopotamia, when he was sent to seek a wife for his lord Isaac to espouse, and who, by means of drawing of the water at the well, didst reveal to him that he should betroth Rebecca: Do Thou, the same Lord, bless also the betrothal of these Thy servants, Anton, and Nadia, and confirm the promise that they have made. Establish them in the holy union which is from Thee. For in the beginning, Thou didst make them male and female, and by Thee the woman is joined unto the man as a helper and for the procreation of the human race. Therefore, O Lord our God, who hast sent forth Thy truth upon Thy inheritance, and Thy covenant unto Thy servants, our fathers, Thine elect from generation to generation: Look upon Thy servant, Anton, and Thy handmaid, Nadia, and establish and make firm their betrothal, in faith and in oneness of mind, in truth and in love.

Amen.

After the vows, Poplowski blessed the rings and asked the couple to place them on each other's outstretched finger. Then he began the service of the crowns by placing a crown on each and then said a final prayer.

May the Father, and the Son, and the Holy Spirit, the all-holy, consubstantial, and life-giving Trinity, one Godhead and one Kingdom, bless you; and grant you length of days, god-fearing children, prosperity in life and faith; and fill you with abundance of all earthly good things, and make you worthy to obtain the blessings of the promise; through the prayers of the holy mother of God and of all the saints.

Amen.

With that, Anton pulled Nadia close and kissed her. But when Poplowski objected that the kiss was too short, he kissed her again until they could stand it no longer and burst into laughter which spread to the other guests who were ready for venison stew, bird-cherry-chocolate-cake, and a steady flow of Chinese vodka.

Chapter 32, KUPALA, JUNE 22, 1803

The irony of the wedding for Anton and Nadia was that it was merely a prelude to the pagan festival of Kupala which would follow later that night. In the eyes and hearts of the wedding couple, they had already been married in spirit if not in the eyes of God and gods when they landed intact on the other side of the bonfire still holding hands three years before. As for gods, the couple had already taken two pagan baptisms when they submerged under the frigid waters of a nameless lake beneath the untamed firmament of the ancients. And now they looked forward to yet another baptism on this night when the rites of Kupala 1803 returned — this time in the snow-melted waters of the Irkut that flowed by of the House of Ilya and past the old Cossack's resting place on an unnamed island further upriver near the Sayans.

The Kupala of 1803 involved an Anton and a Nadia who no longer resembled their former selves. Certainly, their inner spirits were the same as the ones that united in June of 1800. But their outward attributes were utterly different and no longer fit the social labels they were born with. In a country that parsed people according to social rank, they had become strangers in an odd land and were left to forge identities that were true to what they had wrought as they passed through the crucible of life. Of all the places in Russia to land after falling from grace and privilege, they could not have done better than Irkutsk. There, merit mattered more than birthright, and new identities of worth were beaming from the hopeful faces of energetic exiles coming in from all over the far-flung empire. It was a place that Ilya said was full of crazy people, which he meant as a compliment.

As night fell over the House of Ilya, Nadia and Anton put the children to bed and then strolled to the river hand-in-hand.

"Baptism anyone?" asked Nadia as they swung their arms back and forth together.

"I was thinking we might look for fern flowers in the woods. Then baptism."

"What about the bonfire?" asked Nadia with starlight on her face.

"No need. That test is long past." Then turning to look at her. "See, we are still holding hands."

"True - and I love you Anton," to which Anton only felt the need to return a loving smile. Dance with me Anton."

"You know I can't dance."

"Well, then just stand and hold up your arm for me."

With that, they both stood up. Nadia raised her delicate hand to his upraised hand and brushed his fingers as she twirled around him like a top. After each spin, she broke away leaping and jumping like the ballerina she was, but always coming back for another twirl with Anton. It went on like that for some time until Nadia, panting and exhausted, asked:

"Time for a nice cool baptism in the river now?"

After undressing, they dipped into the icy waters of the Irkut until sometime after midnight. Then they sat in an embrace shivering on the riverbank with a quarter-moon painting faint shadows beneath them until their bodies dried in the balmy air. A wolf howled in the distance somewhere in the direction of Ilya's Cairn.

"Want to skip some rocks?"

"You skip, I'll watch," she answered as she sat reminiscing over her first Kupala, the three hard intervening years, and now her wedding.

Nadia tilted her head to the side, rested it on her pulled up knees, and looked fondly at Anton as he skipped rocks across the river.

"You know I'm pregnant?"

"Yes, – a girl."

"How do you know?"

"Anton know."

Anton came over and gave her a gentle kiss. Then they picked up their clothing and walked back to the House of Ilya holding hands. Nadia led the way expertly feeling the way with her feet through the dark. Then they checked on the sleeping girls together. Finding them safe asleep, they went to bed as Kassandrov munched on oats in the livery.

Made in the USA
Middletown, DE
22 September 2022

10841591R00179